Amish Assassin

Ashley Emma

Book 5 of the Covert Police Detectives Unit Series

FACT: There are more slaves now than ever before in history, including over 2 million children trapped in sex slavery. Over 12.3 million people worldwide have become victims. Operation Underground Railroad has rescued over 4,100 children from slavery and has arrested over 2,300 sex traffickers. And yes, slavery is happening in your hometown, and it is the fastest growing criminal industry in the world.

Donate here to join the Abolitionist Club and help support rescue missions to free more children from slavery:

https://my.ourrescue.org/product/DONATE-ONETIME/become-an-abolitionist

OPERATION UNDERGROUND RAILROAD

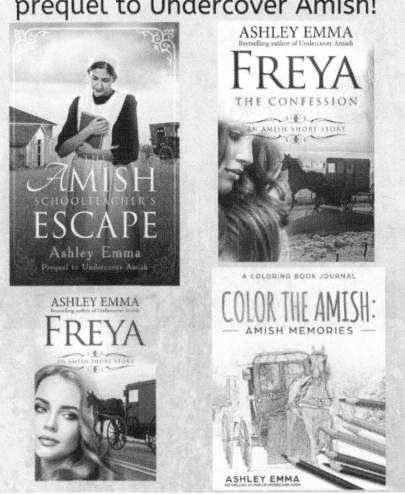

Other books by Ashley Emma on Amazon

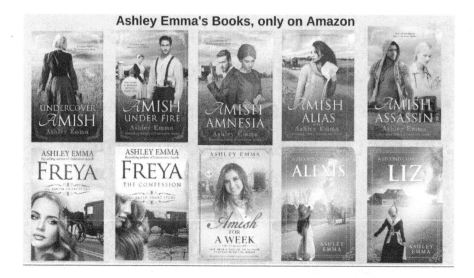

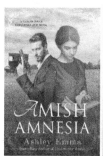 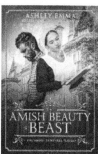  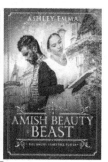

Coming soon:

 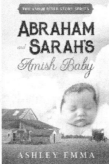

SPECIAL THANKS TO:

Julie

Abigail

Kit

Gail

Robin

Aurelie

There were so many readers from my email list who gave me helpful feedback on this book, so I couldn't list you all here. Thank you so much!

Check out my author Facebook page to see rare photos from when I lived with the Amish in Unity, Maine.

Click here to join my free Facebook group The Amish Book Club where I share free Amish books weekly!

The characters and events in this book are the creation of the author, and any resemblance to actual persons or events are purely coincidental.

AMISH ASSASSIN

AMISH ASSASSIN

Ashley Emma

Table of Contents

Chapter One

What was that?

Anna Hershberger stopped walking and looked around the parking lot, reaching for her pepper spray.

"Help me! Please," a garbled voice pleaded.

Maybe someone truly was in need of help, or maybe someone was using it as a ploy to mug her...or worse. As a young nurse who often worked the night shift at the hospital in Portland, Maine, she'd seen it all. She was no longer the naïve, sheltered Amish girl she had once been in her hometown of Unity, Maine.

She took a few more tentative steps, scanning the dimly lit area.

"Please! Help me." The man's voice was feeble and barely audible.

"Who's there?" she asked.

She heard it again, this time even lower, but it was unmistakably someone in pain. It sounded like the voice was coming from within the rows of parked cars. Anna stepped between the cars and began to search for the source of the noise.

She heard it a third and final time before she found the man lying curled up in a ball on the cement, hidden between two cars. Her brain told her to be cautious; this could be a trick. What was this man doing out here in the middle of the night?

Yet her heart told her to help him.

Clutching her pepper spray, Anna quickly ran to his side. She dropped to her knees beside him as her eyes moved over his body. He looked to be in his early thirties, dressed in black, with brown hair and stubble on his jaw. His eyes fluttered weakly as he looked at her.

"Please help…" He trailed off, the hand clutching his side falling away to reveal his injury, which was a hole the size of a bullet in his side. She checked his back, and there was an exit wound. The cloth he had been holding to it was soaked red, and the wound was still bleeding. He had probably lost a lot of blood. He needed help, and he needed it fast. And in order to do that, she needed to bring him inside the hospital.

"I'll go get help," she told him, returning the cloth to his side and placing his hand on it to apply pressure to the wound. As she rose to her feet, she felt his hand grab weakly at her ankle.

"No hospital. They will find me."

She looked down to see his other hand fall away. His mouth continued to move, but his voice was too weak to hear. Trapped between wanting to hear what he had to say and getting him the help he needed, Anna froze for a second. Then she found herself kneeling to the cement again and placing her ear near his mouth.

"No hospital." His eyes held hers as he looked at her. "Stitch me up here. The bullet went clean through."

Anna's eyes widened. How was she supposed to help him if she couldn't get him into the hospital? She would have to go inside, get supplies and then come back out here. Her coworkers might ask questions. Also, if she stitched up his wound here without proper sterilization, he could get a nasty infection.

She was about to protest when his eyes rolled back in his head and he passed out.

Anna had a choice to make. She called out to the group of EMTs gathered near the ambulance station to come and help her. Hopefully, by the time he woke up, he would be too grateful to be alive to blame her for disregarding his one wish.

Chapter Two

That smell.

That was the first thing that hit Connor as he came out of unconsciousness, his eyes still firmly closed. He had no idea why he would be in the hospital. Yet there was no denying the bitter smell of disinfectant that permeated the air around him.

He hated it, that smell. Thinking seemed like a chore, one that made his head hurt. He slowly lifted his eyelids, his ears also coming awake to the sound of a steady beeping sound in the room. Right above him hung an IV bag. Connor tried to lift his head up and groaned as pain seared his side and the throbbing ache in his head intensified.

For a moment he wondered why he was here, ignoring the ache in his head. Then all his memories came flooding back. He remembered why he hated this smell, the sight of the machines, and all the surrounding white. That made his heart ache with grief from the loss, a pain in his soul worse than the one in his body.

Connor also remembered why he was in the hospital this time, and as his mind went over the events that had occurred just before he had lost consciousness, he found himself frowning in anger.

He had specifically warned the nurse who found him that he couldn't go inside the hospital.

But right now, he had to get out of here as quickly as he could and get as far away from here as possible.

He was about to try to sit up again when he heard the door to his room being pushed open. He closed his eyes and pretended to still be asleep.

*****

Anna walked into the room of the newest patient on her roster, who was still unconscious. Now that her shift was over, she'd changed into her normal clothes, but even though she wasn't on the clock, she wanted to check on John Doe, one of the most intriguing patients she'd ever had.

First, she checked the drip bag hanging above his bed, making sure he was getting the fluids he needed. He had lost a lot of blood due to his injuries. Next, she checked the bandage on his side covering his injury, pleased when she saw that he had not bled through it. She glanced at him, taking in his face.

His light brown hair was cut short on the sides but longer on the top. On him, the choppy look added to the air of mystery and danger that surrounded him. His nose was long and thin, a slight notch at the bridge suggesting it had been broken before and reset. Had he had a violent life? In her line of work, she'd seen it all. Gangs, physical abuse, drug addiction, not to mention human trafficking. Nothing shocked her anymore, even though she'd lived a life separate from the world while growing up.

He was handsome, that was for sure, but it meant nothing to her so long as she did not dwell on those thoughts. But ignoring his looks was almost impossible.

She quickly moved to the foot of the bed, clicking her pen.

"Stop it, Anna. He's cute, but so what? He's a patient," she mumbled under her breath. "And hopefully, he won't be too angry that I brought him here."

Just last week she'd treated a movie star who would have made any other woman swoon. Anna had barely spared him a second glance. In this job, she got hit on all the time, but she'd never been interested in anyone since she'd left her community.

Yet, this man was making her act like one of those nurses fresh out of college and just starting rotation. With his bullet wound and how he'd begged her to not bring him inside, the mystery surrounding him only made him even more intriguing.

Had she made a mistake by bringing him here, inside the hospital? He could have died if she'd left him out there much longer, bleeding out. And how could she have properly treated him out there? Without sterilized tools, if she had stitched him up there, he could have gotten an infection later.

"No. You did the right thing," she told herself softly.

She lifted the clipboard fixed at the foot of the bed and made some notes. For now, all it contained were details on his injuries, the drugs he was taking and other medical information. There was no personal information or identification found on John Doe's person, not even a driver's license or credit card. No pictures or even a piece of paper on him.

After she was done making her notes, she dropped the clipboard and walked around the bed, staring at the heart monitor, happy to see that he seemed to be doing just fine. Then she turned around and found him staring at her.

Her eyes went wide with surprise. Had he heard her? She felt heat creep up her neck and face. Putting on a fake smile, she pretended like nothing had happened. After he left the hospital, she'd never see him again anyway. "Hey, how are you doing?"

He said nothing, and because the awkwardness was overwhelming, Anna just kept on talking, as she usually did when she got nervous. "You should definitely be feeling better than you were when you got here. We stitched you up and gave you blood. I should probably get the doctor if you want to talk about it, but I can assure you that you're doing fine now. You just need to rest and take it easy."

He looked at her blankly.

"Hi, I'm Anna, your nurse. What's your name?" she said.

More staring.

"Okay. Do you remember what happened to you? Who shot you? Was it a robbery?" she asked.

"I'm doing fine."

"That's not what I asked."

She pointed to his side. "How is your side? We stitched it up, of course, so you need to make sure you take it easy."

He said nothing, just looked at her.

"How did you get shot?" she pried.

"I said no hospital," he retorted instead of answering her.

Anna frowned. "Well, I couldn't just leave you there to die, which could have happened if I had tried to help you in the parking lot without the proper supplies and sanitation."

He continued, "In the parking lot, before I lost consciousness, I told you specifically that I don't want to—"

"—be brought into the hospital, I know. I just assumed it was all the blood you lost talking. You sounded a bit delirious." She watched as he scowled at her. "How am I supposed to help you without bringing you into the hospital?"

"You really could have stitched me up there." He glared at her.

"Sure, but not properly. It probably would have gotten infected, at the least. One simply does not stitch up a bullet wound in a parking lot."

Anna frowned at him, angry that she had bothered coming here after her shift had ended to check on him. He was clearly not grateful. She was about to say something when he pushed himself up on the bed and winced in pain. Anger disappearing, she became concerned for him.

"Don't move too much or you'll tear the stitches." She grabbed the remote to the bed and pushed it, so he was sitting up more comfortably.

"Thanks," he said begrudgingly when he was finally sitting up.

"You're welcome."

"And sorry for snapping at you about the hospital thing." He grimaced. "I don't like hospitals."

She looked at him, understanding his irritation a little. She had seen patients who hated hospitals because of bad memories. "You'd risk your life by avoiding going into one when you really needed to?"

He ignored her, looking out the window.

"Okay, then." She walked back to the foot of the bed and picked up the clipboard. "You were not carrying any means of identification on you, so I need some information. I'll also need to know how you got shot. The police are going to need that information."

She looked up to find her audience of one looking less than amused.

"You called the cops?" he said through gritted teeth.

Anna frowned. "Well, you came in with a bullet wound. We are legally bound to let the cops know when we treat a bullet wound. So," she put pen to paper and looked at him, "Your name?"

There was a slight pause, then he replied, "John Blake."

"John Blake." Anna repeated his name as she wrote it down. "I guess we were fifty percent right. The nurses started calling you John Doe when we didn't know your name."

John opened his mouth to say something, but she was already asking him the next question.

"How did you get shot?"

"Mugging attempt on my way back from work. I was alone. And they took my wallet, so that's why I don't have it," he replied, then watched her write that down.

Anna sighed. "Just rest while I go get the doctor. You'll be able to eat after he's done checking up on you. You're probably really hungry."

*****

Connor waited a few seconds after the nurse, Anna, left before he sat up in his bed. Sure, he was hungry.

Hungry to get out of there.

He pulled the needles out of his arm and then placed his legs on the floor. Using his hand on the bed to support himself, he got to his feet and froze, feeling dizzy from his actions. Gritting his teeth, he took several deep breaths then promptly swung into action. His eyes fell on some clothes by his bedside, and somehow he knew that he had the annoying nurse with the beautiful smile to thank for that. His boots were also there, and he quickly took off the hospital gown and changed into the new clothes, grimacing as pain from his bullet wound radiated up his side. The boots were his, so they fit perfectly. But the clothes were a touch too big. He didn't mind, well aware his own clothes had been destroyed. Dressed and ready to move, Connor took his first step towards the door and stopped as someone else stepped in through the door.

Connor ducked behind the bed as the man who'd just entered closed the door behind him and drew the privacy curtain closed. Connor truly wished this was the doctor that the annoying nurse had gone to get. But doctors didn't usually wear dark clothing, baseball hats, and leather jackets in the hospital.

They had found him, and so easily, too. This was why he had been reluctant to come to the hospital.

The man moved in, his face twisting in a smile as he reached for his gun.

"Nowhere to run now, eh?" He pointed his gun at Connor. "So why don't you hand it over, and we can get this over and done with?"

Connor stared at the gun, his mind doing a quick calculation as his eyes shifted to the man behind the gun. "You shoot me now and you'll never get what you want. Besides, there is no way you'll chance shooting me in the hospital."

The man's lips curved in a smile. "You wanna bet?"

The nurse pushed the door open and stepped in. The armed man whirled around and pointed the gun at her.

"Who are you?" he demanded.

Anna's face turned white in fright as she stared at the barrel of the gun in front of her.

"Close the door," the man said, waving at the door with his gun.

Anna froze, her eyes darting from Connor to the gunman.

"I said close the door," the armed man repeated the order.

As Anna rushed to do as he asked, she noticed the metal folding chair beside the door. Her eyes met Connor's, and realization flashed across his face.

"Please don't kill me!" Connor cried dramatically, waving his arms wildly, obviously trying to get the assailant's eyes on him. "What do you want? Money?"

The armed man frowned at him. "You do what I ask you to and maybe I won't kill you. Right now, what I want is for you to shut up. Although," the man pondered, "cash might be a nice bonus."

Anna already had the chair in her hands and was lifting it up higher and higher.

"Sure," Connor said, shifting slightly so the gunman's eyes were drawn even further away from Anna. "We can get it. Then, will you leave us alone?"

A sudden motion from the corner of his eyes alerted the intruder that something was going on, but before he could turn around, Anna brought the chair down on his head with a surprisingly powerful force.

The gunman crumbled to the floor. A rush of adrenaline pumped through Anna, and she wasn't sure whether she should feel guilty or be proud of knocking a man unconscious.

Chapter Three

Connor stared at the woman before him, undeniably impressed by what he'd just seen her do.

"Who is that? What is going on here?" she demanded, dropping the chair.

"I don't know. Nice job knocking that guy out." Connor grabbed the man's gun. He had more than a vague idea of who this man was. But it was none of her business.

"You got shot today, and now this man is trying to shoot you. You really don't know?"

"Just be quiet and let me think."

Anna crouched beside the unconscious man, checking his pulse. "He's probably going to wake up soon," she said.

He had to get out of here with her now. She'd seen too much. Not to mention she'd otherwise be in here alone with the unconscious man when the other man came into the room or when the attacker regained consciousness.

Connor would hate it if she got killed on his account. He opened the door a crack and looked out to see a second gunman walking towards the room wearing a dark jacket, a sinister look in his eye. From the way he hitched one hand to the side, holding his leather jacket to cover his concealed weapon, Connor knew this man was ready to finish the job that the first man had failed to complete.

Grabbing the chair Anna had used to knock out the first armed man, he placed it under the handle of the door. It would probably not last, but it should give them some time. Hopefully, the man wouldn't rattle the door too much to avoid attracting attention.

He ran to the window and looked out, relieved when he saw that it led to a flat roof. "Is there a fire escape out here?"

She nodded. "Yes. It leads to the parking lot right behind the hospital."

Connor grabbed her hand and dragged her toward the window. "You have to leave with me now."

"I will do no such thing," the nurse retorted, slapping his hand away. "Why would I go anywhere with you?"

"We don't have time for this. There's another shooter walking down the hall toward us right now. You've seen my face, and you've seen that guy's face. So, come with me now or he will kill you."

"Let go of me." She shoved him away with surprising force, causing him to hide a grimace as pain flared from his wound. Only the drive to escape kept the pain at bay. Self-preservation was the greatest painkiller of all.

Connor didn't want it to come to this, but he held up the gun. Her eyes went wide. He pulled her again toward the window, and instead of complying, she kicked and fought with more strength and skill than he'd expected. Normally he'd be able to handle it, but this was sapping his strength too much.

"Why should I believe you?" she demanded.

She had barely finished talking when they heard someone jiggle the handle of the door forcefully.

"Let me in," a sinister voice growled.

"Believe me now?" Connor asked.

"Open this door now," the deep voice rumbled on the other side of the door.

Connor was already on the move, and thankfully Anna followed. Grabbing Anna's hand, he pulled her through the window and towards the fire escape, urging her to move faster. They hurried down the fire escape and had reached the ground when they heard a noise above them and looked up to see the gunman at the top of the fire escape.

"Run!" Connor ordered as they ran towards the parking lot, pain searing into his side like fire as his lungs burned from exhaustion. "Where's your car?"

"I don't have a car."

"What? Why?"

"I have my reasons."

"Fine. I'll take one."

"You mean steal one?"

"Uh, yeah. Usually, I'd do this differently, but we're in a hurry." He ran up to a car, picked up a rock, and crashed it through the driver's side rear window.

"Are you kidding me?" she shouted. "Who are you?"

"Just get in!" he snapped, getting in the front passenger seat and preparing to hotwire the car. "You drive in case I have to shoot."

"I can't drive."

"What? Ugh!" Frustration burned through him as he fumbled with the wires. "Fine. I'll drive."

She didn't budge.

"I bet your mom told you not to get in a car with a stranger, but this is life or death here. Get in."

Connor found the wires he needed and touched them together again and again until the car roared to life. He looked out the window at Anna, who was still on the other side of the car. This woman was impossible.

"Get in now!" He hated to do it, but he pointed his gun at her.

*****

At the sight of that gun pointed right at her, Anna took a step back, ready to run. She felt the blood drain from her face, confusion clouding her mind. Why should she trust this man? Was this all one big setup?

What if he was a trafficker and he wanted her to get in the car so he could abduct her? Visions of when she'd been abducted flashed through her mind. She'd been so trusting back then, but she had been overpowered and quickly transported away from her Amish community. Anna still remembered the feeling of the trafficker's hand over her mouth when he'd taken her, shoving her into his buggy.

Anna heard running feet behind her and saw the gunman running towards them in the parking lot, his gun aimed at her.

So many guns. She hated guns.

Anna wanted to crawl under the car and close her eyes. Instead, she grabbed the door handle and jumped into the car on the passenger side. Anna slammed the door closed, and John stomped on the gas, racing the car out of the parking lot. They were almost through the lot when the man lifted his gun and fired twice at the car.

Anna yelped, crouching low in her seat as John got them out of there.

"It's okay," he said, trying to calm her down. "We've gotten away."

Anna slowly lifted her head and turned around to look at him, her eyes wide in shock and fear, then anger. "Who are you?" she asked the man sitting beside her, looking at him as if seeing him for the first time. Fury infused her veins. "And what is going on? You just put me in danger. He could have shot me. And you just stole this car, buster! That makes me an accessory to the crime, I think, or maybe an accomplice. I don't know. But I think I deserve to know what's going on."

John sighed as they rode on, his eyes looking at the rearview mirror from time to time. "It was either break the window and steal the car or we'd be dead. Next time, I'll call for a cab when we're being shot at." He scrubbed his hand over his face.

"Answer my question."

"I can't."

"Seriously? You just led me on a wild bullet chase, and you can't tell me what's going on and who those men are? And who you are?" she demanded.

John—whatever his name was—gripped the steering wheel with white knuckles and looked at his rearview mirror.

"We have to call the cops," Anna said. "I don't have a phone. And you didn't have one on you when you were admitted."

"You mean you don't own a phone or it's not with you?"

"I don't own one."

"No phone and you don't drive. Are you Amish?"

16

"I used to be. Not anymore. And actually, I did own a cell phone, only because I was a midwife and it was necessary."

"Okay." He dragged out the word, nodding slowly. "Whatever. But no cops. Not until I can figure out what is happening."

Chapter Four

Two hours ago, Anna had been fantasizing about ending her shift and baking herself a delicious and decadent chocolate cake that she wouldn't share with anybody else. That seemed like a distant memory.

Now she stared silently out the window, seated beside a man who was a shady criminal at best. And she was still trying to wrap her mind around it. Fortunately, her companion hadn't uttered even one word in the last several minutes. Anna guessed he understood that she needed to ponder recent events.

Now his silence was making her feel tense, and she couldn't handle it anymore. So, she turned in her seat to look at him.

"Why don't you want to go to the cops?" she asked.

"How do you think those men at the hospital knew where to find me?"

Anna opened her mouth to say something, saw his point, and clamped her mouth shut.

"You brought me into the hospital, and they called the cops to report a gunshot injury. Then they show up at the hospital to kill me."

"Why were those men trying to kill you?"

He just stared ahead blankly. This was becoming a habit, and it was annoying.

"Listen, buster, you tell me what's going on right now or I won't take care of your injury anymore," Anna spat out. She knew it was wrong to say that, but she needed to know the truth. Hopefully, he wouldn't know that she was bluffing.

John sighed as they rode on, his eyes looking at the rearview mirror from time to time. "Look, your name is Anna, right? We might be on the run together for a while, so I agree that you should know what happened. First of all, my name isn't John Blake. It's Connor Sinclair."

She nodded. "That's a good start. So, you lied about your name."

"You catch on quick. I'm an undercover field agent for CPDU, the Covert Police Detectives Unit."

She glanced at him. Was he completely making this up?

"I know, I know. I don't have my badge, so I can't prove it. I was undercover. Human trafficking is a big problem in Maine. I was in deep cover with an assassination organization. A big human trafficking leader named Korovin hired the assassination group to take out a woman named Cassidy. She's the founder of Pure Love, a huge nonprofit that rescues and cares for survivors of human trafficking. She has key information on a flash drive that would probably enable us to take down Korovin's entire sex trafficking ring and several others, and that's why he wants her killed.

"I got close enough for the assassination group to trust me, and the CPDU created a cover for me. My fake story was that I was a groomer, or someone who lures people into sex slavery. It's disgusting and horrific. I went to the assassination group saying I wanted to change professions and become an assassin. When I told them that I'd worked for the trafficking ring, they wanted me to be the one to take out Cassidy because of my fake background.

"As soon as I got the kill order, I had the proof we needed, and as a bonus, we were going to protect Cassidy. When the mark turned out to be someone with evidence to bring down Korovin, it was a double win. I left, pretending to go after Cassidy. When they realized I wasn't going to kill her, they went after me and shot me. Cassidy got away. Now I don't know where she is. Anyway, that's why I didn't have any identification on me when you found me."

He fell silent, then looked at her. She could see him from the corner of her eye as she stared at the road ahead. So many questions and emotions somersaulted through her brain, ramming into each other like a chaotic circus.

"Oh, and the reason we can't call the police? Because there is a mole either in the local police station or at the Covert Police Detectives Unit. That's how the assassins knew I was undercover. It happened right after I made the call to CPDU, telling them that Cassidy Hendricks was the target and where she was and that I'd been ordered to kill her. Minutes after I hung up with them, they found me and shot me while I was running, but I got away."

Was this guy legit? Or did he just make all of that up? Was he just telling her not to call the police so they wouldn't arrest him for kidnapping her?

Why on earth had she gotten into this mess with him? She was always so careful, so cautious ever since she'd been kidnapped by the traffickers.

This man could be working for them, trying to lure her into sex slavery again. Anna put her palms over her eyes as if to stop the chaos swirling in her head.

John, or Connor—whatever his name was—chuckled humorlessly. "You probably think I'm crazy or lying. I get it. I would too."

"Uh, yeah."

"And you probably don't trust me one bit."

"What, did you go to mind reader school or something? How did you guess?" she asked sarcastically, wanting to bash her head against the window.

"So, listen. I don't want to make you do anything you don't want to do. If you want to leave me and go on alone, that's fine. But they will come after you eventually."

"What? They're coming after me? I don't know anything!" she cried, anger making her blood pressure rise. She felt the pulse on her wrist. Her heart was racing. Taking deep breaths, she tried to calm down. It wasn't working.

"Sorry. I don't mean to scare you. All I'm saying is you can go on alone, but I do have years of advanced military training and CPDU training. I'm not saying you're weak or not capable of taking care of yourself, but these guys are trained professional assassins. I can keep you safe if you stick with me. If I'm not with you, I can't protect you. Also, to be honest, I really need your medical help. Without you, that wound will get infected. I can't reach the exit wound on my back, so I can't change the bandage myself. And once I get that flash drive from Cassidy Hendricks, we will have the information we need to take Korovin and his trafficking ring down, then your life will go back to how it was before."

Which was completely boring, but how could she complain after this?

"Anna, please. I need your help to shut this sex trafficking ring down."

She shut her eyes for a moment. If he really was telling the truth, how incredible would it be to help him apprehend men who kidnapped and sold young women for a living?

The same type of men who'd kidnapped her.

She could still feel the trafficker's rough hand covering her mouth, the dampness and dustiness of the crowded warehouse…

It was the place where she'd found her calling to be a nurse. But she couldn't let her mind wander back there again. Not now.

Was Connor one of those men?

"Look, I have a gun. If I wanted to kidnap you, I would have by now," he said as if reading her thoughts.

"You pointed that gun at me at the hospital and in the parking lot!"

"You wouldn't get in the car, and that assassin was after us. That was to save our lives. I only did it to get you into the car so we could get away from him and not get shot. You can trust me, Anna. If I wanted to kidnap you, I would have by now."

Trust him? What if he was playing her? "Some traffickers take weeks to talk to the person they're targeting to establish a relationship with them before kidnapping them, luring them in before the victim even knows what's happened," she said.

"You seem to know more about human trafficking than the average person," he observed.

"Yeah, I do."

When she said nothing more, he added, "Anna, you're already in the car with me. I'm trying to show you that it's up to you if you want to stick with me or not. I do have your best interest in mind."

"I didn't ask for this." She glared at him. "I'm supposed to trust you because you dragged me into whatever it is you're involved in? This isn't fair." Anna didn't mean to sound like a child, and she winced at how the words had come out.

Connor glanced at her as if he felt a sliver of pity for her. "Life is not always about being fair." His voice took on a dark tone when he made the statement. Anna looked closely at him only to see the same blank expression on his face. What was he thinking about? What had happened to him?

Anna turned back in her seat and stared out her window. "But why would they want to kill me? I don't know anything; I'm just a nurse."

"The moment you took me into that hospital, you'd already been involved too much. That was part of the reason I asked you not to take me inside. When you saw the first assassin, that sealed the deal. At least you were in your normal clothes, so they might not realize you work there."

"And how long before I can go back to my life?" Anna asked him.

Connor shrugged. "I don't know. Maybe a few days at the very least. Could be a few weeks. I have no idea how long it'll take to get that flash drive and make the arrests."

"I'm going to lose my job. I worked so hard for it," she said dejectedly.

"I'll do my best along with CPDU to explain to the hospital that you were helping me on this mission. I'm sure they won't fire you."

She raised one eyebrow. "Okay. Fine. I'll help you."

"Thank you. I, along with CPDU, appreciate it. I'll make sure you're acknowledged."

"Just seeing those scumbags getting arrested would be great. Can I go home and get some things first?"

"They might know your address, if they've figured out who you are. But maybe not. Hopefully they won't realize you work here because you're not wearing your scrubs. I have no way of knowing. Just to be safe, you shouldn't go back home until this is over."

"Then can I go to the store and get a change of clothes and some other things?"

"Sure. We can go to the nearest department store."

"There's one about ten minutes from here," Anna replied, feeling guilty. She was surprised he didn't see it written all over her face.

"Then sure thing. As long as you get in, grab what you want, and get out in under five minutes. But first, I need to grab my go bag. I have a few stashed in safe places. There's one in a storage unit just a few blocks away from here. I have cash in it, so we'll be able to get what we need."

Anna nodded, just grateful he was allowing her to do this. They stopped at the storage unit, where Connor quickly retrieved his go bag. He got back inside the car and unzipped the bag, revealing bullets, guns, water bottles, beef jerky, a change of clothes, wads of cash, and probably a few other items underneath. Anna saw a candy bar and chuckled. There was also his CPDU badge, which he'd been unable to have on him while he was undercover with the assassins.

"Ah, so there's your badge," Anna observed. "You had nothing on you when I found you in the parking lot."

"Of course not," Connor said. "It would have blown my cover."

Anna peeked in the bag and smiled.

"What?" Connor said.

"A candy bar? Really? Is that a necessity?"

"Yes. Priorities, Anna."

Anna could see the playful smile tugging at the corner of his mouth. Maybe he wasn't so serious all the time after all.

Still, she didn't trust him. Not one bit. Even if he did have a CPDU badge, that didn't prove his innocence. He could still be secretly working along with the assassins or be up to something else that was immoral or illegal.

Connor drove them to the store, then parked in the parking lot. "Just be fast and get back here. You stay too long, and we would be in danger."

She stepped out of the car, nodded at him through the window, and walked away. After waiting a moment, she glanced back to see Connor looking in the opposite direction.

This was her chance. She would not be kidnapped by those monsters again. Of course, he had told her the police had a mole, so that she wouldn't report anything or go to the police for help.

Did he really think she was a complete moron?

Anna had learned a long time ago not to trust anyone when she'd been tied up and transported in a buggy to a dirty warehouse. There, she'd waited to be sold.

Never again.

She walked casually to the store, went around the side of the building, then bolted toward the police station behind the store.

Chapter Five

Anna burst into the police station and quickly headed towards the officer at the front desk.

"I want to report a crime," she said, breathing hard and looking at the cop in front of her whose name tag said *Officer Barrett.* "A man kidnapped me at gunpoint. He's in a stolen car outside. Gunmen were after him at the hospital."

Barrett looked at her, quickly rising from his seat. "You said he is outside? Where?"

"Right there," she said, pointing out the window. She looked closer and realized he was gone. "He was in the parking lot in front of that store. He must have realized I came here and took off." She gave a description of him and the car.

"Rogers, I think we've found him!" the sergeant called. Another officer came into the room.

"You know of him?" Anna asked, worried by how the officer spoke.

"Yes, ma'am," Barrett replied, his eyes on her. "The man you're dealing with is a monster, and it's a good thing you came to us. I need you to fill out this form and then tell me everything that happened. But first, can we go outside so you can show me where he was parked?"

Anna nodded, happy to help.

"Great. Let's go out this way," Barrett said, leading her out the back door.

As they walked out the door to the parking lot, Anna slowed down. Why were they going this way?

She heard a noise and turned to see two men walking toward her. There was something about them that instantly made her wary, and she walked backward to the police station door, shrinking away from them. One of them spoke to Barrett.

"Is this her?"

Barrett nodded, and before Anna could even wrap her head around what was happening, one of them pointed a gun at her. Tears filled her eyes as she realized she'd chosen the wrong side.

Connor had been telling the truth after all.

"You'll come quietly with us if you don't want a bullet in your head."

One roughly grabbed her arm. They pulled her across the small parking lot as she fought to wrench out of his grip, but his grip was like iron.

The parking lot was concealed by other buildings and a fence. No one would see what was happening.

From the corner of her eye, she watched as the other newcomer threw a small envelope in the cop's direction. The sound of it landing in the officer's hand was like a sucker punch to her guts. Connor had warned her that there was a mole at the local police station, and she had refused to listen to him.

Or was she being trafficked again? *No, not again!* she thought.

The very thing she'd been trying to avoid was happening to her again.

27

"Move," the man holding her said as he pushed forward.

Anna struggled to stay on her feet as the two men hustled her into a van behind the station.

No. She couldn't let this happen. She couldn't let them get her into that van.

She kicked, fought, elbowed, and clawed, trying to free herself from their grasp. For a moment, she was free, and she sprinted toward the front of the building.

"Get her!"

She could hear the men's footsteps pounding behind her.

Almost there.

One of them tackled her, wrestling her to the concrete. She landed hard, the wind instantly knocked out of her. Pain scorched her knees, elbows, and ribs as her skin was bruised and scraped. She cried out, then screamed for help as loud as she could.

They shoved her into the van and one climbed in with her while the other went to the driver's seat. Anna watched as the doors slammed closed and the van began to move. Gun still on her, the man sitting near her cuffed her hands and then forced her to sit on the floor.

When Connor had pointed his gun at her, she'd just been angry. Somehow, a small part of her had known he wouldn't hurt her, even though she'd turned on him.

Now, at the sight of this gun pointed at her by these men, she was terrified, searching for a way out.

"Start talking," ordered the one who sat near her. "Or we'll shoot you right here. You're worthless to us."

"But you're police. You should be ashamed of yourselves," Anna spat out.

The man who was driving laughed. "We're not actually police officers, lady."

Anna stared up at the menacing eyes looking down on her and swallowed hard.

They're imposters, Anna thought. *Cowards. Dressing up as police officers to harm innocent women.*

Even though they didn't lay a hand on her, it was clear that should she refuse to answer they wouldn't mind doing that, or even worse.

She started to talk, starting from when she had found Connor in the hospital's parking lot right up until the moment she walked into the police station. When she was done, the two men glanced at each other before turning their attention back to her.

"Did you see a flash drive with him?" the driver asked.

Anna shook her head. "There was nothing on him when I found him. Not a single thing in his pocket or on him. He said he was looking for it, and he didn't know where it was." The last part was a lie, but it was mixed in with enough of the truth that she hoped they wouldn't realize it.

"Am I free to go now?" she asked timidly when they didn't ask her anything for a moment.

"Free?" the one near her chuckled, the sound dry and unpleasant. "Well, if the boss decides not to kill you, maybe. For now, all you are is bait."

Anna stared at him, wondering what he meant by that.

"That man you were with—do you have any idea who he is?"

Anna shook her head, her mouth too dry with fear to reply.

"You are scared of us, but the man you were with is the one you should be scared of."

Anna doubted that but knew better than to say so. She nodded.

The man sitting near her smiled, seeing the look of disbelief on her face. "Do you think we would be chasing after him if he was a nice man living a quiet life with a beautiful wife, a kid, and a white-picket-fence house in the suburbs?" He shook his head, purposely lowering his voice to add gravitas to his tale, even as his eyes danced in laughter. He went on his knees beside her and started to stroke her hair, laughing even more when she struggled in futility. "Knight Clayton is one of the scariest men I've ever seen. He is an assassin. He kills people for money, and he likes it so much, he makes men like us scared of him. When he hears that we have you, he's going to come and try to rescue you. That is how we'll get him."

But would he really care about her at all after she betrayed him?

Laughing, the one who wasn't driving taped her mouth shut then tied her arms and legs together with rope, as the van sped along the road. Tears rolled down Anna's cheeks, the whole situation was so painfully unfair and familiar. How had she gotten mixed up in all of this? She closed her eyes and began to pray silently.

Oh Lord, You said that we should call upon You in our times of trouble and You would hear us. I'm in trouble, Lord, and I'll admit that I am very, very scared. But I also know that You're a God of miracles and that is what I need right now, Lord. A miracle...

Anna prayed until she didn't even know what to say anymore, struggling within herself not to give in to despair. The van suddenly stopped, and the driver got out of the car. The other one went and sat in the passenger seat, playing a game on his phone. Anna stared at the closed side door. The guy in the front seat seemed pretty occupied, and the noises on his game were not exactly quiet.

She began to look around the van for something she could use to free herself.

It didn't take long for her to realize that she was completely stuck. There was no way she could escape. There were no sharp edges. The cuffs and ropes that held her captive gave no indication of being able to be loosened.

Instead, all she could do was try to open that door and get someone to see her, even if it was for only a second until the man in the front seat noticed. She wiggled and inched toward the door, then tried opening it with her elbow. When that didn't work, she tried using her feet.

Anna felt hot tears in her eyes and was ready to give up when she heard a noise at the door of the van. Probably the other man returning from whatever it was he went to do. She scooted backward.

There was a knock on the driver's side door. It was four slow knocks, then two quick ones. The man in the front seat looked, and when Anna craned her neck, she could see that the man had returned. "He's back already?" Anna heard the man in the front seat mumble as he clicked the unlock button.

The doors unlocked, and the other man opened the driver's side door. Anna's eyes opened wide when she realized it was Connor wearing the driver's sweatshirt. Clearly, the man in the passenger seat was too involved in his game to notice that.

Within a half a second, Connor was inside the van and pushed the man's head forward into the dashboard with lightning speed. The phone fell out of the man's hand as he fell unconscious. Connor got back out of the van, then the van jolted down twice. Had Connor just punctured the tires?

The side door opened, and Connor stood there, wearing the driver's clothes and holding a pocketknife. Anna squinted in disbelief.

He didn't say anything, just used the pocketknife to cut the ropes on her wrists and legs. He ripped the duct tape off her mouth, and she winced.

"Let's go," he said gruffly, grabbing her bound hands and helping her out.

Anna was too happy to be surprised, and she quickly followed him out of the van. Was he rescuing her or kidnapping her again?

"Come on," he said, and they quickly jogged across the road toward, presumably, a different stolen car.

Anna followed him, getting in the car and taking the passenger seat beside him. She watched with relief as he started the car and they sped away from the gas station, her heartbeat slowly returning to normal.

When she could no longer see the van, she closed her eyes and said a prayer of gratitude, ashamed to admit that she had been so close to losing faith. Then she turned to the man God had used and knew instantly from the expression on his face that he was mad at her.

And she was angry too. Instead of the tirade of angry complaints she wanted to unleash, she sat in silence until she could compose herself.

"Um, thanks," she managed to squeak out, then shrank into her seat when he turned to look at her.

Nope, he was definitely not happy with her. Not in the least.

Chapter Six

For one moment, Connor had been distracted. Just one moment. A car had pulled up next to him, and a mom and young boy got out of the car. The kid tripped and cried out, and Connor had looked to make sure the boy was okay. It had only been a few seconds. When he looked back where Anna had been, she was gone.

Had she run into the store? Or had she run in another direction? Where was she?

Then he'd seen blonde hair flying as she ran into the police station.

She'd betrayed him. He'd told her why she couldn't go to the cops, and she'd outright turned on him.

After finally rescuing Anna from the two thugs in the van, Connor drove away with her as fast as he could, seething with anger at the woman beside him. Yet, at the same time, he was grateful she was safe now.

"How did you find me?" she asked.

"I saw you run into the police station, then I saw a van with no back windows leave the station a few minutes later, and I figured you were in it. I followed the van until it stopped. When the driver went into the store, I waited until he came out. I asked him if I could buy some drugs off him and he had some on him. It was a hunch, but I was right. He came over to me behind the store, so I knocked him out, stole his clothes, and made a run for the van. The other guy was a fool too, totally distracted by his game. I probably didn't even need to take that guy's clothes to get him to unlock the van."

"I'm sorry for going to the cops. I was scared and I didn't know what to do."

"So, you did the one thing I asked you not to," Connor said through gritted teeth. "I told you why we couldn't trust those cops."

"One officer's name was Officer Paul Barrett. Probably a fake name. I didn't catch the others' names."

"It probably is a fake name. Thanks. I'll let my team know."

"If you knew what I've been through, you would understand why I didn't believe you and why I went to the cops," Anna said with a soft sigh.

He paused, glancing at her. "What do you mean?" he asked cautiously.

Anna turned away, looking out the window. "I don't trust anyone anymore."

"Someone hurt you?"

She nodded.

"Crazy ex-boyfriend?" He knew he was prying, but he was curious.

"No, it's not like that."

He remembered what she'd said earlier about human trafficking and how she knew so much about it. Now that he looked at her closely, she looked so familiar. He had a feeling she might have been one of the Amish women his team had rescued from traffickers in Unity, but he wasn't sure.

He asked quietly, "Were you trafficked, Anna?"

Silence. For the first time since he met her, she said nothing. A single tear trickled down her cheek, telling him all he needed to know.

He looked back at the road, using his own silence to let her know he wasn't going to pry anymore. If she wanted to, maybe she'd eventually want to talk about it, but he doubted it. No wonder she'd gone to the police. She probably thought he was luring her back into sex slavery.

All his anger toward her evaporated, leaving behind genuine pity for this woman whom he barely knew. The anger he felt now was only directed at the scumbags who'd kidnapped her. Hopefully, they'd been arrested, and hadn't evaded the police as they often did.

While working at CPDU, he'd worked on several human trafficking cases. He knew about what the survivors endured and he'd seen the aftermath and destruction of human souls. Women, young boys, little girls, teens, even men. He'd been on missions to rescue them. He'd met survivors, looked into their eyes and could only imagine the horrors they'd been through because he'd never experienced it himself.

He knew that look. The same look that was on Anna's face right now.

Finally, Anna spoke. "My fears, though misguided, were credible. But God used you to get me out of that van."

Her statement had Connor's hand tightening on the steering wheel.

"You think God used me to rescue you?" he asked, his tone like barbed wire. "I rescued you, not God."

"I prayed to God and He sent you."

Not ready to even begin to correct her belief, he fixed his eyes on the steering wheel. For a few moments, Anna was silent again.

"We need to switch cars. It's possible they put a tracker on this, and even if they didn't, they know what car we're driving right now," Connor said.

They pulled into an old gas station parking lot that looked abandoned. While Connor hot-wired a sad and tired-looking old car, Anna stood by silently.

"What? Am I going to prison for this?" she finally blurted.

"No. I'll explain to CPDU that I had to keep switching vehicles so the assassins wouldn't follow us. You won't get in trouble. I'll tell them none of this was your fault."

"That's it? Seriously? So where are we going now?" she asked, letting out a heavy sigh.

He looked at her, then looked away without responding.

She rolled her eyes. "I understand you don't trust me because I went to the cops. But obviously, I know you're telling the truth now. Even though I still don't know who you are, I think you're my best option now."

He chuckled mirthlessly. "What do you think you know?"

"They said your name is Knight Clayton."

"I see those goons became chatty. What else did they tell you?"

"That you kill people for money," Anna replied, watching him as she did, waiting for a hint.

He didn't give one.

"Okay, how about something else about you that is not a lie?" she asked.

This time his head turned slowly towards her. "How about how much I really want you to stop talking? That is one truth."

36

Anna chuckled. "Okay, I get it. You are the big and silent type."

He shrugged slightly.

Anna was unfazed. "Okay, fine. Since we might be stuck together for a while, I might as well tell you about myself."

He didn't reply and she continued talking.

"I'm Anna Hershberger and I am a nurse, but I guess you already know that." She chuckled a little. "I guess some of this seems surreal to me. I mean, I won't say my life has been boring. And yes, you were right. I was kidnapped once before by sex traffickers." She glanced at him, as if looking for a reaction again. "Usually people are either shocked when I say that or have no idea what human trafficking is."

"I figured that had happened to you. And I'm sorry, Anna. Truly."

She nodded slowly. "Thank you. Some of the young women in my Amish community were kidnapped by this sex trafficking ring."

"In Unity? My team worked on that case. I thought you looked familiar."

Anna nodded. "God proved stronger than evil and we were rescued by CPDU before we were…sold."

"I'm so sorry that happened to you, Anna. We rescued so many girls and young women that day. I'm sorry I didn't recognize you at first."

"It's okay, I don't recognize you either. One good thing that came out of that experience, though, was that I discovered what I wanted to do with my life. I was a midwife in the community, but I wanted to do more. There was this girl who got injured when we were with the kidnappers, my friend Liz, and I took care of a cut on her leg. That was when I knew that I wanted to be a nurse. So, I left my community to go to nursing school."

37

Besides not owning a car or phone, there were several other hints that she'd grown up Amish. First, her lack of jewelry and makeup—not that she needed it at all. Then there was her constant mentioning of God. But even more surprising was the fact that he had not realized she had been one of the girls he rescued a few years ago. Now that he thought about it, his mind going over the faces of the girls they had broken out of that warehouse, she did look vaguely familiar.

He imagined she looked much different now, her face holding none of the fear and confusion it had held that night. Like all the other girls and women, she'd been dirty, tired, and some of them had been battered and bruised. In his mind he smiled, wondering what she thought about the fact that he was one of the men who had rescued her. Probably say something about God working in mysterious ways. And it was this train of thought that had his mood turning sour again.

In Connor's opinion, God did not work in mysterious ways. This was something he had learned the hard way. For so long, anger and grief had filled him. As usual, he held onto the anger, dragging it out until it enveloped him and changed him.

"So, do you have any family who might miss you?" Connor asked.

Anna glanced at Connor, surprised as much by the fact that he was talking to her as by the personal nature of the question.

He glanced at her before turning back to the road. "Won't your family be worried if they don't hear from you?"

Anna looked out the window. "My parents died just after I left the Amish. I was an only child. I went home to be with them, and at least I got to see them before they died."

"I'm sorry, Anna." He felt silly for saying it again, but he meant it. "I didn't realize."

"It's okay. My mom called me her miracle baby. They couldn't have children for years before I came along. Even if my parents were still alive, they never had phones in the house, like all the Amish in Unity.

Sometimes it's a few days before they would get a message or missed call. As for everyone else, I kind of lost touch with them once I got really busy with nursing school, then work."

Without her use of a phone, any prolonged absence or lack of communication could be easily explained away.

There was a note of nostalgia in the way she spoke about her family.

At least she had a family at one time, even though they were gone now.

"What about you? Do you have family missing you?" she asked, as if reading his thoughts.

"No." He stared blankly ahead.

"Come on, everyone has family."

"Not me."

"Did they die too?"

"Why do you ask so many questions?" he snapped, and when she frowned and turned away, the sting of regret filled him. "Sorry, I didn't mean to sound like such a jerk."

She stared out the window for a moment before saying softly, "No one deserves being alone."

"I'm fine with being alone," he said. "I'm not much of a people person."

"Oh really?" she asked sarcastically. There, her smile was back.

"Is it that obvious?" He chuckled. "So, do you have friends who will notice you missing?"

"I don't really have a social life or any close friends. Just the nurses at work and maybe my neighbors. For a few days, they might just think I'm sick. But they're going to get worried in a day or two."

"So, were you shunned after you left?"

"No."

"Really? I thought you get cut off completely once you leave the flock."

"A lot of people assume that. I can't count how many times someone looked on me with pity when I informed them I used to be Amish and decided to leave to pursue my dream of being a nurse. They think that means I have been abandoned by my family and friends."

"That's not the truth?"

"No. See, I wasn't baptized. I never officially joined the church. When I decided to leave, I broke no vows. So I'm not shunned. Even still, I'm not sure how people would react if I went back to visit. I haven't returned since my mom died." Anna paused as she seemed lost in thought for a few moments. "Choosing to be baptized Amish is a decision that is never to be taken lightly or forced on anyone. Once you choose that path, you're expected to follow through. Sometimes I wonder if I would have decided to leave to become a nurse after joining the church. Would I have still done it, even though I knew I'd be shunned?" She suddenly looked embarrassed to have revealed something so personal to him.

"Good thing then you didn't have to make that decision. No need to worry about it."

"I guess you're right." She rambled on, talking about her childhood and the difference between the life she used to live and the one she now lived, sometimes laughing at her own jokes. He let her go on and on. It wasn't like he had anything better to do at the moment than listen to her talk.

And for the first time, he didn't mind it.

Not that he enjoyed her talking, but it was tolerable. For a while.

"Are you going to keep on yapping, or can I expect some peace and quiet soon?" His tone was harsher than he'd meant it to be, followed by a quick stab of remorse. To his surprise, rather than take offense and then keep quiet like he expected she would, her lips turned up in a smile.

"Okay, I guess I'm going to need more than a few stories to win your trust." She settled back in her seat. "Too bad I can't cook for you. One taste of my chicken and dumplings or shoofly pie and I bet you'd be in a much better mood. And if that doesn't work, then nothing probably is going to."

Connor looked at her. "Everyone thinks their cooking is the bomb until it all blows up in their face."

His statement was delivered with such a deadpan expression that Anna couldn't help herself. She burst into laughter, her shoulders shaking as she stared at him.

Why did watching her brag about her cooking skills and seeing her face light up with humor have his anger fizzing away?

Grace would have loved her.

The thought was gone as soon as it came, but it had stayed long enough to shake him. He couldn't deny the fact that in so many ways, this beautiful blonde woman reminded him of his late wife. Even though Grace had been a brunette with dark eyes, they shared similar traits: they were both stubborn, sassy, and they both talked way too much.

Shaking his head, he held tightly to the memory of his wife, pushing all thoughts of Anna away and locking them back in the box in his mind that he was earmarking "loud and annoying" for now.

The memories were all he had left of Grace, and he had no plans of ever letting go of them.

Pulling into a parking lot, he stopped the car.

"What are we doing here?" Anna asked, staring at the run-down department store in front of them.

He unclasped his seatbelt, wincing as he slowly motioned for her to get out of the car. "We still need a change of clothes, and we still need food. You'll also need to cut and color your hair. And I should get more medical supplies."

With these words, he pushed the door on his side open and got out of the car.

Anna cocked her head to the side, raising her eyebrows. "Say what now?"

Chapter Seven

For several moments Anna sat still in the car, a shocked expression on her face. By the time she gathered her wits about her, Connor was already halfway to the store. Jumping out of the car and slamming the door closed behind her, she raced after him.

"Why do you think I need to color and cut my hair?"

Connor did not stop walking or even bother to look at her. "Because it's the first thing people recognize when they see you. I don't think you need me to explain to you why now is not a good time for certain people to be recognizing you. They're looking for a woman with long blonde hair, so better to have it short and a different color."

Anna growled in frustration, gathering her long blonde ponytail in her hands. "So what if people remember what my hair looks like? I'm not the only person in the world with blonde hair."

"Not very many people have hair that long." He stopped near the store's entrance.

"It was down to my knees when I left the Amish. I cut over two feet off."

"Seriously?"

Anna nodded. "Amish women don't cut their hair. I mean, they trim it every now and then, but they don't ever cut much length off."

"Look, I understand that you don't want to change the color or cut it. But this is not the time to be vain. You'll get your pretty hair back when you're safe again."

Anna's eyebrows shot up at the unexpected compliment. She would have expected him to say the last bit with a sarcastic tone, but he actually sounded sincere, as though he felt bad about asking her to do this.

"I'm sorry, Anna," he said.

Anna's fists were clenched by her side as she glared at the man who calmly waited and watched her, almost as if he was daring her to make a scene. Taking a deep breath, she decided to give reason a try.

"It's not about vanity. It goes so much beyond that. I've never colored my hair in my life. It's not the Amish way. My hair is one of the last ties I have to my Amish roots. I know you don't care, but do you have any clue how hard it would be to get a dark color out of my hair? Especially a box color? It's not as easy as you think."

"We need to move. We've been here too long. A stupid move on my part."

Grabbing her wrist and ignoring the small gasp of surprise from her, he dragged her into the store. As soon as they were inside, Anna pulled her hand out of his grip and rubbed the area around her wrist. His grip had not been hard or painful at all. His grip had been firm, yet gentle. She had just been surprised by the contact.

"So why don't Amish women cut their hair?" Connor walked quickly, obviously expecting her to follow him.

Anna scrambled to keep up, his long strides forcing her to walk even faster. "In the Bible, it says a woman's hair is her crowning glory. I was always taught to keep it long and never color it."

"Even when you're doing it for your own survival?"

Anna could hear the frown in his voice and didn't blame him for his doubts. "I just really don't feel right about this."

"I guess you're not worried about dying." They entered the clothing section of the store.

Anna stopped walking. "Of course, I am. I'm terrified. Ever considered that?"

The only thing that had stopped her from breaking down up till that point was him. It was crazy to trust someone she just met a few hours ago. Anna knew that God, not Connor, was the one protecting her. It was Him she had faith in to see her through whatever this was. Though, having Connor with her made her feel...safer.

Connor stopped and turned to face her in between racks of clothes. "I'm sorry, Anna. I have considered how you feel about this. I know you must be scared," he said in a quiet voice, almost a whisper. "And again, I'm so sorry you got dragged into this. But we need to do whatever we have to in order to protect ourselves." He reached for her hand again, and this time, she didn't jerk away. Before she could react, he let go. His touch had been warm, gentle, and reassuring.

Her pulse sped up, and when she felt her cheeks heat up, she had to turn away to hide the blush on her face.

Why had his touch affected her like that?

"What about a wig? I could probably find a cheap wig and hide my hair under that. It might not look good close up, but if I wear a hat over it, I think I could make it work," she said, busying herself with sifting through clothes. She then realized she was rifling through men's extra-large shirts.

"Anna, I don't think those will fit you. Not to be forward or anything." He hid a chuckle. "They don't really look like your style."

Her face heated even more with embarrassment. She playfully batted his arm, and he laughed even harder at flustering her. "I know, I

45

know. I guess the women's section would be over there." She gestured toward the women's clothing. As he continued to laugh, she couldn't help but laugh with him. "That's the first time I've heard you really laugh." To be honest, it was a nice change to see this rare mischievous, blithe side of him.

"Don't get used to it," he said sarcastically, still smiling. "Pick whatever you want. Get enough to last a few days. Let's meet back here after."

"Sounds good." Anna hurried toward the women's section. She glanced at the racks of clothes, suddenly confused about what to pick. As she stared at the endless shirts, jeans, and dresses, her mind replayed what had just transpired between Connor and her.

For once, he had seemed happy. For once, all traces of seriousness and the walls he'd built had fallen away. And she had to admit, she liked what had been left: his true, vulnerable self.

She wanted to see more of it. Clearly, he had been through a lot in his life. Maybe grief or hardship had hardened him and made him the way he was.

Annoyed with herself for not being able to focus, Anna grabbed some plaid flannel shirts, two pairs of jeans, two plain t-shirts, and some undergarments. Even after leaving the Amish, Anna hadn't cared that much about fashion. She hadn't gone on shopping sprees like some girls she knew who had left the Amish. When it came to clothing, she had a minimal wardrobe and wore what was practical and comfortable. Besides work, she didn't have much of a social life anyway, except for events at the church she attended in Portland.

Happy with her clothing choices, she made a beeline for the changing rooms.

Maybe as she got to know Connor better, he would let his guard down around her.

*****

46

Connor groaned inwardly, cursing himself for forgetting about women and their shopping habits that wasted time. He figured he'd be waiting for Anna to pick out clothing for a long time.

He remembered the few times he had gone shopping with Grace. The mind-numbing boredom of watching her stare and fawn over outfit after outfit, the tedium only punctuated by the absolute delight of seeing her walk out of the dressing room garbed in whatever dress she was trying on. Of course, even that soon got boring and he always ended up wondering how she had managed to convince him to accompany her. Now he would gladly spend a million years in a shopping mall if he could see his wife again.

Shaking his head and pushing the memories away, he finished picking out his clothing and headed toward the men's changing rooms. Not wanting to stay in one place too long, he scanned the store, making sure there was no threat. Next, his eyes took in all the exits that he could see from here.

After he finished trying on his clothes, he went back to the spot where they'd agreed to meet. Anna was probably going to take forever, and he'd probably have time to go get the groceries while waiting for her.

He was surprised to see her already there, waiting for him. She was admiring a blue flowered sundress, holding it up to herself as if to see if it would fit. "Almost done?" he asked, not sure that it was possible that a woman could finish clothes shopping before him.

She jumped, then quickly put the dress back. "Yeah, I'm done. What took you so long?" she said with a laugh.

"Did you try the clothes on yet?"

"Of course. Ready to go get the food and medical supplies?"

He just smiled at her, impressed. "Wow. You were fast. That's not normal for a woman."

"One thing you should know about me, Connor. I'm not normal at all," she said with a playful smirk, then pivoted and walked toward the food section of the store, that blonde ponytail swishing.

No, she wasn't like any woman he'd ever met. That was official.

"And Connor, I'm not coloring or chopping off my hair," she added over her shoulder. "End of discussion."

Connor couldn't help but grin, shaking his head. She'd get on his last nerve, but he was starting to enjoy her company. He hated to admit it, but he was a little glad she was with him through all of this. Going through this alone would have been lonely, and she made him laugh.

No one had done that in a long time. He'd gotten used to being lonely without even realizing it.

"You coming, buster? Hey, we should get some sunglasses and hats." Anna stopped by the accessories section.

Connor's face heated, embarrassed that he'd been so busy thinking about her effect on him that he'd been lollygagging, and she'd been the one to hurry him along. "You're right. These would look good on you," he said, hurrying over to her and picking up a pair of sunglasses. He carefully put them on her, tucking a piece of hair behind her ear as he did. Realizing what he'd just done, and how close he was standing to her, his heart raced. He couldn't see her eyes now, but he could feel her looking at him, and he took a step back and smiled to cover up his sudden nervousness. "Yup, I was right. You should get those."

She looked in the small mirror on the sunglasses rack. "Thanks," she said shyly, then she grabbed a baseball hat and tossed it to him. "Oh, good. This will help me hide my hair," she said, picking up an oversized hat for herself. "Maybe I can put my hair in a bun and hide it under this."

"I guess that would work. Okay, okay. If you promise to keep it on whenever we're out in public, I won't make you change your hair."

"Thank you!" she said. "Don't worry, I'll be able to make myself look different with this."

"Let's go get some food. We need to get moving."

They made their way toward the food section, and Connor found a stray cart. When he started throwing in chips and other junk food, Anna took over.

"No, no. This won't sustain us. Let me handle this, okay?" she said, taking the cart from him.

He shrugged, not caring enough to argue with her. "Sure. But we can't cook anything on a stove so we can only get ready-to-eat food for now. Just don't get kale or tofu or lentils or other nasty health foods like that, please."

"You don't have to worry about that." She picked out snacks like pistachios, bananas, apples, bottled water, and protein bars, then he threw in some beef jerky and pretzels. "When we get somewhere with a kitchen, I'll make you some real food," she promised.

"I'll hold you to that."

They grabbed some other necessities like medical supplies, toothbrushes, and toiletries, then headed to the checkout. As the cashier was scanning their items, Connor said, "I'll be back in a second." A moment later, Anna's eyes widened when she saw him bring back the blue flowered dress she'd admired, dropping it on the conveyor belt.

She looked at him questioningly.

"I noticed you liked it. It's the least I can do," he said.

She smiled, tilting her head to the side. "Thanks."

After paying, they stopped by the bathrooms to change into their new clothes. He quickly dressed in jeans and a sweatshirt then waited for Anna. Anna walked out of the bathroom in a plaid shirt and jeans with her hair in a bun. He had to admit, as she stood there smiling, she looked pretty.

Beautiful, even.

Someone this annoying should not be saddled with the responsibility of a smile that beautiful.

Anna put on the newsboy hat over her hair, then added the sunglasses. She put her hands on her hips, dramatically posing. "How do I look?"

Grace had taught him that there was only one acceptable reply to the "How do I look" question. But in this case, it didn't really apply.

"Well, you do look different," he said, feeling like an idiot.

"Good. That's what I was going for," she said cheerfully. "Let's hit the road."

They needed to get out of the store and keep moving. By now he was sure Korovin had figured out that the men he had sent to retrieve him were either dead or injured.

More men would be on his trail, ones even more dangerous than the previous ones.

Chapter Eight

Connor pulled the car to a stop and glanced at Anna. She was sleeping, her chest rising and falling rhythmically. He wondered if he had made a mistake in bringing her along. Korovin was wealthy and powerful, but there was no way he had bought every single agent, analyst, police officer or bodyguard in the Covert Police Detectives Unit.

Still, he had no idea who to trust. Not the local police, and regretfully not even the CPDU. There was only one person he could trust, and until he got the signal he was waiting for, he knew he was not safe.

Connor reached into his pocket and retrieved one of the throwaway phones he had bought at the store. Quickly dialing a number, he put the phone to his ear and listened for a few seconds before a voice told him the number was unavailable.

Ending the call, he wondered if Ben Banks had also been compromised, then shook his head. There was no way. Connor trusted Ben like a brother.

The sooner he got the flash drive, the sooner he could get back to his life. He was starting to wonder if it wasn't time to end his career at CPDU. This life was taking its toll on him.

Sighing, he reached out and gently shook Anna.

*****

Anna woke with a start when she felt someone's hand on her. Instant panic rushed through her, and she sat up with a start.

"It's okay, Anna. It's me, Connor."

It took her a moment to realize where she was and who she was with. When she finally did, she looked out the window, her brain still foggy. Her eyes focused on an old motel with chipped paint and a sign with broken letters.

"Where are we?"

"A motel," he answered. "It's late and we need to rest. Come on," he said as he pushed the door on his side open.

"This place looks sketchy. I hope it doesn't have bed bugs." Anna got out of the car, stretching her arms and legs.

"You'll have a bed and a roof over your head. It'll do." He tossed her hat to her. "Don't forget, you promised to wear this whenever we're in public."

"You're right." A bed sounded nice. They collected their bags, and she followed him as he walked into the motel.

At the check-in desk, Connor rang the bell to wake the man sleeping behind the counter. "I'd like a room, please," he said in a gruff voice.

"Two rooms, actually," Anna added.

Connor glared at her. "No, just one, sir."

The man blinked and stared at them in confusion. "We only have one room left anyway."

"One room is fine," Connor replied. "As long as it faces the parking lot. Does it?"

"You're in luck. It does," the man said.

"Sounds great," Connor said.

"No, it certainly is not great," Anna protested. "I'm not staying in the same room as you."

"I thought this would be obvious," Connor whispered to Anna.

"So did I. We need separate rooms," Anna retorted.

"We only got one room left, lady," the man at the desk repeated lethargically. "And there ain't another motel around for miles."

"Look. We're both dead tired, and it's not safe for us to drive all the way to another place. We'll make it work. Don't worry, I'll sleep on the floor," Connor told Anna.

"In the bathroom." She put her hands on her hips.

"Don't push it." Connor turned to the man behind the desk, handing him cash. "We'll take it."

"I'll also need a means of identification," the man said in a monotone voice.

"How about an extra fifty bucks for you and we skip the whole ID process," Connor said, holding out the cash in his hand.

The man glanced at Connor, then his hand darted out and he pocketed the money. Grabbing a key, he handed it to Connor.

"Do you have room service?" Connor asked.

"Not at this time of the night. But there's a pizza place that stays open all night. The number is on the dresser."

"Thank you." Connor reached out, handing the man another fifty-dollar bill. "You'll let me know if anyone comes around asking strange questions, right?"

"Anything for my customers," the man replied.

Connor walked down the hall toward the room, and Anna followed closely behind.

"I'm not spending the night in the same room with you. I'd rather sleep in the car," she persisted.

"It's not safe to sleep in the car." Connor sighed in frustration. "Look, I know what you are thinking. It's not like that. This is about your safety. I assure you, you can trust me. I'm not going to try anything with you. I told you, I'll sleep on the floor. I can even hang a sheet so you have your privacy."

Was he telling the truth? Did he really have good intentions?

"It's our only option, Anna. I'm sorry. Here." He went into the room, dumped his bag on the bed, and pulled out a can of pepper spray and a whistle, handing them to her. She cautiously entered the room. "If you feel like I'm being less than honorable, you have my full permission to mace me in the face. Does that make you feel any better?"

She couldn't help but laugh at the mental image. "Actually, yes. But what about your gun?"

"I would give it to you if I could, but if those guys storm in here, I need it to protect us. I'll sleep here on the floor."

"And what about the knife in your boot?" she asked with one eyebrow raised.

"How did you know about that?" he asked, eyes narrowed.

She shrugged. "Wild guess. I read it in a book once."

Connor laughed out loud. "Don't believe everything you read. Here." He tossed it on the bed. "But you need to give it right back to me if somebody tries to get in here. Sound fair?"

"Not really. But fine. Seriously, if I so much as see you walking toward me, I really will mace you in the face."

"I don't doubt it. Look, I'm tired and hungry. I know you are too. All I want to do is order pizza and sleep until morning. What do you think?"

"Sounds heavenly." Anna knew deep down that he would never do anything to hurt her. However, she had promised herself a long time ago that she'd never trust anyone else again.

She'd still keep the pepper spray, whistle and knife in her hands tonight while she slept. She was a light sleeper. The slightest noise or movement would wake her up in an instant. If he did try anything, she'd be ready, even if she didn't think he would.

Connor walked to the dresser and picked up the flyer for the pizza place.

"Do you like Hawaiian pizza?" she asked. "It's my favorite."

"Gross. No. Pineapple has no business being on a pizza," Connor said, shaking his head. "How about we get half Hawaiian and half pepperoni?"

"Sure." She shrugged. Anna was so hungry right now, she didn't care what he ordered.

He quickly placed the order and then sat down on the single chair in the room. Anna sat on the edge of the bed, still a little uneasy to be alone with him. Funny, she had been alone with him in his hospital room and in the car and had felt no awkwardness then. Why did she now?

She watched as he took a thin extra blanket and used rope from his bag to hang it across the room. He attached one end to a light fixture, and on the other end of the room, he attached it to another light fixture.

"How's that?" he asked, clearly proud of himself.

"Nice job. Thank you. I appreciate it."

He acted like he was relaxed, but Anna knew better. She could see the way his ears seemed to perk up at every sound that came from outside the room and knew he was still at full alert. Like her, he had changed clothes at the mall and was now wearing a flannel shirt and jeans tucked into his old boots. Her eyes drifted to his face, taking in the hard lines of his jaw and the blank look in his eyes as he flipped through a magazine she knew he was not reading.

Just a little imagination was all she needed to picture him as the killer they said he was. Still, the picture would not form. Oh, he was far from being a perfect man, and Anna knew it was not hard to imagine that he had killed one or two people in the past. But killers didn't go out of their way to save clueless women who had lied to them and put them in danger. Why he had put himself in danger to rescue her was something Anna was still struggling to figure out.

His hand moved as he changed pages, and Anna swallowed as she realized she had been staring at him for a while.

She turned away and took a look around the room. It was not as clean as she would like it to be, but it wasn't too bad either. The sheets were fresh and there was no dust on the dresser or any of the surfaces. It was sparse in furnishing, just the bed, dresser, and the single chair where Connor was sitting. On the bed there were two pillows and a set of folded blankets. The hat he had bought for her was on the dresser, the remaining shopping bags on the floor beside the dresser.

Maybe she would have been nicer to him if he wasn't the one who had put her in this situation in the first place. She couldn't deny he had and still was going out of his way to help her. If they'd met under different circumstances, maybe they'd get along better. In a different situation, she might even...like him.

Maybe from now on, she would try to be nicer to him.

"You want to ask me something," Connor said without lifting his head.

"Yes. I was wondering exactly when it would be okay for me to go back home."

"When the guys who want to put a bullet in our heads have been taken care of." He closed the magazine and turned his attention to her, surprised to see that she looked really worried. He sighed as he leaned forward in his seat. "Look, I've already talked to some buddies of mine, and they're dealing with the situation. A few days more, hopefully, and you can go back to changing bedpans and sticking needles in people."

Anna glared at him. "I'll let you know that I like my job very much, and it is very much more than changing sheets and cleaning up after people."

"Sorry, I didn't mean to make it sound like that. Of course, you like your job, and you're good at it. Look, I'm sorry for what I said. It's just…" He paused and mulled his words in his head before continuing. "Not all of us leave hospitals with good memories."

What was that supposed to mean?

"About your earlier question. Like I said, hopefully, very soon all of this will be taken care of. In the meantime, you need this." He reached into his pocket, stood up, and dropped a phone onto the bed. "Here. It's a burner phone."

Anna stared at the phone and didn't move to get it.

Connor frowned. "It's a phone, Anna, not a bomb."

"I just don't think I need it."

"Of course, you do. I need to make sure you can reach me in case of an emergency. And that I can reach you too. You do understand that there are people out there who want to kill us, right?"

Anna stared at the phone, not really knowing why she was finding it hard to collect it from him. She had done without one for so long, even though she had learned after leaving the settlement that technology was not as evil as she used to think it was.

This was about her survival. She grabbed the phone and stared at the screen. "In Unity, there's a phone shanty at the end of the lane. I remember following my dad when he wanted to call our relatives. I used to be fascinated by it. I had a cell phone when I was a midwife there, but it was a very basic, old flip phone, only for emergencies. It died a while back."

"Then why didn't you get a new one after you left the community?"

"Because phones now do more than what is necessary. Music, pictures, videos, even the internet. It's so much more than just allowing you to talk to people. Of course, I told myself I could get one and just not use it to do those other things. But the best way to avoid sin is to avoid temptation. So I didn't get one at all."

Connor scoffed. "I think you have more self-control than that. Besides, it would be up to you how you'd use it. This is for emergencies. I've programmed my number into the phone. If anything happens, call and wait for me to reply. If I don't reply or someone else answers my phone, end the call immediately and call the second number I programmed into the phone. The one that says emergency option. My contact should answer and help you."

"Thank you. So, where are we going?"

"Right now, I'm trying to get in touch with my friends who work at CPDU, Ben Banks and Jefferson Martin. We can trust them. I'm hoping one of them will call me back by tomorrow. In the meantime, I'm just trying to confuse the people who want to kill us by staying on the move," he replied. "I'm hoping he can help us."

"Ben Banks?" Anna chuckled.

"What, you know him?"

"He was Maria Mast's bodyguard in Unity. Maria is one of my best friends from home. I went on a date with him, but I guess we didn't really have a connection because we lost touch after that. He went back to CPDU, and I left and went to nursing school."

"You went on a date with Ben?" Connor laughed out loud. "Oh, this is too good."

"It was one date, and there was no spark. We had nothing in common."

Connor looked at her thoughtfully but didn't ask anything more about it. "And Maria Mast is your friend? I know her. She married my friend Derek Turner. We worked at CPDU together for years," Connor said. "I mean, I shouldn't be surprised. It's a small community."

"Oh, of course! I've been friends with Maria since we were little, and I know Derek, too. Maria's parents, Mary and Gideon, were like second parents to me. I was at their house all the time growing up, and they took me under their wing after my parents died." There was a hint of a smile on her face as she reminisced, then Anna's eyes lit up. "What about Derek? Couldn't he help us? Like you said, he was a CPDU agent."

"No way. I couldn't ask him that. They have their son Carter and a baby now, too." Connor shook his head. "Derek and I were close when he worked at CPDU, and I visited him a few times in Unity. But I can't ask him to shelter us."

"Just call him tomorrow. See what he says."

Connor grumbled. "I guess I could try calling him. He might at least know someone trustworthy who could help us."

"Can you tell me what is on the flash drive?"

"The information on the drive is enough to convict dozens of traffickers. But it's best for you if you don't know what is on it exactly. Then you won't need to lie if something happens."

"If something happens? What, if they kidnap me again?"

"Anna, that's why I'm sticking with you. I'm doing everything I can do to keep that from happening. You need to learn how to drive and how to shoot, just in case something happens to me."

It took Anna a few seconds to find her voice.

"No," she squeaked. She cleared her throat and repeated herself more firmly. "No, I'll do nothing of the sort."

"Is that a no to both?"

He had to be joking, Anna thought to herself as she stared across the table at him. "Of course, no to both. I don't want to know how to drive, and I definitely don't want to know how to shoot a gun."

Connor stared at her for a few seconds, mulling something over in his head. "All right, I guess I can see why you think you don't want to know how to shoot. I don't understand the driving part though. Why don't you want to learn how to drive if you left Unity?"

"Just because I left the community doesn't mean I've forgotten everything I learned when I was there. In fact, out here, I should be even more careful."

Connor didn't accept her argument, and he was already shaking his head before she even finished talking. "Look, I can understand the argument for why you don't use phones, don't want to shoot guns, and even for why you don't wear certain clothes. I mean, how can driving a car serve as a temptation for you? I don't think driving is a sin."

"I don't want to talk about this." Anna crossed her arms.

"I normally wouldn't care. I'm trying to protect you here. Why is driving such a big deal?"

"I'm scared of driving!" Anna suddenly blurted and then lowered her head in shame.

"Wait, what?" Connor stared at the woman across from him, unable to believe she was scared of anything. "You're scared of driving? Why?"

"I don't want to talk about it," Anna replied.

Connor said nothing, just waited for her to finally lift her head and look at him.

"I don't know," Anna finally said. "It's just, you have all those pedals, and then there is the steering and I don't have any idea how I could maneuver something so big…" she trailed off. "Hey, you know, I should change your bandage." She rummaged around in the bags and found the medical supplies.

Anna lifted her head to see that Connor was silently laughing at her. Glaring at him, she folded her arms across her chest. "Make fun of me if you want to."

"I'm not making fun of you. I just find the current situation a little bit funny, that's all." He paused and realized she was truly embarrassed about her admission.

Anna knelt next to where he was sitting. "Hold still." She lifted his shirt and removed the bandages from the front and back.

"I had this buddy while I was in the Marines—" he said.

"You were in the Marines?" Anna interrupted, a little shocked to hear something so personal about his history.

Connor paused, realizing he had revealed something about himself he didn't want to, then he shrugged it off.

61

"You want to ask questions or listen to my story?" he asked with a scowl.

"Pardon my curiosity, oh great one. Please continue." She began to clean his wound.

"Nice to see you have a sense of humor," he shot back, rolling his eyes when Anna grinned at him. "Like I was saying, when I was in the Marines, I had a friend who freaked out one day when he saw a spider in his pack. I'm talking about someone who had no problem doing a drop-off in the middle of a desert or running into a room full of men with guns. And a small, eight-legged critter had him screaming like a banshee. What I'm trying to say is that fears are irrational and sometimes they have no rhyme or reason. What I do know is that fears can be overcome if you see just how harmless what you are scared of is."

Anna looked up at him. "You won't stop pestering me until I agree to learn how to drive, will you?"

"Nope."

Anna thought about it. Then she nodded her head.

"All right, I'll try once and if I'm not comfortable with it, we stop and we don't talk about this ever. There, I'm done." She stood up and gathered the medical supplies.

"Thank you." Connor appeared to ponder her proposition. "But you know, I don't think I can pass up the chance to make fun of you for being scared of something my nana did."

Anna stared at him for a few seconds before she burst into laughter.

"What?" Connor asked, wondering what amused her.

"You said 'nana'." She giggled like a school girl, and Connor couldn't help but crack a smile.

"So?"

"I don't know of any grown man who says that besides you."

"Of course, there are," Connor replied sheepishly. He paused, then asked, "So, what you were saying before about how you left, does that mean you're not Amish now?

Anna sat down in the chair at the opposite end of the room. "Not anymore."

"Then why do you still live like you're Amish?"

"What?"

"Your hair, the way you talk about God. You don't own a car or cell phone. I'll even bet that you don't have a TV in your house and have never seen a movie."

Anna scowled at him, the camaraderie that had developed a few seconds ago now destroyed.

"I don't need a TV or a phone. And yes, I talk about God, but that doesn't make someone Amish. I use electricity now, I wear pants. I would not be living this way if I were still Amish." The fact that he was right about her not owning a TV or having ever seen a movie irked her.

"Didn't say there was anything wrong with it. Just making an observation."

Anna just snorted and settled back into her seat.

"All right, sorry if I sound so judgmental. It's just hard for me to understand how you guys do without some of these things."

"Simple. We understand that by not using modern technology, we don't become as distracted from our relationships with God and our families. You should try it yourself, a week without any of those things. You'd be surprised by how much of the world is passing you by."

"Is there nothing you want to do but can't because it goes against the beliefs you're hanging onto?"

"No," Anna replied just as quickly. But she'd always wanted to fly on an airplane to some place far away. If she was being honest, she'd like to watch a movie sometime, too. Then she remembered the sundress still in the shopping bag and her voice dropped. Firming her shoulders, she told herself that a few seconds of wishful thinking didn't equal doubting her faith. "No, I am perfectly happy with the way I am."

"Come on. There's got to be something you want to do."

Anna sighed, knowing he'd keep bugging her until she told him. "Okay, okay. I want to fly on a plane someday. I've always wanted to go to Germany or someplace tropical like Hawaii."

"Why haven't you?"

"Well, it's expensive. But I guess there's a part of me that still feels like flying on a plane would be wrong."

"Well, if you really want to, you should do it sometime. Anything else?"

"You were right. I've never seen a movie."

"What? I was kidding about that. You've never seen a movie before? Seriously?"

"Seriously."

He leaned forward. "When this is all over, Anna Hershberger, I promise I will take you to see your first movie ever."

Anna's heart leapt. What did he mean by that? Did he mean…like a date?

Did she want it to be? She hardly knew this man.

"I mean, you know, as a way to thank you. If that's okay with you," he said sheepishly. "If you want to go. As friends. As my way of saying sorry for dragging you into this."

Anna felt her lips curve upwards in a smile. Date or not, she'd take the offer. "I'd love to."

There was a knock on the door, and Connor quickly looked through the peephole, holding his gun. "It's the pizza guy," he said, putting the gun in his holster, but still keeping one hand near it as he paid the man and took the pizza, just in case it was a trick. Carrying the box into the room, he dropped it on the bed, and Anna breathed a sigh of relief.

"Eat," he said to Anna as he grabbed a slice for himself and retreated back to his chair. "Ew. Pineapple."

Anna reached for the box and grabbed a slice for herself, laughing. "We can't agree on anything, can we?"

*****

Connor listened as Anna's breathing finally fell into the easy rhythm of someone asleep. Aware that she would never be comfortable with him awake in the room, he had pretended to sleep so she could feel at ease enough to fall asleep. He had not expected to hear her crying, and the sounds of her sobbing quietly into her pillow drifted towards him. Feeling guilty for the role he had played in creating those tears, he listened, hands fisted around his blanket as she cried. When she finally stopped crying and fell asleep, he closed his eyes.

Connor reminded himself that morning would come soon enough along with a chance to do things better.

Chapter Nine

It was a sixth sense honed by years of warfare and combat situations that woke Connor up from his sleep. He wasn't sure if he'd heard anything or not, but his hand immediately went under his pillow to retrieve the gun.

At the same time, he was jumping to his feet and shaking Anna awake. A peek out the window at the parking lot revealed a truck that had not been there when he went to sleep.

She blinked her eyes open, a little groggy before she came fully awake and stared at him in fear. Then her eyes opened wide and she held up the pepper spray.

"Hey, buster, I told you—"

"Shhh. They're here." He put one finger to his lips and then pointed at the bathroom. "Get in there and lock the door behind you. Don't open the door for anyone."

She got up and ran to do as he had said, and he was grateful she hadn't argued with him for once. Connor quickly stuffed pillows in her bed to make it look like she was still sleeping there, and he did the same to where he had been sleeping.

Grabbing a lamp off the desk and unplugging it, he stood behind the door as footsteps sounded down the hallway. The door opened easily, slowly. They must have had a key. Had the man working behind the desk ratted them out?

Connor silently cursed the motel manager for giving him up. Had they paid him off or maybe even beat it out of him?

Staying quiet and still, the two men shot two bullets at the bed where Anna had been lying a few minutes ago. Muffled pinging sounds told him the guns were silenced, though they were still quite loud. Loud enough for other people in the motel to hear.

Enough for someone to call the police.

Connor crept forward and landed a blow on the nearest attacker's skull with a satisfying *thwack*. By the time the unconscious body hit the floor with a thud, he had already repeated the action on the second intruder.

*****

As Anna hid in the bathroom, clutching her pepper spray, her heart and stomach sank when she heard a pinging gunshot.

Had they killed him? Was Connor dead?

If they had killed him, she knew they'd kill her too.

She then heard two dull thuds, each sound followed by what sounded like someone crumpling to the floor.

After a few more agonizing seconds of muffled movement on the other side of the door, it stopped.

Silence.

Anna jumped when someone knocked on the door. "Anna, open the door; it's me."

Could it really be him? "Connor?" she asked tentatively. Was this some kind of trick?

"Hurry, Anna. Open the door. It's okay."

Anna remained near the opposite wall, her pepper-spray held out in her trembling hand as a weapon.

"Are they gone?" she demanded.

"They're unconscious, but not for long. I knocked them out with a lamp. Come on, Anna, we need to go right now."

Hearing the urgency in his voice propelled her forward, and she unlocked the door to let him in.

"I heard gunshots," she replied, her eyes filling with tears. "I thought you were dead."

"I made it look like we were still sleeping. Come on," he said again, taking her hand and leading her out. "We have to get out of here before they send more people, and especially before the cops show up."

When they came out of the bathroom, Anna stopped when she saw two men on the floor, unmoving. Were they dead?

Did he lie about them being unconscious?

She bent down and checked both of their pulses. They were definitely not dead, but indeed unconscious. He'd been telling the truth after all.

Why had she wanted to believe he'd killed them, that he really was a cold-blooded assassin?

"Anna, we don't have time for this. We have to go right now," Connor urged.

They grabbed their bags and hurried out of the motel.

They drove for a few moments, tension in the air. Would he ask her about it? Did he realize she'd thought he lied?

"You thought I killed them, didn't you?" Connor eventually asked. "Is that why you checked their pulses?"

"No. Well, yes. I don't know. Look, I didn't ask for any of this. I was just doing my job the day I met you, trying to be kind to someone I met dying in the parking lot. I don't know you, and I don't know what you're capable of."

"Look, I know none of this is fair."

"Fair!" she shouted. "This has gone way past the point of being unfair. I don't even know who you are, why we are running, or where we are going. For all I know you may even be the one I should be running from."

"I've told you everything. You just don't want to believe me because it's easier to see me as the bad guy."

In her line of work, Anna was used to seeing blood and death. In the ER, she had seen stab wounds, bullet wounds, and domestic violence injuries. She'd seen people die in the hospital; she'd seen the bodies.

When she'd seen those men on the floor, all those memories came rushing back, and she'd truly thought they were dead.

"I'm no assassin, Anna," Connor whispered. "I just wish you'd believe me."

*****

As the sun came up, Connor pulled up in front of a nearby diner and stopped the car. Anna lifted her head and looked up at him before looking around her.

70

After he'd risked his life to rescue her from the van, and after the stories they'd shared at the motel, Anna wanted to trust him. She wanted to convince herself that this man truly was innocent and that he was undercover for CPDU. That he wasn't an assassin or some other criminal who was just lying to her.

Now she had no idea what to think.

Connor said, "I'm just wondering how they found us so fast. In the van, do you think the men put anything on you, like a tracker or something? Did they touch you at all?"

Anna was quick to shake her head. Then she stopped and really considered his question. "No. Thank God. The only thing they did was tie me up and threaten me."

"We already threw your clothes away, so if they had pinned anything to your clothes that would be gone by now. I switched cars after I rescued you, so they couldn't have put a tracker on the car yesterday. I'll get a new car after this just to be safe." He paused as he mulled the situation over in his head. "I've just been wondering how the men knew we were at the motel. I would have noticed them following us if they had tried."

Anna shrugged. "Maybe they did follow us and you really didn't notice."

Connor rolled his eyes. "No. I think the motel employee was working with them or somehow ratted us out to them. I'm going to check the car one more time for a tracker, just to be safe," he said, getting out of the car and searching it carefully.

What felt like only a few minutes later, Anna jumped when Connor got back in the car. She'd been so engrossed in the suspenseful story she was reading, she hadn't noticed him at first.

"I found something," he said.

She looked at the small tracker in his hand.

"When I checked last night, it wasn't there. I'm positive. But it's here now. I bet they put it on the car before they came into the motel last night, just in case we got away, which we did. But since they didn't use this to find us at the motel, I wonder how they found us there. Maybe the police located this stolen vehicle in the motel parking lot, and one of the corrupt officers alerted the assassins. Maybe they threatened or paid off the man working behind the desk, or maybe he's been working with them or is somehow connected to them. We might never know. At least I caught it now rather than later."

Anna suddenly realized something and dropped her voice to a whisper. "Can they hear us?"

Connor couldn't help himself as his lips turned up in amusement. "No, they can't. It's not a listening device. It's just a simple GPS tracker, and the range is not very wide."

"So, they are close by?"

"Close enough. They know I'll pick up any tail they have on me. So, they'll probably keep their distance for now and wait for us to stop somewhere for the night. Then they'll make their move on us. Just like they did last night. They don't know our exact location, but it gives them a general area."

"Then it was my fault we were attacked, wasn't it?" Anna asked, frowning.

"No. Not at all, Anna. None of this is your fault. If anything, I should have thought of this earlier. Please, don't feel bad."

She nodded. "I'll try."

"Good thing we found it early enough. Now we can use it to buy us some time."

She wondered what he meant by that. She smiled as she watched him get out of the car and drop the tracker in the back of a truck parked in the parking lot of the diner.

"That should keep them busy enough," Connor said as he let himself back into the car. "At least until the battery dies. Now, once that guy leaves, we can go have some breakfast."

A few minutes later, an elderly man with a trucker hat and mustache got into the truck and drove away.

"We'll eat here and then get back on the road," Connor said as he walked toward the diner. "Don't forget your hat."

In the diner, they sat down in a booth situated near the emergency exit at the back where Conner could have his back against a wall and a good view of the front door. While they waited for the waitress to bring their food, Anna found herself doing everything she could not to look at him. Suddenly realizing how silly it was to try to ignore him forever, she looked at him.

"I hope I don't get into trouble at work for not giving formal notice before I left," she said.

"As I said before, when this is over, I, along with CPDU, will tell them why we needed your help. Also, I haven't really thanked you for saving my life when you found me in the parking lot, I just realized."

"You're just now realizing that?"

"I know, I've been a dolt about it. Thank you for helping me, even though you took me inside the hospital when I specifically told you not to." He noticed her glare and let out the rest of his words in a hurry. "But you did what you thought was right. I am sorry for everything that's happened. I had no intention of dragging you into this."

"Of course, you didn't. You've made it clear since the moment we left the hospital that I was an unwelcome distraction." Anna did nothing to tamp down her anger except making sure she wasn't too effusive in her expressions. "You even blamed me for everything—"

"I did nothing of the—"

"Yes, you did, when you accused me of taking you into the hospital instead of finding a way to help you that wouldn't have involved calling the cops."

"I know I haven't exactly been a bundle of joy. I haven't been fun to be around in a long time, ever since…" He trailed off and sighed, leaving Anna surprised at his sincere tone. She'd been expecting a sarcastic retort. "I actually used to be a nice guy. A lot more fun than I am now. You don't deserve any of this. I just hope with your help I can get the information we need to shut down this trafficking ring."

Ever since what? What was he referring to? Anna stared at him as he fiddled with his fork. She wanted to ask, but couldn't find the words for once. He really could be sweet when he wanted to be. Sometimes. When he wasn't being sarcastic, stubborn, or annoying, which was a lot.

Maybe he did have a heart.

She was saved from having to come up with a response to his surprising answer when the waitress returned with their food.

"Thank you very much," Connor said with a wide smile. Then turning that smile on Anna, he grabbed his fork and began to eat with gusto. Feeling better than she had when they'd arrived, she also began to eat.

After they finished, Connor reached into his pocket and dropped enough money to cover their food and a nice tip. They headed for the door.

"I have to change your bandage before we go," Anna said. She grabbed the medical supplies, and they got in the backseat of the car. "Try not to move too much," Anna said, removing his bandages from his abdomen and back. Being this close to him in such a small space, she was more aware of him now than she had ever been. She could feel her heart beating wildly in her chest as the scent of him wrapped around her like a warm blanket on a cold night. Changing the bandages was a simple enough task, but for some reason, she was having great difficulty focusing.

There was nothing to feel awkward about, she reminded herself. She was just trying to keep his wound clean. She'd done similar tasks a thousand times for her patients.

It had never felt like this before, though. And, if she was honest with herself, it felt good to be this close to someone. After everything she had been through, it was a reminder she was still human after all.

Chapter Ten

They mostly drove in circles for a while before Connor pulled onto the highway and continued his journey to a destination Anna still didn't know, taking her further and further away from where she called home and everything she knew.

Now that they'd found the bug, Anna called HR at the hospital to let them know she was sick and wouldn't come into work for a few days. It bought her some time, but not much.

Late that night he pulled up into another motel. This time she didn't argue with him when he paid for only one room. She declined his offer of food and crawled under the covers, not surprised when he grabbed the blanket and prepared a place for himself on the floor between the bed and the door. This time, she didn't bother asking him to hang up a sheet. She could see how tired he was.

Anna could have asked him to share the bed with her, but that would have been completely inappropriate and against her beliefs, even though it was a big enough bed and she knew she was safe with him. A few moments later, she heard him snoring lightly.

For a long time, she stared at the ceiling of the room, thinking about how much her life had changed in the last forty-eight hours. A part of her wondered if she had done the right thing by stopping to help him. Then she chided herself for even thinking like that. She had done the right thing, and she should be proud of that, no matter that it had turned out to be the most dangerous decision she'd ever made.

Anna wondered if she would ever see her coworkers again or get to visit her friends back home.

Would she survive this? Or would these assassins take them out at their next stop?

Tears rolled down her face, but she was too distraught to wipe them off. Turning around, she buried her face in her pillow and wept silently until she was too exhausted to do anything but fall asleep.

As she often did, Anna dreamed of home. In Unity, Maine, the birds sang more, the grass was greener, and the air was purer.

In her dream, Anna had just walked out of Maria Mast's house. She'd been checking on Derek Turner and Ben Banks' injuries.

"Excuse me, ma'am, would you mind helping my horse for a second?" a man had asked, standing near his buggy, which was next to Anna's buggy.

"Actually, I have an appointment to get to," Anna said, gripping the handle of her medical bag. She quickly walked away.

"Are you a doctor? My horse cut his leg. Would you mind looking at it, maybe bandaging it up?" he persisted.

Anna set her medical bag and cell phone on the front seat of the buggy and climbed up onto it, taking hold of the reins. She clicked her tongue, signaling the horse to begin walking. "Sorry, sir, I'm not an animal doctor. I'm a midwife."

"Close enough," the man said. He stepped forward and grabbed her reins, desperation in his eyes. "Please, just look at it for a moment? Please? I can tell she's in a lot of pain."

Anna looked over at the horse. She did have a few moments. Maybe she could take a quick look at the horse's leg. If she didn't, she knew she'd feel guilty.

"I guess I can, but I only have a minute," she said and climbed down from the buggy. She walked over to the horse. "Which leg?"

"The front left one," the man said.

Anna lifted the horse's leg gently. "Looks fine to me. There's no cut here."

"Oh, sorry. The right leg," the man said, taking a step closer to her.

Anna inspected that leg as well. "No cut here either. She's fine," Anna said, turning and walking away. The way he kept on walking closer to her set her on edge, making the hairs on the back of her neck rise. "Just have her take it easy, sir. Have a nice day. I have to go."

Suddenly, the man was standing in front of her, and he grabbed her wrist.

What was he doing? Panic flooded through her as she tried to dart away, but he stepped in front of her again.

"This is going to be harder than I thought," he sneered through clenched teeth.

He raised up a small white cloth, and Anna knew instantly it was chloroform. Once he got it on her mouth, she'd be knocked unconscious.

Anna screamed as loud as she could. Maria, Derek, and Ben were definitely close enough to hear her.

"Shut up!" the man cried, trying to get the cloth onto Anna's mouth.

Every nerve in her body was alive with adrenaline, every cell in her screaming to get away from him. Anna fought, clawed, kicked, and punched him as hard as she could, but he was so much bigger and stronger than she was. Even with her massive effort, he still got the cloth onto her mouth.

As she held her breath, she continued to struggle, but after a few seconds, she stopped moving and closed her eyes, going motionless and falling to the ground. Hopefully, she'd tricked the man into thinking she'd gone unconscious.

He moved the cloth away from her mouth and let go of her for a split second. In that moment, she kicked him in the face, rolled, and stood. She bolted away from him, sprinting toward Maria's house where her friends could help her.

The man was surprisingly fast, catching up to her within seconds and tackling her to the gravelly ground. This time he held the cloth onto her mouth until she couldn't hold her breath any longer, and even though she didn't want to, her body screamed for oxygen and breathed in.

Darkness overtook her.

"No!" Anna screamed as she woke up, sitting up in the motel bed.

"What's wrong?" Connor said, instantly standing, gun in hand. He looked around the room, his eyes darting quickly.

"Just a nightmare." Anna gripped her blanket tightly, taking deep breaths to slow her racing heart rate. "I'm sorry. I get them sometimes."

Connor put his gun down. "From when you were abducted?"

Anna squinted at him in the dark. "How did you know?"

"Just a guess." He shrugged. "I get nightmares too, about Iraq."

Anna slowly nodded. So, maybe they did have something in common, even though their nightmares were about totally different things. And she was sure she hadn't lived through nearly as many atrocities as he had, and she couldn't imagine the horrors of war.

Still, the day she was kidnapped haunted her like it had been yesterday.

"Sorry I made you think something happened," Anna said, settling back down on her pillow.

Connor got back down on his makeshift bed on the floor. "You have nothing to apologize for, Anna," came his voice in the dark. From here, she couldn't see him.

After a few seconds of silence, she asked, "Do the nightmares ever go away?"

"No, not for me. Not yet. They've become a part of me, I guess. Something I've learned to live with."

Anna took a deep breath. "Me too."

*****

Anna opened her eyes and knew immediately that she was alone, even before she lifted her head up to look at the floor where Connor had slept. The bathroom door was open, and she could hear no one inside. Realizing he had abandoned her, she jumped off the bed, took a step toward the door, then stopped as her eyes fell on a piece of paper propped up on the dresser. She sighed in relief as she read the note Connor had left for her.

I'm sitting in the hallway, so you're safe. Clean up, get dressed, and when you're ready, meet me in the car so we can get on the road. The cup of coffee on the dresser should still be hot if you need a pick-me-up.

Anna couldn't resist smiling, her hand leaning on the dresser as relief swept over her to learn he had not abandoned her. She reached for the cup of coffee on the dresser and found it hot like he had said it was. Taking a sip, she found that he had gone with more sugar and cream than she was used to. Still, it felt good to feel the heat of the beverage warm her up. And it was the thought that counted.

Rummaging through her bag, she looked for a change of clothes. For a moment she stared at the sundress, the one Connor bought her. She slowly reached for it and held it against herself as she stared into the mirror. It was easy to imagine how she would look in it, and Anna wished she had the courage to wear it. After a few seconds, she dropped the dress back in the bag and opted instead for one of the outfits she had picked herself, a flannel shirt and jeans.

*****

As he stood in the motel hallway, Connor ended the call he was making and pushed the phone into his pocket.

He couldn't reach Ben, Derek, or Jeff, and Connor was starting to get worried. Connor was hoping Ben or Jeff would help him because they had more than a business relationship from working together. They'd been close friends for years.

Connor remembered when Grace's condition became so bad, it was clear she was not going to make it. His CPDU buddies had rallied around to console him. Their presence was the only thing that had kept him from going crazy with the grief of knowing he was going to lose his soulmate.

Of course, there was nothing anyone could do to stop him from finally losing his mind when Grace died. Connor had lost himself in the only thing he knew how to do well, which was work. He'd gone back to Afghanistan for a year, then spent over a year in Iraq. In the desert, fighting for survival and hunting terrorists with his closest military friends kept him from thinking about her too much.

It was when they all went to sleep, when it was quiet, that was the most dangerous time of day for him. That was when his mind would be consumed by thoughts of Grace and he'd be crippled by loneliness.

Even more dangerous than being shot at by terrorists, those were the times he'd thought about taking his own life. Some days he wished one of the terrorists would just shoot him or he'd die in an explosion.

Then the pain would stop.

But now he was going to make everything right, and when he was done, he would say goodbye to this life altogether. Working in the military, and then law enforcement, for all these years had drained him. He needed to go somewhere and start all over again. For now, though, there was the matter of Anna Hershberger to take care of.

Connor looked up when he heard the door to the motel room open, and Anna walked out, holding her bag in her hand.

"Good morning," she said with a small smile at him.

"Morning. Hope you slept well."

"Yes. Thank you for asking."

He nodded. "Let me guess. You were scared when you woke up and found yourself alone. I was here the whole time."

Maybe it was the fact that Anna was really not used to seeing him being this friendly or that he had managed to read her so easily, but she found herself frowning at him.

"Of course, I was scared. I thought you'd left me behind."

If he noticed the bite to her tone, he didn't show it, just smiled at her as he replied.

"I won't leave you, Anna. That would go against everything I am."

Her heart warmed at his words. She knew he meant he wouldn't leave her only until this situation was resolved.

What would it feel like to hear him say that to her in a different context?

Like a romantic context?

She shook her head, silently chiding herself. *He doesn't mean it like that at all. We barely know each other,* she thought. Why was her mind thinking these things?

For once, Connor misread her expression. "You didn't have to worry," he said. "I was right here by the door. The window is too high and small for anyone to fit through. There was no way anyone would have gotten in without me knowing."

Anna glared at him. "How about if they sent a really small person that could fit in through the window in the bathroom? How would you have known that I was being attacked then?"

Connor's eyes widened. Then he lifted his head and burst into laughter, his chest rumbling with the force of it. A few seconds later Anna couldn't help herself as she joined him in laughter.

"Wow. With that imagination of yours, you should consider writing a book."

Connor's phone rang.

"Hello?" Connor said, walking down the hallway, away from Anna.

"It's Derek."

"Thank God. I was hoping you'd call me back this morning."

"Sorry. I don't have a phone in the house, and you called my business number, so I didn't see it until I went into work this morning. Is this line secure?"

Connor couldn't help but grin a little. Derek sounded just like he used to back in the day when they'd worked together at CPDU. "Yes."

"Are you okay?" Derek asked.

"Well, I was shot, but Anna has been taking care of me."

"You need to get here. We can take care of you here."

"I really hate to impose on you, especially with the baby."

"Connor, you'd do the same for me. We want you here. I have so much to tell you. But first, do they know who Anna is?"

"No. She wasn't wearing her scrubs at the hospital. I don't think they know who she is."

"Then get here as soon as you can," Derek said. "Because two teenage sisters in the community went missing last night. Their family realized they were gone early this morning. Their names are Lilly and Katie Holt. I know them well."

"It could be two young Amish girls who snuck out for a few days. Or it could be Korovin's group. The timing is too coincidental. Do you know anything else about what happened?"

"This is where it gets weird. Their younger sister, Debra, said that she overheard them talking late one night about meeting up with a young man in the community who was going to set them up with dates. This happened the night before they went missing, but she didn't know who they were talking about."

"Set them up with dates?" Connor shook his head. "That can't be right. An Amish man wouldn't do this."

"Exactly. Something went wrong somewhere. We need to find out who this young man is."

"Let me guess. They didn't report it to the police."

84

"No. The Amish don't report crimes. And in this case, it might be a good thing. If it gets reported, the mole at CPDU might realize that someone is suspicious of kidnapping or trafficking and is investigating. Whoever this young man is could find out and leave town, then we'd lose our lead," Derek explained. "Right now, most people here think they jumped the fence for a few days and will be back soon."

"What about Anna? It's okay for her to come back?"

"Well, it might be a bit awkward for her, but you'd be surprised how many people would want to see her. And Connor, there's one more thing. I know because of the circumstances you want to stay at our house with Anna so you can protect her. Just in case anything happens."

"Right."

"Well, that won't sit well with the community. I mean, when I came here and stayed in Maria's house to protect her from her stalker, everyone knew I was an undercover bodyguard. They knew I had to be in the same house as her. But this is different. No one can know you're working undercover or else the two leads could get spooked and leave."

"What are you saying?"

"I think you and Anna should pretend to be a married couple so you can stay in the same house together. Otherwise, it would be scandalous. People will be talking enough about Anna returning, and we don't want people to get the wrong idea, if you know what I mean. This is to protect her reputation. Not to mention, word would get around really fast and the trafficker would find out. After this is over, you can tell everyone the truth."

"Are you kidding me? We don't even get along that well. How can we pull this off?"

Derek sounded unamused. "Come on, Connor. Do it for Anna. Please?"

Connor gave an exasperated sigh. *Why me?* "Ugh. Fine. But she's not going to like it. We're on our way."

Connor hung up the phone and turned to see Anna walking up to him, staring at him. "Was that Derek? What did they just say to you? Were you talking about me? I'm not going to like what?"

"Wow. That's a lot of questions." He'd get to that part later. He already had enough to tell her. "That was Derek, yes," Connor said, and filled her in on the conversation, leaving that last bit out.

"Lilly and Katie Holt? I've known them since they were babies," Anna said. "It's not like them to just leave. They aren't like that. They're devout and wouldn't leave their families or make them worry. At least, they were devout when I left. That was a long time ago."

"So, I know this is probably a lot to ask, but will you go to Unity with me and stay with Derek and Maria? I can't investigate there without you. I need you to be my eyes and ears."

"Katie and Lilly are my friends, along with their older sister, Ella Ruth. Traffickers could be targeting more of the girls there. Of course." Anna nodded, suppressing her rising anxiety. "I'll go with you."

"Thank you. I know it might be hard for you. So I really appreciate this, and of course, you'll be helping shut down a sex trafficking ring."

Anna smiled in satisfaction. "Honestly, I'd love nothing more than that." She knew first-hand how traumatic and terrifying it was to be kidnapped by those monsters. If she could help prevent one girl from being taken or help even one girl be rescued, she would do anything.

"Maybe you can talk to Debra and Ella Ruth to see if they remember anything else. Do they know you well?" Connor asked.

"Well, I haven't seen them in a while, but yes, I know all of them well. I think they trust me. But Debra is young and shy. I'm not sure if she'd tell me anything."

"You've got to try."

"Okay. I'll try."

"And do you think you can ask around and try to figure out who this supposedly Amish man is? I can't exactly go around the community asking nosy questions. The guy doesn't know who I am. But he'd trust you and would be a lot more willing to talk to you."

"I think I could, yes."

Connor continued, "I think this man might be a groomer, or a young man who gets girls to meet up with traffickers at a certain place and time. They develop a friendship with young women and get them to trust them, then lure them into trafficking before the girls realize what's happening. The young man might not even realize the full extent of what he is doing, but he was probably promised a lot of money. He might think he is setting up regular dates. But they are not regular dates. These girls are being sold," Connor explained, then winced, touching her shoulder. "I'm sorry. That was blunt. I know they're your friends. Are you okay?"

Anna's eyes reddened with tears and she swiped the moisture away. "It's not just that. You know traffickers have targeted Unity before."

Connor nodded solemnly.

"This is bringing up terrible memories. But I want to help," she said, determination rising in her voice. "I'll do anything to help."

His eyes were understanding, and he didn't pry. "That's the spirit. Let's go to Unity."

After Anna changed his bandages again, they made their way out of the motel and toward the car, the knot of dread grew within Anna's belly with every step. Unity was where she'd had her heart broken by Isaac Troyer, who married Olivia Mast, one of Anna's best friends. It was where her parents had died, and where she'd been abducted.

But Unity also held good memories. Unity brought back happy memories of her childhood and teenage years, like going to Maria's house to play when she was a child, or going to Singings and work frolics, canning applesauce, and attending church and school as she grew up. She hadn't left Unity because she couldn't wait to leave. Leaving was the hardest thing she'd ever done. Her calling to be a nurse was stronger than her fear of leaving home. And after her parents died and Isaac told her he was in love with Olivia, she'd felt like nothing was stopping her anymore.

Still, she hadn't seen her community in so long. What would people say? Would they judge her for leaving? Or would they be happy to see her?

Doubt and fear crept in as she imagined no one wanting to talk to her and people talking about her behind her back. Or worse, mocking her outright.

"Anna, are you okay?" Connor asked again as he started the car and began driving. "You're quiet. And that never happens. It's weird."

Anna nodded. "I just don't know how people will react to me coming back. I'm nervous."

"Um, there's one more thing I need to tell you."

Anna gave him a sideways look. "I already know I'm going to hate this."

Yes, she was.

"We have to pretend to be married," he blurted out. Now he wished he would have pulled over, just in case she punched him while he was driving.

"What?" she roared. "Are you kidding me? Why?"

"Well, think about it. I need to stay at Derek's house with you to keep you safe, just in case anything happens. I can't tell anyone I'm working undercover or else the groomer might leave before we can figure out who he is. Do you really want people getting the wrong idea about us, especially with you coming back? They'll have enough to talk about already."

Anna took in his words, nodding slowly. He was right. The Amish gossiped too, just like anyone else. "This stinks."

"I know. I'm sorry. I mean, we don't have to. I'm just thinking about your reputation. It's up to you."

"Ugh." She covered her face with her hands. "If I come home as an *Englisher* and stay in the same house with a man I'm not married to, it would look bad. Yeah." She shook her head. "I can't believe I'm saying this, but you're right. We have to pretend to be married."

"Once the investigation is over and the trafficking ring is shut down, you can tell everyone the truth. They'll understand why we had to lie, right?" Connor asked, sounding way more optimistic than he felt.

"I hope so. When Olivia had to lie to everyone, pretending to become Amish again when she was investigating a murder, we were hurt. But we understood why she had to do it. Hopefully, the community will understand this time, too."

"Right. Exactly. Don't worry, you'll get back to the hospital, back to your life." He looked solemnly at her. "I'll make sure of that."

Anna nodded, realizing that she believed him when he said he would keep her safe. Of course, it was not him she was counting on, but it still felt odd to see who God was using to keep her safe.

But at that moment, what she feared the most—even more than getting shot at or being chased down by the assassins—was how her community would react to her return.

Chapter Eleven

As they drove through the town of Unity, before they even reached the Amish community, they caught glimpses of some Amish people on the street in their distinctive clothing.

Connor opened his mouth to ask something, then saw that Anna looked a little nervous. "As long as they don't make me wear that funny hat, I don't think I'll mind anything else they can make me do."

"They won't make you do anything." Anna smiled. "But that's too bad about the hat. I think it would look good on you."

Connor chuckled, then turned serious. "You nervous?"

"Yup," Anna replied.

"Don't worry; I'm right here with you."

She nodded gratefully for his reassurance then realized what he'd just said. He was offering emotional support. Anna looked at him, surprised by his sudden show of kindness.

He caught her looking at him. "What? I mean it. I'm here for you. Especially after all you've done for me, and how you're willing to help me. It's the least I can do."

She nodded. "Thank you." Her heart smiled at his sincerity, and she wished she'd see more of that side of him.

They drove past the yellow diamond-shaped sign with a black buggy on it, warning drivers to look out for buggies. They were getting close.

Anna found that people often expected the Amish community to be separate from the rest of the town, a smattering of farms and white houses clustered together, gated and closed off from the rest of the world. But the Amish homes were spread out throughout the area and ranged in color from maroon to tan or gray, but none of them had shutters or power lines. Anna's childhood home had been next to a group of several other Amish homes, only a short buggy drive away from the church that doubled as the schoolhouse. Since her parents had died, she'd sold the house to a nice Amish family. The place had brought so many memories of her parents anyway, making her miss them even more.

"There are some bad memories I have of this place, but they are mostly good. I had a wonderful childhood, and I always had friends and family around. One thing that I've really been missing is the church here."

"Why?" He'd blurted out the question, then wished he hadn't.

Anna looked at him. "Because it feeds my soul. I love worshipping the Lord, listening to the sermon, and enjoying the fellowship. I mean, I go to a church in Portland, but it's not the same. It's so different from the one here I grew up in. So, you don't go to church, I'm guessing?"

"Not anymore," he replied as he settled back into his seat. "Not in a very long time."

"Well, maybe you'll want to go with me this Sunday. It's not that far from Maria's house."

"Not going to church with you, Anna." He stared resolutely at the road in front of him, his face not inviting any further discussion on the matter.

"But we will be telling people we are thinking of joining the Amish church. Won't it seem odd if you don't go to church?" Anna argued.

"I'll tell them I wasn't feeling well if anyone asks."

Anna would have dropped it if she did not feel so strongly that going to church would do him a lot of good.

"I'm not saying you have to decide now or anything, just saying you should think about it. Besides, don't you want to get to know people and ask questions? That's the best place to do it," she said.

"All right, that's it. I already told you I'm not going to church, and I don't like you pushing the matter. I've made up my mind, and that's it."

She blinked in shock. He didn't want to go, even just to talk with people and see what they knew? "Sure, yeah." She swallowed and cleared her throat in the hopes that her voice would stop shaking. "Suit yourself. My soul needs it, so I'm going. It's up to you if you want to come. I'm sorry for pushing it."

"Look, I'm really sorry for lashing out at you like that. It's just..." He took a deep breath. "Look, I can't go into why, and to be honest, I don't feel like I need to. You know the people better anyway, and you'll find out a lot more than I would. I'll probably just sit outside. I'd like to be nearby, just in case. I'm sorry."

Anna stayed silent, trying to figure out what had just happened. Why did he hate church so much?

"Turn left here," she said as they came upon the Unity Community Store, a small Amish store owned by her friends Irvin and Esther. The car jostled down the dirt lane, approaching the Amish homes behind the store.

As they slowly drove past the wide fields of crops, Anna saw a few men stop their work to glance at them before continuing. She recognized some of them and knew the exact moment they recognized her, too. She saw curiosity on their faces, followed by wariness, and if she was being honest with herself, it hurt a little seeing the guarded looks in their eyes. She turned her eyes toward her destination.

As they neared the end of the lane, Anna saw Mrs. Baker and Mrs. Johnson walking down the lane, two women who were known to gossip. When they saw Anna in the car as Connor drove past, their eyebrows raised in shock.

"Was that Anna?" she heard one of them say as she passed.

There was no turning back now. Soon the whole community would know she was here.

"We should stop here and tell the bishop I'm here before rumors spread," Anna said.

"Want me to go with you?"

"Well, if you're going to be my husband, yes. They'll want to meet you." Anna couldn't help the trace of bitterness that showed through her words. She hated lying but knew it had to be done in this case.

Anna took a deep breath, got out of the car, and walked up to a woman washing clothes in the backyard.

"Good afternoon, Marta," Anna greeted the woman, recognizing the wife of Bishop Byler.

Marta recognized Anna and her eyes widened, and she grinned, hurrying over to give Anna a hug. "Anna! It is great to see you."

"Thank you. I'm glad to see you, too. It's good to be back." Relief washed over Anna at Marta's kind welcome.

"Are you staying?"

"Visiting. I'm here with my husband." Anna tried not to wince as she said the words, guilt filling her as she lied.

"Ah! Husband?" Marta said enthusiastically. "I had no idea you got married. What wonderful news."

"Thank you," Anna said. "This is Connor."

Connor gave a half-wave and a fake smile. "Hi. Nice to meet you." He must have known the women here didn't shake men's hands because he didn't offer her his hand.

"I'm so happy to meet you," Marta said. "We're glad to have you here."

"May I speak with Bishop Byler? Is he home?" Anna asked.

The door to the house opened, and a man stepped out. A jolly looking elderly man with a long gray beard approached them. He was a much more forgiving and understanding man than their former bishop had been. "Anna," he said jovially. "What a wonderful surprise."

Anna introduced him to Connor, and they greeted each other.

"I just wanted to let you know we will be staying with Derek and Maria for a short time. I know word will spread quickly, and I wanted you to be the first to know."

"Thank you for letting me know."

"Also," Anna glanced at Connor. "I'm thinking about rejoining the Amish, and Connor is considering joining." Connor smiled uncomfortably, but Marta and the bishop didn't seem to notice.

"That is good to hear. We hope to welcome you into the church soon," the bishop said.

She suddenly heard a commotion behind her and turned around to see familiar faces running towards her. It was Maria, Derek, and their son Carter, who looked about eight or nine, but Anna wasn't great at guessing ages. Even from this distance, Anna saw Derek still had a limp. When he'd been Maria's bodyguard, back when he worked for

CPDU, he'd been shot in the leg while rescuing Maria, Anna, and their friend Liz from the traffickers who'd kidnapped them.

Anna smiled as Maria caught up to her and immediately wrapped her arm around her in a very tight hug. In Maria's other arm, she held a baby on her hip.

"I'm so glad you're here!" Maria cried, somehow squeezing Anna even tighter, even with one arm.

"I'm so glad to be here! So, this is Rebecca?" Anna asked, taking a step back to look at the child. "Can I hold her? How old is she now?"

"Of course!" Maria carefully handed Anna the baby who was now looking up at Anna with big, blue eyes and reaching up at her with pudgy fingers. "She's a year old now, but she thinks she's sixteen sometimes."

"Wow!" Anna said. "A year old? That went by so fast. I'm sorry I wasn't here to help when she was born." Anna looked down at the sweet baby, guilt filling her. "Even a year ago, it was too hard for me to come back, because of the memories of my parents." Anna smiled at Rebecca, who said something in gibberish. "I'm sorry, Maria."

"I totally understand," Maria said. "Actually, I had to go to the hospital anyway. There were some complications, but once we got there and everything was sorted out, she was born safe and healthy."

"I'm glad to hear that."

"Derek." Connor beamed, pulling his friend into a big hug. "Good to see you, man."

"You, too," Derek said. "It'll be great to spend time together." Anna caught a twinkle in his eye. Did Derek miss his former occupation with CPDU? Maybe he was looking forward to investigating again.

"They can stay with us," Derek said to the bishop.

"Good." Bishop Byler turned back to Anna. "We still pray for you and hope you will change your mind and come back to the church. For what it's worth, it's great to see that you're well. Hopefully, you'll have a lovely enough time here that you'll truly consider staying."

After saying goodbye, Maria pulled on Anna's hand as they left.

"You know you didn't need to ask for Bishop Byler's permission or anything, right?" Maria said to Anna. "We would have put you up no matter what he said."

"I know," Anna replied. "I just felt like it was the right thing to do before he heard about it through the grapevine."

"True. Anyway, I'm so excited you're here."

So far, it had been a much warmer welcome that she'd anticipated. She relaxed a bit, taking a deep breath. She told herself everything would be fine.

At least for now, they were safe.

Chapter Twelve

"I still can't believe I'm standing in the same room with you," Maria said to Anna as she handed her a few changes of clothing.

Anna smiled. This was the third time Maria had said that, and it reminded Anna just how much she missed her friend.

Rebecca toddled around the living room, playing with books and puzzles, while Carter read a book nearby. He was always reading.

"Connor, this is for you. You and Derek are about the same size, so it should fit," Maria said, handing Connor a stack of plain Amish pants, shirts, and suspenders with a black hat on top.

"Awesome," Connor said, smiling as he held up the hat. "I've always wanted to wear one of these."

"Well, hurry up and change, then I'll show you my new cabinet shop," Derek said to Connor.

Anna went upstairs to the room she'd be using and quickly changed. As though no time had passed since she'd last worn an Amish dress and prayer *kapp,* her fingers deftly worked the pins on the dress that held it in place. She swept her hair up into a bun, pinned it in place, and put her prayer *kapp* over it, letting the white ribbons whisper against her shoulders.

She glanced in the mirror over the dresser, not sure what to feel besides guilty about pretending to want to be Amish again.

No, she'd left this life behind. It just wasn't for her. Saving lives, working on the front lines of health care was where she belonged.

Anna hurried down the steps into the kitchen where Connor stood talking with Derek near the kitchen table. Anna smiled at the sight of Connor in his dark pants, white shirt, and suspenders.

"What?" Connor caught her looking at him. "I look nice, huh?"

"Yes, actually. But don't let it go to your head," she said with a smirk.

Connor just smiled and nodded at her. "You look pretty nice yourself, Hershberger."

"All right, let's go," Derek said with a laugh, pulling Connor toward the door to show him his new cabinet shop. Connor was clearly happy to spend time with Derek.

They were among friends now.

"It's great to see you, too. It's much better seeing that you're truly doing great than reading it in your letters," Anna said to Maria.

"You'll always be family to me. You know that, right?" Maria said.

Anna nodded. "Of course, I do. I'm sorry I waited until I really needed to before coming here."

"Hey, I'm just glad to see you. It's so weird how you and Connor met like you did. He's been Derek's friend for years, and you've been my friend for years. What are the odds that you'd meet that way?"

"You mean him pointing a gun at me and making me get in a car with him so an assassin wouldn't kill us? Yeah. Maybe it was fate."

"You're going to have to tell me all about that. I want to know the whole story. All I've gotten so far is Derek telling me what Connor told him over the phone. But I want your side of the story."

99

Anna filled Maria in on all the details from how she'd met him in the parking lot to how he'd offered her his emotional support when they'd arrived in Unity.

"See? He is a nice guy," Maria said. "I mean, he always was when he came to visit. He used to even go to church with Grace. Although, that was before—" Maria stopped mid-sentence.

"Who is Grace?"

"Oh," Maria's face paled. "I'm so sorry, I thought you knew about her."

"Knew what?" Anna persisted.

"I shouldn't say anything more about it. Connor should tell you, not me. I'm sorry."

"Oh. Okay. Well, maybe I'll ask him."

"No, you should wait until he's ready to tell you. It's hard for him to talk about."

Wow, something terrible must have happened, Anna thought. Was that why Connor was so prickly and cold when she'd first met him?

"You know, when we walked through the door, you could almost see his brain working, trying to figure out escape routes," Maria said, clearly trying to change the subject.

"He's promised to keep me safe." Anna couldn't help but smile. "You know, when I told him I've never seen a movie before, he offered to take me to the movies to see my first one after all this is over."

"No way." Maria gasped, dropping the potato she'd been peeling. "Like on a date?"

"I don't know," Anna said. "I can't read him most of the time. At first, he was so prickly and ornery, and now he's kind of sweet. Sometimes. When he wants to be."

"You like him." Maria grinned like a child about to sneak into the cookie jar.

"No! He's too annoying."

"What? Come on! Don't lie to yourself." Maria playfully shoved Anna, making her drop her own potato. Maria smiled at Anna. "The first time I saw both of you, the first thing that popped in my head was how good you look together."

"What do you mean by that?"

Maria shrugged. "I don't know. Maybe it was how he stood close to you, how he looks at you, and how you look at him like—"

"I do not look at him like anything."

"Sure. But not only that. How you also seem ready to jump to his defense." She reached out and took Anna's hand. "It's not just that. He looked comfortable in your presence and you in his. He's not like that with just anyone."

"Really? It's not even that," Anna said, her smile fading. "I don't know if I can trust him. I don't know him very well. He told me he's innocent, but sometimes I wonder if those assassins are after him because he really was an assassin."

"I've known Connor since Derek and I got married, and Derek has known him for years. Derek trusts him. He's a good man. He's not an assassin. He was undercover."

"I don't know what to believe," Anna sighed. "He puts up walls and won't let me in. And I know I do that too, and I have ever since I was abducted. I just feel like it's so hard to get to know him. I wish he'd give me some type of hint about how he feels about me."

"Connor is like that. Don't worry, he just needs some time."

"Enough about me. So, what has changed since the last time you wrote to me?"

Maria shrugged. "Nothing much. Liz and Simon finally got married. Remember I told you he was courting her?"

Anna nodded. "I remember that. Wow, Liz has gotten married. I hope I get to see her before I leave."

"Of course, you will. We could even go over to her place tomorrow and pay her a visit. I'm sure she'll be delighted to see you."

Anna knew that was true. She and Liz had stayed in touch after she left the community until a few years ago when their letters became farther and farther between as they both got busy. She still asked about her from Maria and sent her well wishes. But her reservation was not because she was afraid of how Liz would receive her. "I'm just not sure how people will react to me being here."

Maria smiled and took a pot and filled it with running water from the sink. "You'd be surprised by how many people will be glad to see you."

Anna was still unsure. "I don't know. They weren't exactly thrilled the first time I left."

"Of course, they weren't. You were rejecting them and what they stood for. Besides, it would not be wise to show any encouragement to someone leaving the faith. But that was a long time ago, and they've had time to think about it."

"I'll believe that when I see it," Anna said as she swept up the peelings. "What about Connor? I mean, he's a strange face. No one knows him."

Maria glanced at her friend, noting the concern in her voice and the look in her eyes. "He'll be fine. Don't worry. He's not the first strange face they have seen around here. Besides, everyone will think you're married."

Anna resumed sweeping. "I guess so."

"Like I said, times are changing here. Let's just say we're no longer as strict as we used to be. Last week in church the men even talked about opening a bed-and-breakfast inside the community and catering to people who would like to see what it's like to live Amish."

Anna's eyes widened in surprise. "Really? Wow, that's really progressive."

"Not really. They didn't get enough votes to pass the idea," Maria said with a chuckle. "But Derek said that it was hotly contested. So, progress, but not exactly progressive, yet."

Anna smiled. "Well, I guess we should be happy for what we do have."

"That's the point," Maria replied as she put the potatoes on the woodstove. "It's so great to see you, Anna. I've missed you."

She'd said it four times now, but Anna understood, and she grinned at her friend.

"I've missed you, too."

*****

"Thank you again so much for letting us stay with you," Connor said to Derek as they entered Derek's new cabinet shop. "Wow, this is a nice place."

"Thanks. The community helped me remodel it after Gideon retired and passed the business onto me." Derek walked back to the counter and leaned on it. "We're thrilled to have you here. Maria is ecstatic to have you both stay with us."

"We don't want to be a bother to anyone. And I know it might be weird for Anna to be back here."

"If you know anything about Anna by now, you'll know she is a truly great person. Everyone loves her. Sure, we were unhappy to see her leave, but most of us understood that she would have been unhappy if she had stayed here. I think most people will be happy to see her."

"Good. So, are you still loving the Amish life?"

"Absolutely. I wouldn't trade it for anything. Haven't regretted it for a second."

"I mean, the buggy and hat are cute. I just don't understand how you left everything behind and adapted to this lifestyle."

Derek shrugged. "Because I understood that what I was gaining was more important to me than what I was losing, which wasn't much." He grinned. "I love Maria, and trust me, I would do anything to be with her. This was nothing."

"Sure, but maybe it would have been easier convincing Maria to leave with you."

Derek smiled. "Then you don't know my wife. Or me, for that matter. Being Amish is not something we measure in terms of convenience or see as a sacrifice. We are happy here. Happy to live this lifestyle because it lets us concentrate on things that are truly important. Like God and family. It helps us grow personally every day and also teaches us to love our community and that material things don't really matter in the pursuit of happiness." He shrugged with a small grin. "Now, there are cases where the things you want in life are unfortunately not available here. Like in Anna's case. Then you have to decide what you want to do about that. Even for her, it wasn't easy to leave."

Connor knew that. Just like he knew Anna was definitely happy to be back, and seeing her with Maria, he knew he had never seen her this happy in the short amount of time he'd known her.

She deserved to be happy. To meet someone who would love her the way Derek loved Maria and to protect her. He knew very well that person was not him.

As long as she was safe and happy, he would be okay with that. Even if it meant leaving her. Connor pushed his mind to focus on what was important. Making sure she was safe from Korovin and his goons, even if he had to risk his life to make sure of that.

"I'm sorry I stopped coming to visit you after Grace died. I shut everyone out when I needed you most. I'm sorry," Connor said, leaning on the counter beside Derek.

"I get it," Derek said. "I was the same way when my first wife Natalia was murdered by those traffickers. After that, it felt like nothing mattered anymore. I threw myself into my work. My life was empty until I met Maria. We tried to contact you, but when you didn't respond, we figured you would come to us when you were ready."

"Yeah, sorry about that too. I ignored your calls and letters. I just wasn't in the right frame of mind to really talk to anyone."

"Well, you seem happier now, which is kind of weird, considering you have assassins chasing after you. Maybe it's Anna. Maybe she's had a good influence on you. She's pretty funny, huh?"

"Funny? I don't think that's the right word. Stubborn, annoying, pestering—"

"Devoted, loyal, brave…" Derek countered. "Come on. You can be honest with me. What do you really think of her? Is there anything going on with you two?"

"No," Connor blurted, a bit louder than he'd intended. "I mean, she's pretty. I won't deny that. But she thinks I'm an assassin or some type of criminal. She doesn't trust me. How can anything happen between us if she doesn't trust me?"

"Well, that can change, my friend. Give it some time. Dinner should be just about ready," Derek said, pushing himself away from the counter. "Time to head home."

Connor waited as Derek locked up. Then both of them made their way back to the house.

Chapter Thirteen

Derek, Maria, Anna, Carter, Connor, and baby Rebecca arrived at the Holts' house. A few seconds after Anna knocked, Esther Holt opened the door and wrapped Anna in a hug.

"I'm so glad to see you," Esther said. "It does my heart good."

"I'm glad to see you, too," Anna said, squeezing her friend tighter. "And I'm so sorry for what happened to your daughters."

Esther pulled away. "God is watching over them. We pray they will be home soon. Come in, come in."

The group entered the house and took off their shoes and jackets. Carter ran off to play outside.

"Have you called the police?" Anna asked quietly. Hopefully, they hadn't.

"No, we are trusting the Lord," Irvin Holt explained. "If it is His will, He will bring them home. We pray for them constantly."

"I just wish there was more we could do," Anna said, relieved they hadn't called the police.

"Pray. That's all we can do." Esther nodded solemnly.

"We brought you this," Maria said, handing them a loaf of her homemade banana bread and a casserole.

"Oh, thank you. We so appreciate how the community has been taking care of us in our time of need," Esther said. "I won't need to cook for days." She attempted a weak smile, but it didn't crinkle the fine lines near her eyes.

"That's what community is for. You are family to all of us," Maria added.

As Maria continued to chat with Esther and Derek introduced Irvin to Connor, Anna saw young Debra coming down the stairs, peering at them shyly. Anna slowly approached her.

"Hi, Debra. Remember me?"

Debra shook her head.

"I've known you since you were a baby. But you haven't seen me since you were very little. We came today to visit you and your family. I bet you've been having a lot of visitors lately."

The girl nodded again.

Anna sat on the bottom steps. "I bet you miss Katie and Lilly."

"*Ja*," Debra said, then sat down next to Anna.

"I want you to know I'm doing everything I can to bring them back home to you," Anna assured her, and the child's eyes lit up. "But I need your help, Debra. Can you help me?"

Debra nodded enthusiastically.

"You share a room with Katie and Lilly, right?" Anna asked.

"*Ja*."

"So, before Katie and Lilly went away, did you hear anything they talked about at night in your room? Maybe when you were supposed to be sleeping?"

Debra furrowed her brow and looked at the wood floor. She looked back at Anna, unsure.

"It's okay, Debra. I'm trying to help your sisters. I'm a friend. You can tell me."

Debra scooted closer, her dark eyes wide. "They said they were going on a date," she whispered.

Progress. "Oh, really? Did they say who asked them to go on the date?"

Debra leaned even closer. "A handsome young Amish man."

"Wow. You have a very good memory, Debra."

The child smiled.

"Do you remember anything else they said? Did they say his name?" Anna asked.

Debra paused again. "They didn't say his name. They talked about what to wear."

"Did they say they were going to wear Amish clothing or *Englisher* clothing?"

"Amish clothing."

"Hmmm." Interesting. "You have been so helpful, Debra. Do you remember anything else they said? Did they say what the men's names are?"

Debra shook her head. "I was sleepy. I don't remember anymore."

"That's okay, Debra. You've helped me very much." Anna patted her hand. "I am praying that God brings your sisters home safe."

"*Bitte*." Debra thanked her. "I'm going to *spiele* now."

"Have fun playing."

Debra hurried back up the stairs.

Anna sighed. She wished the young girl had remembered more, but this was a start. Anna was surprised to hear the girls wore Amish clothing on their date. Perhaps they had planned on changing into *Englisher* clothes after leaving the house. When sneaking out, Amish girls sometimes wore *Englisher* clothes.

Who was this young Amish man? Anna thought through all the young Amish men in the community. She'd known them all since they were babies. And they were all still here in Unity, as far as she knew. So if any of them did take Katie and Lilly on dates, they came home even when the girls didn't.

Would any of them take a young woman on a date with evil intentions?

Anna stood up from the steps, heading back into the kitchen. She could see Irvin, Connor, and Derek talking outside.

"When we woke up to find them missing, I cried and cried," Esther told Maria as Anna approached.

"I can't even imagine. I would have outright panicked," Maria said, patting Esther's arm. Anna couldn't relate as much because she didn't have children yet, but she knew she would probably also panic if one of her own children went missing. Hopefully, that would never happen.

"I know God tells us not to worry, but..." Esther covered her face and succumbed to a fit of sobs, and Anna and Maria wrapped their arms around her. Anna's own eyes stung with tears as Maria wept with Esther.

Please, God. Help us get the information we need to shut this trafficking ring down and bring the girls home. Please protect them.

And even if they weren't trafficked, please bring them home, Anna prayed.

Ella Ruth came through the front door and took off her jacket, looking concerned for her mother. Anna patted Esther's back and released her. Leaving Maria to comfort the older woman, Anna approached Ella Ruth while Esther was preoccupied.

"Hi, Anna. It's great to have you back. How are you?" Ella Ruth asked.

"I'm good, but I'm more concerned about you and your family. I know this has been hard on all of you. I'm truly sorry."

Ella Ruth lowered her eyes.

"You must be close to Lilly and Katie. Did they tell you anything about the young Amish man who set them up with dates? Do you know his name?" Anna asked.

Ella Ruth shook her head. "No, they didn't tell me anything. I think they thought I was going to tell on them. And to be honest, I probably would have told on them. I can be overprotective sometimes."

"Of course. I understand. I'm sure the police will want to know the name. I'm just curious. If there are young men here with impure intentions, the other young women should know."

"Right." Ella Ruth sighed. "They were so set on going, and there probably would have been no way to change their minds."

Anna lowered her voice to a whisper. "What if he asks out other girls?" Anna didn't have to say the rest for Ella Ruth to have a look of realization cross her face.

"I know you're trying to protect the other girls. I wish I knew more, but I don't. They don't share everything with me. I'm just the goody-two-shoes older sister." Ella Ruth slowly shook her head. "I wish they could see how I'm just trying to protect them."

Anna reached for Ella Ruth's arm. "Sometimes we can't change someone's mind, even if we know what's best for them. Ultimately, they have to make their own decisions, and there's nothing we can do about that. None of this is your fault."

Ella Ruth's eyes reddened with unshed tears. She looked away, swiping her sleeve across her face. Her feet shifted her weight restlessly.

Was Ella Ruth holding something back?

"Ella Ruth, is there anything else you want to tell me?"

"What? No," she spluttered. "Really, I don't know anything else. I'm sorry. I wish I knew."

"Okay. Well, if you think of anything, please come by and tell me anytime. And if you need someone to talk to as a friend, I'm always here for you." Anna pulled Ella Ruth into a hug.

"Thanks, Anna."

"We better get going, Anna. Rebecca will need her nap soon," Maria said, her eyes still red from crying.

Anna took one last look at Ella Ruth before leaving, just in time to see her scurry up the stairs like a frightened child, even though she was a young woman of about twenty years.

Now Anna was sure of it. Ella Ruth was hiding something.

*****

Late that night, as Connor lay awake in bed, he began to think back about what Anna had said in the car about church.

He knew she was right. Not only should he be going to church for his soul but also to gather intel.

He still wasn't sure he was going to do it, though. Praying hadn't helped Grace. Still, he knew if Grace were here, she would have found a way to convince him to go. She managed to do it the first time, and when they were together, he really started to enjoy going to church. The sense of kinship and fellowship he felt with his fellow church members, the strange peace and calm that followed a good prayer session, the joy of singing hymns in church. He used to love that.

After Grace died, he told himself that she was the reason why he used to enjoy church. He wondered what she would say now if she were alive.

What would Grace say about Anna if she were still alive?

Thinking so much about Anna made him feel guilty, like he was somehow betraying Grace, even though he wasn't.

Trying to distract himself, he reached into his pocket for his phone. Still no call and no messages from Ben or Jeff.

Anna was going to go to church, and there would be no stopping her. If she insisted on going, he knew he should be nearby, in case he needed to protect her or Derek's family.

Maybe it would be enough to just sit outside the church door and wait for the end of the service.

*****

"Thank you," Connor said as Maria cleared the plates in front of him.

The four of them had just finished breakfast, and it was the best breakfast he had eaten in a long time. Only politeness stopped him from asking for thirds. The food was just that good. Although he was pretty sure it was not just the food that had Anna grinning as she joined him at the table, setting her medical supplies down. And once again he was reminded of what a truly happy Anna looked like.

"Nice to see you in a good mood," he said to her as he rested both elbows on the table and leaned forward.

"What do you mean?" she asked as she changed his bandages.

"That I've never seen you so happy in the short amount of time we've known each other."

"Well, that is to be expected. It's great to catch up with friends I haven't seen in a long time." She nodded at him. "Besides, you seem pretty happy yourself."

He almost cracked a smile.

"Okay. I'm done," she said after changing the bandages, putting her medical supplies away.

"You ready?" Maria asked, looking at Anna.

"Yes."

"Where are you going?" Connor asked.

"We're going to visit our friend Liz."

"Maybe this Liz knows something about the groomer. Can I come?"

"Sure," Anna said. "We can definitely ask her. She's friends with many of the younger Amish girls."

"I'll come too," Derek said.

114

"Sounds like a plan." Connor put on his black hat. He turned to Anna and waggled his eyebrows, making her laugh.

Chapter Fourteen

Anna stood behind Maria as they knocked on Liz and Simon's door. Maria, Derek, Carter, and Rebecca were also with them, but Carter ran to the backyard to play.

As Anna waited for someone to answer, she took a look around. It was clear it was just newly built, and she loved the quaint but charming design. As per Amish custom, she knew everyone in the community had chipped in to help with the building, and she remembered what that felt like. All the men worked together to help one of their own start his family.

Anna remembered attending many work frolics growing up, the talking and laughing as they worked, and how they would all join in when one of them raised up a spontaneous hymn from the *Ausbund,* the Amish song book. The women would bring baskets of food for the men during their break. Children would run and laugh as they helped their mothers serve the men, and some of the older ones were even roped into helping. Suddenly feeling nostalgic, she realized there was a lot she missed about living in the community.

The sound of someone behind the door brought her out of her reverie, and she stood up straight when she saw that it was Liz who had come to the door.

"Morning, Maria." Liz greeted Maria, then she saw Anna behind her. Her eyes widened in shock as she rushed forward and hugged her hard. "They said you came in yesterday. I can't believe it!"

Anna smiled as she hugged her friend back, too emotional to say anything. After a few seconds, both friends separated but still held hands. Simon wandered over to the door, wondering what the commotion was all about. Then he saw Anna, and he looked just as surprised and happy as his wife.

"Would you believe that?" he asked with a wide grin. "Liz was just talking about going over to Maria's place to pay you a visit. Hi, Derek. Who's this?"

"This is Connor, my husband," Anna said, still feeling the sting of guilt.

Simon shook Connor's hand. "Nice to meet you, and great to see you too, Anna." He took a step back from the door. "Come on in!"

"Let's go make a pot of tea," Liz said to Anna and Maria as the men were chatting and laughing. "May I hold Rebecca?" she asked Maria.

"Of course." Maria handed the baby to Liz.

"I still can't believe you got married," Anna said, grinning at her.

"I could say the same about you. Actually, I was just thinking maybe you can help me deliver my own baby in about six months," Liz said, shifting Rebecca in her arms.

Anna's eyes widened. "Wait, what?"

Maria looked just as shocked. "You're pregnant?"

Liz nodded, practically glowing with pride. "Yes, I am pregnant. I haven't told many people yet. Do you think you could help me deliver my baby?"

Anna was touched by the faith that was being placed in her, and she was filled with an odd combination of happiness and guilt. "I don't know if I will still be here then."

Liz sighed. "I would have loved for you to do it." She suddenly had tears in her eyes. "I still remember how you helped me with my leg injury at the warehouse when we were abducted."

"You would have been fine," Anna said, squeezing her hand reassuringly. "All I did was treat a cut."

"Maybe, but it was more than just treating a wound. It was how you stayed with me, talking to me and making sure I wasn't panicking." She used the back of her hand to wipe her tears away. "I'm sorry. I can't seem to stop crying. Must be hormones."

Maria waved her apology away. "Don't worry about it. After the news you just shared, a few tears are not only expected, but welcome."

Anna nodded. "I'm so happy for you, Liz. Marriage suits you."

"I'm so happy, and Simon is simply the best husband." Liz sat at the table and leaned forward. "But I want to know about you. So, tell me about Connor. How did you two meet?"

"Uh…" Anna's heart rate spiked. She hadn't thought about this. Anna glanced at Maria, who only shrugged. "We met at the hospital where I work."

"Oh! Was he a patient?"

"Well, yes."

"How romantic," Liz murmured. "So you took care of him as his nurse and you fell in love?"

"Ha. Something like that," Anna said with a nervous laugh.

This was ridiculous. She couldn't lie to one of her best friends like this.

I have to tell her the truth.

"I'm sorry, Liz. I can't lie to you. That story isn't true."

"Anna!" Maria whispered with caution.

"Actually, that was true. He was my patient, and I took care of him, and I might have developed feelings for him at that time, but there's a whole lot more to the story than that," Anna said all in one breath.

Liz stared at Anna, eyes wide and mouth agape. "I want to know everything. Please. I won't tell anyone, I promise. I can keep a secret."

Maria rolled her eyes and shrugged. "Well, she can. She's kept plenty of my secrets over the years. You might as well tell her. Maybe she can help us more if she knows the truth."

Anna told Liz the whole story, all in a hushed whisper so Connor wouldn't hear. "So, have you heard anything about this young Amish man, this groomer? Or anything about Lilly and Katie's disappearances?"

"I don't know anything more than what you know. I know they went missing the night before last, and I heard they had mysterious boyfriends, but nothing more than that. I don't know if they were Amish or not. Most people are guessing the boyfriends are not Amish and that they convinced the girls to jump the fence for a few days. They think they'll be back soon, or hope so, at least," Liz explained. "But you think it's much more serious than that, don't you?"

"Yes, I think they were taken by traffickers. But we have no proof at all, and we can't ask the police or CPDU for help because of the mole, or moles. Right now, I really need information from people here," Anna said. "So, if you can ask around and see what people know, that would be great. Maybe because I haven't been here in a while, people might not be telling me everything they know."

"Of course, I'll ask around," Liz said with an enthusiastic nod. "And what about you and Connor? Are you together?"

"No. It's not like that." She shook her head. "I'm helping Connor with the case and with his bullet wound. That's all."

Maria raised a brow. "You sure about that? You two looked absolutely sweet on each other this morning."

Anna blushed. "No, we did not. Connor's just a friend, nothing more."

"Why?" Liz asked.

"It's very complicated. When the right man comes along, I'll know."

"And how do you reckon you'll know when the right man comes along?" Maria asked. "I mean, it's not like they write these things on their forehead."

Liz chuckled. "Now, wouldn't that be a sight? If you see a man walking around with 'Anna's man' written on his forehead, then you'll know."

Anna laughed. "I don't know. I think I'll just pray and ask God to guide me to the man He chooses for me." Anna shrugged. "Isn't that how it is supposed to happen?"

"Yes, sometimes." Maria smiled. "But you have to be careful when you pray that you're not waiting for the answer you want instead of the answer He chooses for you."

"So you think God has chosen Connor for me?" Anna asked, wondering how they had ended up talking about this.

"I have no idea, silly. All I'm saying is if a good man makes your heart sing, then maybe that is the sign you've been waiting for," Maria said.

Liz took Anna's hand. "Don't mind Maria. You know how she's always liked playing matchmaker."

Anna turned to Liz with a big grin on her face. "All right, I want to hear everything about you and Simon. How did you two end up together?"

Liz beamed, and it was clear she was about to talk about something she loved. Anna settled down to catch up with her friends, grateful for the chance to be with them.

One of the men opened the front door, and they heard the sounds of someone coming in, a young woman's voice.

Ella Ruth Holt stepped into the kitchen, holding a large container of soup. "Hello," she said. "They told me I'd find you in here. My mother wanted me to bring you this in case you don't feel like cooking. Or eating, for that matter."

Liz chuckled. "Oh, Esther. I told her I was pregnant the other day. Tell her I said thank you. And she's right, I don't feel like cooking or eating much. Simon will appreciate this too." Liz took the container from Ella Ruth. "But really, I should be the one bringing your family food with everything that's happened."

"No, no, don't worry. We have plenty. Again, it's great to see you back, Anna," Ella Ruth said, clearly putting on an artificial smile. "Sorry I didn't get to talk to you much last night with all that was going on."

"Thank you. Yes, and I'm sure it's been a lot for your family. Again, I'm so sorry. I don't have siblings, but I can't even imagine. You know we are praying for all of you," Anna said, her heart breaking for the Holt family.

Ella Ruth nodded, her eyes filling with tears. "I worry about them all the time. And..." When she choked out a sob, all three women gathered around her to comfort her.

Anna patted Ella Ruth on the back. "Ella Ruth, if you know something, anything at all, you can tell us. It would be good to talk about it." Anna's eyes met Maria's, and they exchanged a knowing look.

"I feel like it's partly my fault!" Ella Ruth cried, wiping her tears with her sleeve.

"Why, dear?" Liz asked.

"Because I knew about the date and didn't tell my parents. My parents wouldn't have let them go and they'd still be here."

Liz, Maria, and Anna looked at each other. Ella Ruth had told her that Katie and Lilly hadn't told her anything about the date. Why hadn't Ella Ruth told Anna this last night?

"Well, I'm glad you told us. And it's not your fault. They might have still sneaked out without your parents knowing," Anna said. She wanted to get more information out of Ella Ruth, but had to do it cautiously. "Is there anything else on your mind?"

"Well, I'm a little scared. I know you want information so we can alert the other girls in town. There is a young man who asked Katie and Lilly on dates. The night Katie and Lilly went on their dates, both girls went missing."

A young Amish man, just as Debra had said. Anna wanted to pepper Ella Ruth with questions and had to take in a deep breath to calm herself down. If she became too persistent or pushy, Ella Ruth might shy away. "Why are you scared? Who is he?"

"Liz and Maria, remember the new man you met at church, Moses? The traveling salesman?"

Maria and Liz nodded eagerly, eyebrows raised in anticipation.

"Of course," Liz said. "He seemed a bit odd to me."

"It's him," Ella Ruth said. "And yes, he is a bit odd. He doesn't know much Pennsylvania Dutch, only a little. He says he comes from a less traditional community in New York where they don't speak it anymore. He's been coming and going here for several months now, saying he travels for work."

Anna wanted to dash out of the room and shout Connor's name, but she held still. "Why are you scared of him, Ella Ruth?"

"Because he asked me on a date, too."

"Would you excuse me for a second? I'll be right back." Anna slipped out of the room and hurried to find Connor. The men were in the barn.

"Connor? I need to talk to you!" Anna called, and Connor walked over to her.

"I found out something." Anna told him what Ella Ruth revealed. "She could help us. I think we should tell her everything."

*****

Connor drew his brows together in thought. The more people who knew about this, the messier it could get. "How well do you know her? Would she tell anyone?"

"I don't think she'd tell anyone. Her parents are worried enough, and she'd do anything to protect her sisters. She feels terrible, like it's her fault."

123

"Maybe we could use her as bait," Connor said, pondering the options.

"What?" Anna all but shouted. "No way!"

"Hear me out. If this guy asked her on a date, she can agree to go and we can watch them from a distance the entire time."

"And what if something happens?"

"Derek and I have years of training for these types of situations. Of course, now it's different, because we can't rely on the police or CPDU for help this time. If he does kidnap her, we will follow them, and he might lead us to the traffickers. If he hurts her, I'll make him wish he hadn't. But it's up to her. We have to ask her. Maybe we can get Ben or one of the other guys to come help us. I hope Derek wants to help with this. Now that he's Amish, I don't know for sure if he will, but I'll ask him. Beg him."

"Okay. And, Connor, there's one more thing." Anna winced. "I kind of told Liz everything."

Connor looked like he was about to unleash a hot retort, then he closed his mouth and reconsidered. "Actually, that might be a good thing. She can help us ask around and see if any of the other girls were approached by our suspect. She can keep a secret too, right?"

"Definitely. We've been friends for years, and she never told any of my secrets."

Connor waggled his eyebrows. "Oh, really? What kind of secrets?"

Anna playfully punched him in the arm. "The kind of secrets I'll never tell you."

"Ow. Go easy on the injured guy. How old is she?"

"I think she's about twenty or twenty-one. I'll ask her."

"Let me know what she says. Hopefully she's over twenty-one."

Anna was already walking back toward the house, eagerly anticipating Ella Ruth's response. She burst through the door. "Ella Ruth, how old are you?"

"I'm twenty-one. Why?"

"Good. You're an adult. Well, we need your help."

"Me? What do you mean? I told you everything I know this time, honest." Ella Ruth stared at her with wide eyes.

"No, there's something else you can do. But before I tell you what it is, I need to know a few things. Do you want to help your sisters, even if it puts you in danger?"

Liz gasped. "Anna, what are you talking about?"

"Yeah, what's happening?" Maria asked. "I thought no one was supposed to know about this."

"I just talked to Connor. We need her. She could really help us," Anna said, gesturing to Ella Ruth. "If you want to help us, Ella Ruth."

"Yes, yes, of course! I want to help, even if it's dangerous. I feel responsible for this, so I want to do everything I can to get them home," Ella Ruth insisted. "And I won't tell anyone, not even my parents. Just tell me what I need to do."

Anna explained the plan to Ella Ruth, expecting her to back out at any moment. Ella Ruth listened intently with wide eyes as her face paled.

Once Anna was finished explaining, Ella Ruth nodded. "I'm in. I'll do it."

"Really? Thank you, Ella Ruth. If this guy is working with the traffickers, I think with your help, we might get the information we need to take them down. And Connor won't let anything happen to you," Anna assured her.

"So what do I do now? Moses asked me on a date, but I said no. So, now should I tell him I changed my mind, then let you know when the date is?" Ella Ruth asked.

"Just act friendly and interested toward him. If he's a groomer, he will ask again."

"I don't know where Moses lives, and I don't have his phone number. I'm not even sure if anyone knows what his last name is. It's probably a fake name, right?" Ella Ruth asked.

"Probably," Anna said.

Ella Ruth sighed. "Well, I guess I'll have to wait until the Singing to talk to him then. It's tomorrow night."

"Okay. I'd go with you, but since everyone thinks I'm married to Connor now, I wouldn't really fit in. How about you let us know after? We can wait nearby, just in case he tries anything on you or the others." The Amish Singings in Unity were for the young singles in the community, so married couples didn't usually go. "And maybe we can follow him home from there."

"Sounds like a plan."

Chapter Fifteen

After leaving Liz's house, they walked back to Derek and Maria's house. As the women and children went inside, Connor spoke up.

"Derek, can I talk to you out here for a minute?"

"Sure," Derek said and sat on the bench on the porch.

"Do you by any chance still have any of your guns?" Connor asked, sitting beside him.

"I just have one gun, but it's a rifle I use only for hunting. Lots of Amish men around here have guns for hunting, and we never intend to use them for self-defense. Why?" Derek looked at Connor hard. "What's going on? What are you about to ask me?"

Connor told him what Anna had learned from Ella Ruth. "We could be getting close. If this guy is a groomer helping the traffickers, we could follow him during the date, and he might lead us right to where they are keeping the other girls. There are only a few people I trust with this. I think Jeff, Isaac, and Olivia are busy tracking down Cassidy Hendricks, so I don't know if they can come up here and help with this. Even if they can, if the traffickers find out more outsiders have come here, it might make them suspicious, and they might run."

Derek nodded slowly.

"I need your help, Derek. I know you left your police work behind when you joined the Amish, and I've already asked so much of you, but would you help me with this? Will you help me follow him?" Connor's eyes pleaded with his friend, and he waited anxiously for an answer.

"No. I'm sorry."

"What? Really?" Connor hadn't known what to expect to hear from his friend, but the answer still shocked him.

Would he really say no to helping rescue innocent girls?

"I left all my old ways behind when I joined the Amish. I won't pick up a gun in self-defense ever again. I'm done with violence. I chose this peaceful life, I love it, and I don't want it to change. I don't want anything to change," Derek admitted, looking at his hands in his lap. "I don't want Maria to think I'm going to leave the Amish."

"But you won't! I just need help this one time. This isn't for me. You could be helping rescue several innocent girls. It's just this one time."

"You say that, but this one thing will lead to more. I know what will happen if I say yes to this. I'll be involved until the end. And I can't do that. I just can't." Derek stood up and stomped into the house, leaving Connor sitting on the porch alone, stunned.

Derek was different now, that was for sure. Connor would have to get in touch with Jeff or Ben and see if either of them or one of the others could help him instead.

For now, he had to teach Anna to drive so he could help her follow Moses tonight. One of them might have to walk ahead of the car, because they would drive with the headlights off. The car would periodically pull over to let the buggy get ahead, and right now, Anna was the only one who could help him.

*****

128

Later that day, there was a loud screeching sound as the car came to a sudden stop.

Anna's heart came all the way up to her throat. Her grip on the steering wheel was so tight, her knuckles had turned white.

Then she turned to Connor sitting beside her and found him looking as cool and unfazed as ever.

"I guess you get points for finally figuring out that to stop the car you press the brakes," he said, looking around at the empty road. "Good thing we're on a back road. Otherwise, someone might call the cops reporting a reckless driver."

Anna took several seconds to get her breath under control. "This is why I didn't want to do this," she panted. "It's too hard."

"And how many times did you say that when you were in nursing school?" Connor shook his head. "I can't believe that a woman who has no problem poking a man with a big sharp needle is balking at driving."

Anna paused, realizing that he was right. Sure, it kind of looked daunting now. Just like it had been when she realized that learning to be a nurse was not as glamorous as she imagined it would be. But, oh, how she loved it.

Still, she did not give up, thinking instead of what her reward was going to be if she just persevered and got the result she wanted. The joy of passing her nursing exams. How happy she was when she saw a patient leave the hospital, healed and happy.

"At least there is a point to studying. If I didn't read, I failed." She scowled at the steering wheel. "I don't see why I need to learn how to drive. I can always take the bus or catch a cab."

"Okay." Connor nodded, pretending to agree with her. "I mean, just because you're too chicken to do something doesn't mean you should do that thing anyway. Besides, if something happens and I am shot again or something, thank God you went to nursing school. You can do your nurse magic and heal the wound instantly so I can continue driving."

Anna narrowed her eyes at him. "I know what you're doing, and I can tell you it's not going to work."

"Sure, I know that." He placed his hand on the handle of the door. "Switch seats so I can drive us home."

Anna growled inwardly, telling herself several times that she didn't need to do this, didn't need to prove any point to him. Then she placed her hand on the steering wheel.

"All right, I'll try one more time. We try this one more time, and after that I don't want to hear about it."

"Remember to put the car in reverse and check your mirrors before you try to drive," Connor simply replied.

Thirty minutes later, Anna's grip on the steering wheel was still as tight as ever. But she had managed to drive to the end of the street and back three times.

"So," Connor asked after they were parked back in the driveway, "how does it feel to finally conquer your dreams?"

Anna's face had the widest grin he had ever seen when she turned to him.

"Thanks, Connor, for making me do this." She paused as she twisted her hands in her lap. "I think I can admit now that this was more about my fear of driving than it had ever been about me growing up Amish."

*****

That evening, Connor and Anna waited in Connor's car under some trees for the Singing to end. As they watched people leave the house where the Singing had been held, they saw Ella Ruth walk out with a young man—the suspected groomer.

They spoke for several minutes, but from this distance, Anna couldn't hear at all what they were saying. Finally, they parted ways, and the man drove away in his buggy. By then, everyone else had gone their own ways, so Ella Ruth walked over to the trees where she knew Anna and Connor were waiting in the car.

"Our date is tomorrow night at seven," she told them. "I wish we didn't have to wait so long for the date. I'm so worried about my sisters."

"I know," Anna said. "And we had to wait for the Singing just to talk to him. Does anyone know where he's staying?"

"No. No one knows where he lives," Ella Ruth said.

"He probably has a place outside the community," Connor said. "Anyway, we will be at your house tomorrow night waiting for him to pick you up so we can follow you. And right now, we need to go follow him." His eyes watched the buggy slowly amble down the lane, still in sight. They still had time to let it get ahead so he wouldn't notice their car.

"I'll be ready," Ella Ruth said. "See you tomorrow night."

"Let's go," Connor said, starting the car, and slowly driving it behind some trees, keeping the lights off. He waited until the buggy went around the corner, then drove the car down the lane. "If he heads

131

downtown, we won't be as easily spotted. I won't make you drive tonight, but you might have to get out of the car and walk to see where he goes so I can hang back in the car."

Anna nodded.

They followed him down several streets, only about two miles outside the Amish community, where he stopped at a horse boarding barn. They watched as he led the horse inside, left the buggy parked outside, paid the owner some cash, then got in a beat-up car and drove away.

"Ha," Anna spat. "I mean, we knew he wasn't Amish, but now we know how he got the horse. He must have bought the buggy locally and is leaving it there when he's not using it."

Connor snapped some photos with his phone. "Just in case the Amish girls aren't convinced he's a fake, this should convince them."

They followed him a few more miles downtown until Moses stopped at a dingy apartment building. Moses got out of the car, then walked up the steps to the second-floor balcony. Because the stairs and door were clearly visible and exposed, Connor could see which apartment Moses went into.

"So, this is it. Well, I seriously doubt anything is up there, and if I have Ben or Jeff search it with a warrant, he could get spooked and leave town. Then we'd lose our lead." Connor glanced at some trash barrels on the curb. "I have an idea. Wait here, okay?"

"Okay," Anna said. "What are you doing?"

"Delivering a pizza," Connor said with a laugh, pointing at an empty pizza box on top of a recycling barrel. He was wearing his regular street clothes now, luckily, and not his borrowed Amish ones.

Connor got out of the car, grabbed the box, and headed up to the second floor, where Moses lived. He knocked on the door, pulling his baseball cap low over his eyes. "Pizza delivery."

A moment later, Moses opened the door. "I think you have the wrong apartment number, man. I didn't order pizza."

"You sure?" Connor asked. "Hold on, maybe I got it wrong." Connor turned quickly, as if to check the number on the apartment door. He fell on the balcony floor hard, then grabbed his ankle in mock pain. "Ow! My ankle."

"You okay, man?" Moses asked, kneeling down to help Connor up.

"Oh, yeah, yeah, I'm fine." Connor tried to get up, then cried out, as if his ankle had been twisted. "I think I twisted it. I'm not sure if I can walk. Do you have any ice?"

"Yeah, dude. Just wait a second," Moses said, walking inside his apartment.

Connor bolted up, dashed silently from the open door into the living room, then peered into the bedroom. He also looked around for anything with the man's name on it, maybe some mail or something on the wall, but didn't find anything in those few moments.

Connor made it back to the doorway before Moses came back. He sat on the floor near the door.

The apartment was teeny tiny, definitely not a place where several missing girls would fit.

"Here's an ice pack," Moses said. "Want me to call somebody?"

"Nah, I'll be fine in a minute. Just gotta sit here for a few minutes and I'll be fine."

"Want to come inside and sit on the couch?"

Connors eyebrows shot up. He hadn't expected the guy to ask him to come in. "I don't want to put you out, but that would be really great."

"Come on in," Moses said, helping Connor up and helping him hop to the couch. All the while, Connor held onto the pizza box, just in case Moses got nosey and peeked inside. That would be a dead giveaway.

Either this guy was really great at pretending to be nice, or he actually was a nice guy caught up with the wrong people, maybe desperate for money.

How could he not know what he was doing by bringing girls to the traffickers? He had to know.

No. Moses was not truly a nice guy at all.

"Thanks," Connor said as Moses helped him ease down onto the couch.

"No problem. Want a soda or water or something?"

Wow. What service.

"No, that's okay. I'll be out of here in a minute. I gotta get this pizza to the right person."

"Okay. I'm just going to watch the game," Moses said, turning on a football game on TV.

With Moses sitting right there, Connor couldn't exactly get up and look around, unless he asked to go to the bathroom, but Moses would probably help him there and back anyway. He watched the game for a few minutes, just to play along, then set the ice down.

"I think I'm okay to walk now," Connor said, moving his foot. "I don't think I actually twisted it. It's probably just bruised."

"Okay, do you need help?"

"No, I'll see myself out. Thanks a lot, man," Connor said, limping out of the living room to the door. Moses followed him politely.

"Okay, have a good night," Moses said, opening the door for him.

"You, too," Connor said, then walked out the door. Just for show, he limped all the way down the stairs and to his car, just in case Moses was watching out the window.

"What happened?" Anna asked in the car.

"There aren't any girls up there," Connor said, driving down the street. "But he was nice. It was weird." Connor told her about how Moses had offered him the ice and let him sit inside.

"Wow. So, he's great at pretending to be something he's not. That's why everyone thinks he's actually an Amish man."

"Exactly."

Chapter Sixteen

Late that night, Connor's phone buzzed. Connor let out a breath, relieved to see it was Ben. Finally.

"Hello?"

There were a few seconds of silence before Ben finally spoke. "Is this line secure?"

"What do you think?" Connor replied impatiently.

"There is a reason why we set up these protocols, and you of all people should know how important it is to ensure we follow them."

There he goes again, acting like a know-it-all. Typical Ben. "Yes, the line is secure, Ben," Connor said. "I've been trying to reach you. Where have you been?"

"I'm so sorry," Ben said. "Jeff, Olivia, Isaac, and I have been trying to track down Cassidy Hendricks ever since you warned her the assassins were after her. We think she went to South America and then on to Africa. I've been here with Tucker and Davis, trying to find out who the moles are in CPDU. This line is separate from my normal cell phone, and I didn't have it on me while I was at CPDU since you've been trying to reach me. I'm sorry. I didn't want them to know about it."

"It's okay," Connor said. "I have a lot to catch you up on." Connor explained everything that had happened so far.

"It's been harder than you think, especially since we are doing this on our own." Ben sighed. "To be honest, if it wasn't for Anna, I would have said you should report for debriefing. Your presence here may force the mole out of hiding. Sounds like she's been a tremendous help."

"Absolutely. Today she got some information, and we are setting up something." Connor explained how Anna got Ella Ruth to agree to use her as bait. "We're going to have Anna follow them on their date, and I will be waiting nearby if something happens. We are hoping eventually the groomer, if that's who he is, will lead us to the headquarters. We followed him to his apartment tonight, but nothing was there." Connor explained how he got in with the pizza delivery charade.

"Anna is impressive. Her Amish roots could help us a lot more than we expected. You should keep her around. I remember Anna. I asked her on a date after Derek and I finished our assignment while protecting Maria Mast. We went on one date, but it didn't go anywhere."

"Yeah, I bet. She told me all about your date," Connor teased.

"Oh, stop. That was forever ago. She's great, but I don't think we had a connection."

"I know, she told me that too. You know, I really hate putting her in danger. Even though she knows the risks and still wants to help. I asked Derek to help me follow them, but he said no. I think if we had one of you come here to help me, it might make the traffickers suspicious to have another outsider come here, since Anna and I are already here. What do you think? Do you think it's a bad idea if one of you come here to help me out?"

"Like I said, we are tracking down Hendricks, and Tucker and Davis are busy at CPDU trying to find out who the mole is, and I'm pretty busy helping them. If I leave, the moles at CPDU will notice. It would be better if it was only you and Derek, because like you said, if I show up too, it might seem suspicious. It's not common for outsiders to be there as it is. Can you ask Derek to reconsider? I'm surprised he said no. It's not like him to turn down something like this."

"He's different now. He's Amish."

"Still, we need him. And about Anna, I know she's useful, but if you change your mind, we could move her to a secure location. Maybe we could arrange to transport her to a safe house that would be known by only both of us and a few selected people we know we can absolutely trust. But setting up such an operation without the knowledge of the higher-ups is very difficult, and it sounds like we really need her help."

Connor couldn't argue with that. Still, he knew something had to change and soon, too. Anna had a life she needed to get back to. Plus, he couldn't protect her forever. Every day Korovin remained free, Anna's life was in danger.

"Is anyone else working with you?" Connor asked.

"No," Ben replied. "It's just us. I don't trust anyone else at CPDU. Even Tucker and Davis don't know the full specifics. Jeff, Olivia, and Isaac know everything though."

Connor had no problem with Ben trusting them. They were like family.

"Tucker and Davis don't know about Anna yet?"

"No."

Connor leaned against the wall of the house. "So, what's going to happen now?"

"Give it one more week or so and if nothing turns up, you come in with what you have, we put your woman in witness protection and hope we wade out of this mess with our hands still clean. But it sounds like with Anna's help, you'll make a lot of progress quickly."

Connor sighed. "I don't know. I've got this bad feeling, this itch between my shoulder blades that I can't seem to scratch."

"You think you've been compromised?" Ben inquired hesitantly.

"No." Connor paused. "No one knows where I am."

"I don't think I need to tell you how important it is to listen to your instincts in this kind of situation."

"I know, and I don't think it is anything like that. I think I feel like I'm more relaxed than I should be."

"Do you think this has anything to do with the fact that for the first time since Grace died that you're spending time with a woman?" There was a pause. "Anna's beautiful."

"Anna?" Connor snorted, trying to hide the fact that his face heated. It was a good thing Ben couldn't see his face now or he never would have heard the end of it. "Nah. Anna is nice enough, I guess. More annoying than anything."

"Oh, really?" Ben's voice had a smile in it and Connor found himself gritting his teeth. "Hey, you know, Jeff's wife was Amish."

"Yeah, that's true," Connor replied, wondering how his mind had skipped over the fact that Jeff's wife was also Amish. "But Anna isn't Amish anymore. Hey, how easy was it to teach his wife to shoot?"

"Actually, she picked up on it well. In fact, you remember what happened when her attacker finally came for her. Why?"

"Oh, nothing."

"Are you trying to teach Anna to shoot?"

"Trying. She won't let me."

"It's because of how they were raised. The Amish don't believe in self-defense. Lucy fought it hard at first, but she agreed later once she realized it was necessary."

"Anna did agree to let me teach her how to drive, so we're making big progress."

"There's a start. I'll keep an eye out here and if we can resolve this soon, we'll do so. Otherwise, she goes into witness protection. That drive is encrypted, but nothing the cyber team at CPDU can't hack. Hendricks said she didn't want it to fall into just anyone's hands, and she knows Korovin wants her dead."

Connor said, "I have no reason to doubt her. Sorry, I've got to go. Call if anything happens."

"Will do," Ben replied. "And if Derek still refuses to help you follow the groomers, let me know. I'll try to be there. At least I could wait at one end of town in my car and you can let me know when they are headed my way. Then you could drop back slightly and not seem like a tail. Let me know."

They ended the conversation and the line went dead in his hand. He took the phone away from his ear. For a few moments, he just stood where he was.

Maybe there was still a chance for redemption.

Maybe there was still hope that Connor could take a step back from the darkness slowly covering him.

*****

The next morning, over two cups of coffee, Connor told Derek about his conversation with Ben last night and how Olivia and Isaac were helping them.

"I'm sorry about last night, Connor. I overreacted," Derek said. "I was up all night thinking about what I should do."

"I understand if you don't want to, Derek. You did leave your old life behind to become Amish. I get it. Ben is worried that if he leaves CPDU to come here, even for a day, the moles will take notice and so will the groomer and traffickers. We both agree it would be better if you did it, so we don't raise suspicion by bringing in another outsider, but we can make it work."

"I know. I keep thinking about those girls. If something ever happened to my children and someone had the choice to help them, I hope that person would help them, no matter the cost. I know I vowed to never use violence again, and I hope it doesn't come to that, but if I need to in order to help those girls, I will."

Connor could hardly believe what he was hearing. "You'll do it? You'll help me?"

"Yes, Connor. I'll help you follow them."

"Oh, wow, thank you." Connor stood up and gave his friend a hug, slapping him on the back. "You probably won't even need to use a weapon. I just need you as backup. Maybe to contact someone if I get hurt. I'll do my best to keep you out of harm. If we're successful, we'll only follow them, then once I know where the headquarters is, I'll call in for backup and you can go home. That's it."

"Whatever you need from me, I'll do it. But we have to keep this between us. I talked to Maria about it, and she was totally in agreement, but we both know I could get shunned if anyone finds out," Derek warned.

"I understand. Thank you, Derek. I'll call Ben and let him know."

*****

Connor drove Derek, Anna, and Maria in his car to the Holts' house to speak with Ella Ruth about their plan before the date. As he drove, Connor updated Anna about what Ben had told him. Carter and Rebecca were staying with Mary and Gideon.

"You must know Olivia Troyer, right, Anna?" Connor asked. "And her husband, Isaac? Her name was Olivia Mast before she got married. I know she's your cousin, Maria."

"Of course!" Anna cried. "We've been friends since we were babies. And besides, Maria and Olivia are more like sisters."

"Everyone calls her Liv. After her family died in the fire, she came to live with us. She really is more like a sister to me," Maria said, then grinned at Anna. "And so are you."

"Well, Olivia and Isaac are working with Ben and Jeff to track down Cassidy Hendricks. They think she might be in Africa," Connor told them. "If they find her, they'll probably let her know it's safe for her to stay with them, then maybe they can come back here and help us out."

"Wow. I hope they get back here safely," Anna said.

"We're here," Connor said, parking the car down the lane from Ella Ruth's house so her parents wouldn't see it. They walked the rest of the way and secretly met her in the barn.

"Thank you again so much for doing this," Anna said to Ella Ruth in the Holt's barn, away from where her parents could hear them.

Anna and Maria wore *Englisher* clothes, so they'd blend in with the other people in the restaurant where the date was set to take place, and hopefully Moses wouldn't recognize them. Anna wore her hat and some fake glasses, and Maria also wore fake glasses. Hopefully, it would be enough without going over the top, considering they hadn't officially met Moses yet.

"We really do appreciate it," Connor added. "This is very brave of you."

"I just hate lying to my parents about it. I told them I'm going on a date with Moses, but they think he's a nice, innocent Amish man, of course. And they believed me, because I've never lied to them. I'm supposed to be the 'good girl'. I just hope they'll understand why I'm doing this and I don't lose their trust forever," Ella Ruth said, twisting her apron in her hands.

"They will understand, especially if this helps find your sisters. Don't worry. We will talk to them after this is all over," Maria said, patting Ella Ruth's arm.

"Thank you. Well, he should be here to pick me up any moment," Ella Ruth said.

"We will be waiting in my car," Connor told her. "We will follow you to the restaurant. Anna and Maria will be at a nearby table the whole time. If he takes you somewhere else, we will follow. I'm not going to put a wire on you, in case he looks for one, but Anna will be wearing one. If she thinks there's immediate danger, she's going to say the code word: cake."

"Cake? Really?" Anna said, scrunching up her nose at Connor.

"Why not? I like cake," Connor stated, smiling. "Ella Ruth, if you feel like you're in danger at all or want to get out of there, just look at Anna and Maria and scratch your head."

"Okay. Okay," she said, probably more to herself than anyone else, as if she was trying to reassure herself she could do this.

"Don't worry, Ella Ruth. We will be right there. If anything happens, we will be there in seconds. We won't let anything happen to you," Derek said, as if reading her thoughts. "Connor and I have been doing this for years. I'm a bit out of practice, but I think it will be like riding a bike." He gave a half-smile.

"If he takes you to where the other girls are being kept, we will follow you there. Then we will know where your sisters are, and we will call for backup. We'll get you out. I know it's scary. But we've got you covered."

"I know, I know. I'm just nervous." Ella Ruth shifted her feet.

Why had Connor just told Ella Ruth that they would call for backup if she was taken to where the other girls were being held, making it sound as though she'd be rescued immediately? Anna didn't know much about police operations, but she guessed it might take some time for CPDU to gather personnel and make plans for such a tactical response.

"Hold on," Anna said. "Even if you call for backup, wouldn't it take a while for CPDU to respond? They don't know what we know, and we'd have to catch them up. I don't know much about CPDU, but wouldn't it take them a while to plan how they would storm a building and rescue the girls? At least a few hours?"

"Well, it depends," Connor said. "If Moses does take her to the other girls, we will have to call for backup. Ella Ruth," he said, turning to her, "we will get you and the others out as soon as we can."

144

"That's our only option, Anna," Derek said. "We're hoping for the best here."

"Ella Ruth, you know what you're signing up for, right?" Maria said.

"Yes. I understand if he takes me, you might not be able to get me out right away. I don't care. I told you I'd do anything to get my sisters back, and I mean that. I still want to do this," Ella Ruth said, nodding.

Anna crossed her arms. She didn't like this, not one bit.

"Let's pray," Anna said, then took Connor and Maria's hands. Everyone held hands in a circle, and she prayed, "Lord, please give Ella Ruth peace tonight. Please give us the information we need to find Katie, Lilly, and the other girls. Please keep us alert and keep us all safe. In Your name, Amen."

"Amen," everyone repeated.

Anna didn't want to let go of Connor's warm hand in hers. And did he just rub his thumb along her knuckles, or had she imagined it?

She quickly let go and crossed her arms, hoping no one noticed how flustered she was.

"We better get in my car before Moses—whatever his name is— shows up," Connor said, and they all hurried out of the barn.

Rain drizzled, coating the starlit fields with a coat of water that glistened in the moonlight as the four ran to Connor's car. It was parked behind some trees near Ella Ruth's house so they could see when Moses picked up Ella Ruth while remaining concealed.

About twenty minutes later, a buggy pulled up near the barn. Another few minutes later, the buggy ambled down the dirt lane. Connor followed at a distance with his headlights off, often pulling over on the side of the road to give it time to get ahead. Derek also got out of the car and walked ahead to help Connor navigate.

It was definitely not ideal, and a trained professional would notice the car following, but Connor hoped Moses wouldn't notice. Normally, CPDU would use several cars to follow a suspect and avoid suspicion, but Connor's car was all they had right now.

What seemed like hours later, they arrived at Little Italy, the most expensive restaurant in town, where Ella Ruth was going on her date with Moses.

Ella Ruth and Moses walked inside, and they waited a moment before going in.

"Remember," Connor said before they got out of the car, "if you feel like you or Ella Ruth are in danger, the code word is cake."

Anna nodded. "Got it." Before she slammed the door shut, she caught Connor's gaze. He looked at her intently with concern in his eyes.

"Be careful, Anna."

She gulped, her heart rate quickening. Was it from the way Connor was looking at her or the fact that she was about to go undercover with zero experience? "I will."

Chapter Seventeen

Anna shut the car door and hurried inside the restaurant with Maria where the smells of Italian food and the clinking of wine glasses greeted them. They looked around and saw Ella Ruth and Moses sitting at a table in the right corner.

When the hostess came to seat them, Anna said, "Can we sit at a table near that corner? On this side of the room?" Anna gestured to an area that was behind Moses and Ella Ruth. Anna knew they might not get a table right next to them, but she hoped they would be close enough so she and Maria could try to listen to their conversation.

"Of course. Right this way," the woman said. They followed her to a table that was two tables behind Moses and Ella Ruth.

"So, we're just two friends having a girls' night out," Anna whispered as they sat down. "You know, if Moses happens to see us and talk to us."

"Right. Be cool." Maria picked up a menu, then shook her head. "Should we even order anything? I'm too nervous to read this menu."

"We should or else it will look suspicious. Who goes to a restaurant and doesn't order anything?" Anna whispered, reading her own menu. Then she said in her normal voice, "Let's split fettuccine Alfredo."

"Sure. Sounds good. I love fettuccine Alfredo." Maria shifted in her seat, looking over at Ella Ruth.

"Stop staring," Anna whispered.

Maria quickly looked away.

It took willpower for Anna to not glance over. They made mindless small talk while trying to listen to Ella Ruth's conversation with Moses.

"I know we have only met a few times," Moses was saying, "but I am falling for you, Ella Ruth. You're kind, smart, and beautiful. Any guy would be lucky just to talk to you."

Anna rolled her eyes. He'd probably been trained to say that.

"Really?" Ella Ruth said, sounding nervous.

"Of course." From where Anna sat, she could see Moses reach for Ella Ruth's hand across the table. He said, "I want to take you out again. You deserve to be treated like a princess. I can buy you jewelry, clothes, a car, anything you'd like."

"I'm Amish. I don't want any of those things," Ella Ruth said. "They don't matter to me."

"Really? There isn't a small part of you that wants to wear jewelry or wear normal clothes? I can give them to you. I can give you anything you want. What would you like?"

"I like books," Ella Ruth said shyly.

"Then I will buy you a mountain of books."

Wow. What a schmooze.

"You are the most beautiful woman I've ever met, Ella Ruth. I'm falling in love with you," Moses said to her.

Ella Ruth paused and almost met Anna's eyes, then quickly looked back at Moses. Nice save. "I'm falling in love with you too," she said in a shaky voice.

Good. She was playing the part.

For the rest of the meal, Moses showered Ella Ruth with compliments, promising her the world. The waiter came to take their drink order, then Maria and Anna pretended to chat while listening to what Moses was saying. "If you could go anywhere in the world, where would you like to go?" he asked.

"Um…" Ella Ruth hesitated again, looking down at her lap. Ella Ruth had probably never even left the state of Maine before. "Anywhere in Europe."

"I will take you there, my darling. I promise. And soon."

"Really?" she asked, and even Anna was convinced that Ella Ruth was excited about it.

"I promise."

A few minutes later, the waiter brought Anna and Maria their food. They ate absentmindedly, occasionally talking about this and that while still listening to Ella Ruth and Moses.

"Well, I should take you home," Moses told Ella Ruth. "I don't want your parents to get worried."

Maria looked at Anna with wide eyes. Anna raised her eyebrows, silently telling Maria to keep calm.

Moses led Ella Ruth out of the restaurant, but not before placing a one-hundred-dollar bill on the table. Moses watched for Ella Ruth's reaction.

"Moses, that's too much, isn't it?" she said sheepishly.

"I always like to leave a big tip," Moses said arrogantly. "Just to spread some kindness."

Anna wanted to vomit.

As the couple walked by, Anna and Maria bent their heads over their plates. Anna let out a sigh of relief when they continued walking out of the building.

"Wow. He just paid with a one-hundred-dollar bill. There's no way the meal cost even half that much," Anna said so Connor and Derek could hear.

It only confirmed their suspicions.

"Come on. Let's go." Anna slapped some cash on the table and they walked out, keeping a good distance.

As Anna and Maria stood in the entryway, they looked out the window to see Moses help Ella Ruth into the buggy. He unhitched the horses and drove away, then Anna and Maria hurried to Connor's car where Derek was also waiting.

"Well, that guy is a sleazebag, I'll tell you that. But nothing happened," Anna said as they got in.

"The night isn't over yet. Let's see if he's really taking her home," Connor said, and they followed slowly behind the buggy all the way back to Ella Ruth's house. Connor parked behind some trees in the shadows.

"That's it? He's really taking her home?" Anna spat. "I really thought he'd try something."

"He could be doing this to get her to trust him," Derek said. "He's keeping his word. He thinks that will make her trust him more. It will make him seem honorable."

"I wonder what they're talking about," Maria said as they watched the couple talk inside the buggy for a few minutes. Then, without so much as a kiss goodbye, Moses helped Ella Ruth out of the buggy. She waited until Moses drove away, then crept through the back door.

"Wow. That was uneventful," Maria said. "I mean, I'm glad she's not hurt, but I was hoping we'd find the girls tonight."

"Me too," Anna said, feeling the exact same way.

"Well, let's follow him again. We can talk to Ella Ruth tomorrow and see if Moses asked her on another date," Connor said.

"From the way he was talking to her, I'm sure he did," Anna said in agreement.

Connor drove the car slowly down the lane to follow Moses again.

*****

The next morning, someone knocked on the door after breakfast as Maria and Anna cleared the table with Carter.

"I'll get it!" Carter said enthusiastically, racing for the door.

"Hold on there, Tiger. Let me see who it is first," Maria said, looking out the window. "It's Ella Ruth."

Anna walked over as Ella Ruth came inside.

"Carter, go play for a minute, okay?" Maria said, and Carter dashed off to the living room and pulled a puzzle down from the shelf that was quite advanced for his age.

"You did great last night," Maria said to Ella Ruth.

"Really? I was so nervous."

"You played the part well, even if you were nervous. It seemed genuine," Anna added.

Derek and Connor came inside from doing chores in the barn.

"We saw you walk up. Great job last night," Connor said. "Did Moses ask you on another date? And did he try anything on you that we missed? We followed him again last night after the date, but he only went to his apartment again, which was a disappointment."

"He was a perfect gentleman. Or at least he acted like one. He didn't even try to kiss me. But yes, he asked me on another date. He wants to take me to the movies. I've never been, but secretly I've always wanted to go, so I agreed."

"Good. You did the right thing," Connor said. "Now he thinks he can get you to do things that are against the rules. When is the next date?"

"The day after tomorrow at seven in the evening."

"Can't he do tomorrow night instead?" Anna asked.

"No, he said he'd be working. The soonest he could do it is the day after tomorrow," Ella Ruth explained.

"Well, we will be there. Same routine," Derek said.

"Good. Well, I better get going. I told my mom I was visiting Lydia at the bakery, so I should be on my way there. I'll see you later," Ella Ruth said, then let herself out.

"She's a brave young woman," Anna said with a sigh, watching Ella Ruth walk down the lane. "Braver than I could ever be," she added under her breath.

Anna hardly noticed that Maria and Derek had gone into the kitchen, leaving her alone with Connor in the entryway. She jumped when she turned and realized how close he was standing next to her.

"We both know you're the bravest woman I know, Anna Hershberger," Connor whispered into her ear, making her shiver as she took a quick step back. Why did he have to do things like that, flustering her?

Uncomfortable with his rare compliment, she was about to dash away when he gently took hold of her wrist. "When you prayed for Ella Ruth last night in the barn..." He sighed. "It was wonderful. I don't know about anyone else, but I felt at peace."

"Really?" she asked, tucking a stray blonde hair back into her *kapp*.

He nodded. "It reminded me how it felt to pray again. Thanks for that."

"I'm glad," she said, all too aware that he was still grasping her wrist. His touch sent heat radiating up her arm, like sparks from a fire. She pulled away awkwardly, made an excuse about helping Maria with the dishes, and darted away before she could do something foolish.

As she walked away, she couldn't suppress the smile that spread across her face, thankful he couldn't see it.

Chapter Eighteen

That evening, as Anna washed dishes, she was not surprised when Connor joined her at the sink to help her dry and put them away.

"Dinner was great," he said after several seconds of silence between them. "You were right. You are a great cook."

"Thanks." Anna couldn't hide her smile.

"You ready to practice driving again?"

"Well, I'm not sure I'm ready to drive on any major roads yet."

Connor nodded in conciliatory agreement. Then with a sly grin, he added, "Of course I'm sure you'll get over that fear quickly enough when you have people shooting at us."

"Yeah," she said awkwardly, unable to meet his eyes.

"You okay?" he asked gently.

Anna nodded. "Sorry. I just realized that a few weeks ago I was complaining about how hectic my roster for that week was. Now I'm wondering if I'll be shot at."

Connor was quiet. He didn't know how to respond to this or what he could say to make everything better. Especially since the only way to make things better was for her to get back to work and to the life she knew. Connor couldn't promise either of those. Again, he felt the weight of the burden he had placed on her and couldn't help but feel guilty.

"How about you go to bed," he finally said. "I'll finish here."

Anna looked at the sink and all the work that still needed to be done. But she was too distraught to refuse his offer.

"Thank you," she said, drying her hands on a towel before heading to her room.

At midnight, Anna's eyes were still wide open.

Despite all his crude manners and flaws, Connor had gone out of his way several times to keep her safe. Even when she had managed to get herself in trouble by going to the police, he didn't hold it against her. Considering how they'd met, he was also nicer and gentler than she was expecting.

But that was what she liked about him.

*****

There are few places where the history of a town can be more poignantly felt than in the location chosen to bury its dead. The Amish burial plot was no different. Though Connor had accompanied Anna to the cemetery so he could watch over her, he gave her space.

"We should go, Anna. I don't like being out in the open like this," he said, feeling a bit uneasy. He'd personally rather let her visit her parents alone, but he was still wary about letting her out of his sight, especially out here in a field.

Anna nodded. "All right, give me just a few minutes more."

He nodded.

155

There was barely enough light to read what was written on the gravestones, given the lack of artificial light in the graveyard. But Connor squinted his eyes and barely managed to read the names on the tombstone she stood in front of. On each tombstone, all that was written were the names, birth dates, and dates of death. There were no epitaphs.

He took another respectful step back and looked around him, his eyes moving from one stone to another.

Connor remembered when he had to choose what would be engraved on Grace's tombstone. He had spent days agonizing over what he would write. In the end, he realized that no words would ever be able to capture the essence of who she was to him or the people she had blessed with her life.

Sometimes, the most important tributes are not the ones written on tombstones, but the ones inscribed on hearts. Maybe the Amish felt the same way. Most of their customs were inspired by their faith and not emotions. As if she had read his mind, Anna answered his unasked question.

"We don't see a need for fancy tombstones." She spoke without taking her eyes off the tombstones. "Here in Unity, we believe that when a person dies, if they had a relationship with God, then they go to heaven to be with God. In other communities, maybe they focus more on following rules to get into heaven. We believe the only way we can go to heaven is through God's gift of salvation, not by good works. We could never be good enough on our own."

Connor nodded in agreement.

There were a few seconds of silence between them and he wondered if he should ask about her parents.

"My father and mother," she said without taking her eyes off the two tombstones before her. "They had me at a late age after being told by doctors for years that they would never have children. Right after I left the community, my mother got pneumonia. She'd always had asthma to begin with, so we were always careful about preventing her from getting sick. I put school on hold and came home to be with her, and she died from the sickness. My father died only a few days later when he got careless on the farm and got behind an unsettled horse. I think after my mother died, he became very distracted, like he wanted to go to be with her. After that, I left for good and haven't been back since. I miss them both every day. Sometimes, I wonder if I had gone to nursing school before then, maybe I could have saved them."

"Would you have been able to?"

She shrugged. "I don't know. My mother was always a bit fragile. Maybe if she had gotten to a hospital sooner, if I had recognized the signs and had tests done earlier, maybe I could have saved her. And if I had saved *Maam*, then I would have saved *Daed*."

"Was that why you left?"

She glanced at him. "I had already left before she got sick. I would have left either way. I wanted to become a nurse and care for people in their time of need. I wanted to save lives. Taking care of my mother when she fell ill only reaffirmed that, but by then I'd already made up my mind."

"I think they would have been proud of you and who you are now," he said, his voice barely above a whisper, memories of his own grief assailing him once more.

Anna looked surprised by the compliment from him and how he'd broken his tough facade. "Thank you, Connor. That means a lot. Have you ever lost anyone close to you?"

"Yes, I have. I understand what it's like. I know people say they're still with you in your heart and that they're not really gone, but nothing can fill the void they leave. People just say that stuff to be nice, or maybe because they know nothing they can say will make it any better. Sometimes, it's best to just say nothing at all and just be there for the person." Connor didn't know why he was babbling so much as he stared at the sunset in the distance.

"Who did you lose?" Anna asked, turning to him.

He wanted to tell her about his late wife, but the words wouldn't form.

After a few more agonizing seconds, he finally realized he couldn't do it. He couldn't find the right words that would do Grace's death any justice, so he'd say nothing about it at all.

"Was it your family? Your parents?" Anna asked.

"Actually," he said, surprised by how easily he was telling her about this when he couldn't speak to her about his wife yet. But this had happened years before he'd lost Grace, so he'd had more time to heal. "My parents died when I was nine, then my grandmother, Nana, raised me. I didn't have any other relatives who would take me in. She was a wonderful woman. She died when I was eighteen, and that's when I joined the military." He turned away, pushing the painful memories of his parents' death out of his mind.

"Oh, Connor." Anna felt the sting of guilt as she hid her face. "And I made fun of you for saying 'Nana.' I'm so sorry."

No, he didn't want her sympathy. "Don't be sorry, Anna. I was making fun of you, too, at the moment, if you remember."

He was right, but now was not the time to reminisce about their jokes. "How did your parents die?"

"They went on a hiking trip one weekend and got lost in the woods for several days. By the time they were found, it was too late," he said, not bothering to hide the sadness in his voice. "They were the

158

best parents. I hope I can be like them one day. If I ever have children, I'd do anything for them. I'd always put their needs before my own."

"I'm so sorry, Connor." Anna came closer and touched his arm.

He looked up at her. "Even though your parents are gone, you have no idea how lucky you were to have them for so long. And everyone else here is like family to you. At least you have them. When I joined the military at eighteen and then joined CPDU later on, the friends I made there were more of a family to me than anyone else ever was— Jeff, Ben, and Derek. They're like family. When I joined, I figured no one would miss me if I died. Then I met them, and they helped me through some dark times of my life."

"Genetics don't always matter. You don't have to be related to someone to call them family."

Connor nodded, looking at Anna's parents' tombstones. "I hope one day I'll know what it's like to have family. I mean a real, biological family."

"I'm confident you will. Thank you for telling me all this, Connor. I know sometimes it's hard for you to talk about certain things." She smiled. "You know you can tell me anything." She hoped this would encourage him to tell her more about his past, but she didn't want to pry. She was feeling too honored by his uncharacteristic openness to reach out for more than he was willing to offer just then.

Connor smiled back, suddenly realizing just how close she was standing to him. His heart raced, and he took a fumbling step back. Why did she have this effect on him?

"Come on," he said, turning and walking away awkwardly. "We should go."

*****

Anna stared at Connor in confusion as he walked away from the cemetery, then she followed him.

What had that been all about? He had started to pour his heart out to her, then just as though someone had bent a garden hose in half, the flow of words had abruptly stopped.

She wished he'd feel comfortable enough around her to speak freely. Maybe that would never happen. Didn't he know she wouldn't judge him, that she'd understand?

Anna had a feeling they had more in common than they realized.

Later that evening, Derek, Connor, Anna, and Maria waited again at Ella Ruth's house when Moses picked her up for her date. They followed them to another restaurant, where Anna and Maria sat at a table nearby them again. Like last time, Moses showered Ella Ruth with compliments and promised her the world. Then they followed them to a movie theater, but afterward, Moses brought her home, still acting like the perfect gentleman.

This time, he did kiss her on the cheek when he dropped her off at home, and Anna imagined how hard Ella Ruth must have tried not to cringe or back away.

The four of them watched from Connor's car as Ella Ruth waved while Moses' buggy drove away, then she walked to the barn, glancing in their direction.

"Come on, let's go talk to her," Connor said, and they piled out.

They crept along the shadows on their way to the barn so no neighbors nor the Holts would see them. As they stepped inside the barn, Anna asked, "What happened? Anything?"

160

"Nothing important that you didn't see. You heard how he fawned over me at the restaurant. I can't believe that works on some girls," Ella Ruth said, snickering. "And at the movies, he just held my hand. It was two hours of torture, just imagining what he might have done to my sisters and how he helped in their disappearance. But he just brought me back to the buggy after, drove me home, and kissed me on the cheek. Ew."

Ella Ruth scrunched up her nose in disgust. "I guess he must have done his research, that the Amish don't normally kiss on the lips until marriage. He asked me on another date for tomorrow night. And he gave me this." Ella Ruth held up an expensive art supply case and opened it up to reveal paint brushes, pencils, and tubes of paint. "I told him before I like to paint. He wanted to buy me a diamond necklace, but I told him I don't wear jewelry."

"Well, I'm not surprised," Connor said. "That's a really nice art case. He's using expensive gifts to make you feel like you owe him later on when he asks you to sleep with his 'friends.'"

"Yeah. He's just trying to get you to trust him and feel comfortable around him by not trying anything physical with you right now. He wants you to really think he's Amish."

"And if I didn't know any better, I would think that," Ella Ruth said. She threw the art case down on the hay-covered floor. "I'll never be able to use that without wanting to vomit."

Anna nodded. "I don't blame you. Burn it."

Ella Ruth raised one eyebrow. "I want to."

"You know, he might not even ask anything of you for a few more dates at least," Connor said. "And we can't wait around much longer. Maybe you should amp things up on the next date. Can you tell him you love him and you want him to take you away from here?"

161

"Ugh," Ella Ruth groaned. "I don't want to, but I can do it. Why? Do you think it might make him take me to the other girls sooner?"

"Yes," Derek said. "It might work if he doesn't see through it."

"No, I won't let him. I'll make it believable. I'll even kiss him if I have to." Ella Ruth scrunched up her nose again. "Not exactly how I imagined my first kiss, but I'll do anything to get my sisters back."

Maria patted Ella Ruth's arm. "Don't worry. It won't be real, so you don't have to count it."

"True. Well, I better get back inside. I'll see you tomorrow night."

"And hopefully," Connor said, "this date will be the last."

Chapter Nineteen

"Good morning." Anna greeted Connor with a smile, wondering if he'd made up his mind to come to church with her.

"Morning," he replied as he got to his feet, filling her with hope when he grabbed his car keys from the table. "You ready?"

Anna nodded her head. "So, you are coming?"

"I'm driving you there," he replied as he walked her out and held the door open for her.

"Any particular reason why you changed your mind?" Anna asked, unable to keep the grin off her face.

"I said I was driving you to church so I can watch over you; I didn't say anything about attending the service." He nodded to a paperback novel on the dashboard as they got in the car. "While you're in church, I'll be catching up on my reading."

"Oh." Anna could not hide her disappointment. "It really will seem odd to people if you don't come inside."

Connor sighed. "I told you, we can say I'm not feeling well if anyone asks. I'm only going to keep an eye on you and Derek's family, and I'll be right outside. I did promise to protect you, and I don't think the Holy Spirit is in the habit of stopping bullets."

Anna reared back, a little shocked by his words. "The Lord still performs miracles."

Connor scoffed. He'd prayed for a miracle for days in that hospital, but he'd never gotten one.

"You used to go to church with Grace, right?" Anna said.

It was years of practice and self-control that had been honed that stopped Connor from showing any reaction to Anna mentioning Grace's name.

"Who told you about Grace?" he asked, unable to keep the bite out of his voice.

"Grace?" Anna frowned, feeling the change in his demeanor but not quite able to see the difference. "Maria. She said you used to go to church together."

A part of Connor had known Anna would find out about Grace soon enough. He just had not been ready to hear Anna say her name. She had no right to mention Grace's name, no right to gain access to that part of him. Especially when she seemed to be waltzing all over every part of him that he held close. And as he pressed down on the gas to get them to church faster, he couldn't silence the voice that what he was feeling was guilt and not anger.

He stopped the car in front of the church and waited for Anna to get out. She took her time with it and then leaned in through the window.

"You sure you don't want to come in?" she asked.

"I already told you, Anna," he replied through gritted teeth. "Stop pestering me about this."

"Wouldn't Grace want you to go to church?"

"Don't ever mention her name again," Connor suddenly bit back, forcing the words through gritted teeth.

Anna gulped, shocked to see him so furious. She immediately took a step back from the car, hurt by his actions. She looked up to see a group of people smiling as they walked into the church and took a deep breath.

Then she climbed up the steps that led to the church and made her way into the presence of God.

Now her soul definitely needed it.

*****

Anna would have preferred if Maria allowed her to sit alone in the back of the service, but her friend had been insistent on sitting with Anna right in the middle of the congregation. Anna's mind kept wandering to her conversation with Connor about Grace.

Silently castigating herself for letting her mind wander, she concentrated on the service.

The congregation was singing hymns, and even though most people held the *Ausbund* songbook in their hands, very few of them actually needed it. They had grown up with these songs, had learned most of them by heart already. She had learned to speak this form of German before she'd learned English, like all the Amish children in Unity. As she opened her mouth and sang, her heart was full of joy.

She missed this, singing with her church family. No drums, no piano, no guitars. No music other than the voices of the worshipers, harmonized by the fact that they actually believed the words they sang. This was how the Amish worshipped God.

Anna sang with everyone around her, eyes closed as she slowly swayed to the music. A feeling of calm settled around her as it usually did when she was in church, even the church she went to in Portland. But this calm was different. This one felt just a tad bit

165

warmer, memories of services just like this in her childhood wrapped around her soul like a cozy blanket around her shoulders.

There was a sudden dip in the volume of the songs, enough that Anna turned around wondering what had caused it. She was shocked to see Connor walk in and sit on a bench at the back of the room. The distraction lasted barely a second before everyone was singing normally again. Anna turned around and continued singing, but even though the hymn being sung was solemn, she couldn't help the big smile on her face.

*****

Connor sat in his car, staring at the church as the sound of the singing voices wafted into his car like a smell he couldn't get away from.

The German words of the song washed over him as he closed his eyes. He only knew a few words here and there that he had picked up while visiting in the past, but they still drew him in.

The words the congregation sang tugged at him. If one thing could restore his heart, it would be this.

Like a strong magnetic force, Connor couldn't resist the pull of the singing any longer. He got out of the car and sat on the church steps.

He'd sit here, only so he could hear better. That was all. He wouldn't go inside.

The words from another familiar song came rushing back to him, a song that he used to sing with Grace in their old church.

"Prone to wander, Lord, I feel it, prone to leave the God I love…"

Yes, he was prone to wander. That much was clear. He'd been wandering, lost, ever since Grace had died.

The words were like water to his parched soul. Even just sitting here, listening to singing in German, he felt revival in his heart.

He squeezed his eyes shut.

Go inside. Go inside, a voice inside his heart whispered.

"No," he muttered.

Go.

What was happening? Why did part of him want to go inside when every other cell in his body screamed not to?

As if his body was being controlled by invisible puppet strings, Connor begrudgingly got up and walked into the church.

It had been a long time since Connor had stepped into a church. The last time he'd stepped foot in this building he'd been here with Grace while visiting Derek.

As he opened the door and walked into the room, several people quieted their singing to glance his way, then they continued singing again. He noticed Anna eyeing him, but he quickly averted his eyes and sat down in the back of the room.

And as he stared at the familiar setting of an Amish church, it was clear this was nothing like any other church he had ever attended. Everyone sat on backless benches, and one half of the room was separated by a wall divider. Before coming here, he'd always heard that the Amish held services in their home, and he'd been surprised to see that this community had built their own combination school and church building.

And as he sat down and sang along, something odd happened. Even though there were no accompanying instruments, the songs spoke to him and reminded him of all the times he had gone to church with Grace and of the times he had gone alone and, just as equally, enjoyed himself.

It was like the music spoke to him in an elevated language that rose above the lyrics, touching his heart and bringing a measure of peace to him in a way that years of pent-up emotions couldn't.

By the time Bishop Byler rose up to preach, he had Connor's full attention, and even made brief eye contact with him.

Derek came over and sat next to Connor. "I'll translate for you, but some words I might not know yet. I'm still learning." Derek had learned the language after marrying Maria and joining the Amish, unlike the others who had grown up speaking it.

"Thank you," Connor said, knowing the sermon would be in Pennsylvania Dutch, a form of German. Yes, he knew a few words, but not enough to grasp a whole sermon.

"We must surrender to God's will in everything. In every situation, God has a plan," the bishop said. "God does not stray from us. We stray from Him. If you ask for forgiveness, He will always forgive, no matter what. We are prone to wander, but if you seek Him, He will draw you back to Him."

Connor felt as though the bishop was speaking only to him. How had he known to say that part about how we are prone to wander?

It was just like the line of the song that had come to Connor's mind earlier.

God, is this a sign? Connor wondered, but he knew the answer.

It was something Connor had heard a hundred times, but for the first time, he truly heard it.

In that church, a little seed of hope was planted in his heart. A chance for a new beginning. And when he kneeled down to pray at the end of the service, he closed his eyes, and for the first time in a long time talked to God again and got an answer back, at least one that he recognized.

*****

"Anna!" Leah, who was Katie and Lilly's older sister, and also a friend Anna had grown up with, called out. "I heard you're married. Congratulations."

"Thank you," Anna said. "We came to your house the day we got here to offer our help to your family, but I heard you were away."

"Yes, I have been away staying with relatives in Pennsylvania for several months. I have been doing a lot of soul searching and I had to get away, and I got a job out there. But when I heard my sisters went missing..." Leah's eyes filled with tears, and she took a deep breath. "I came back right away."

Anna nodded with understanding, knowing what the Holt family had gone through even before Katie and Lilly disappeared. "Of course, Leah. I hope you don't feel like any of this is your fault, because it isn't."

"I just keep thinking, maybe if I had been there, I might have noticed what was going on and stopped them before it was too late." Leah tried to contain her sobs by placing a hand over her mouth. Anna quickly pulled her into a hug.

"This is not your fault, Leah. Please know that," Anna said, patting her friend's back.

Leah sniffed, finally pulling away. "I just keep praying, every minute of every day."

Anna nodded.

"Anyway, enough about me. I want to know all about how you met your husband. Is that him?" Leah asked, wiping her eyes and gesturing to Connor.

"Yes."

"So, how did you meet?"

Connor walked over, coming to her rescue.

"We met at the hospital. I got into an accident and she helped me recover as my nurse," Connor explained.

"Oh, how romantic!" Leah cried, putting a hand over her heart. "That is so sweet."

Mary Mast walked over and added, "I didn't know that. What a lovely story. So, I heard you're planning on joining the Amish officially?"

"Well, yes," Connor said, leaving Anna relieved she didn't have to come up with the lies.

"That's great news," Mrs. Johnson said, who had been standing nearby and clearly eavesdropping as usual. "So, where will you live? Will you build a house or buy one?"

"Probably buy one," Connor said with a nod. "We aren't too picky."

"Well, we are so glad to meet you, Connor, and congratulations on your wedding," Leah said, and the other two women nodded.

"Well, we have to get going," Anna said, looping her arm through Connor's, guilt bubbling up within her for lying right to her friends' faces. Hopefully, they would understand and forgive her. "And Leah, please let me know if there is anything I can do."

"Thank you, Anna. Right now, all we can do is pray."

Anna turned away with Connor. While she heartily agreed prayer was the most important thing they could do, all she could think of was the next time they would follow Moses.

Chapter Twenty

Later that afternoon, Maria said to Anna, "It was really nice seeing you in church. I was shocked to see Connor there."

"Well, I tried to convince him to join me. At first, he refused. I guess he changed his mind after."

"I'm glad he did. As far as I know, he was a strong Christian until Grace died."

"Really?" Anna said. "Wait. Grace died?"

Maria sighed. "I'm sorry, I said too much again."

"So, who was this Grace? There's more to the story? Please, I'm dying to know. Connor won't say anything about it. Is that why he's so closed off?"

"Well, I think he blames God for taking her. After she died, we tried inviting him over a few times to come visit and go to church, but he always said he couldn't make it. We haven't seen much of him since then. He shut everyone out, I heard, not just us. He met Grace at church, and of course, as if losing her wasn't enough—" Maria suddenly stopped.

"Wait," Anna said, pausing when realization fell on her like a bucket of ice water. "Was he married? Was Grace his wife?"

"I'm so sorry. It's not my place to tell you what happened. He will when he's ready."

Maria leaned down and gently rocked the handcrafted wooden cradle that held her baby. "Anna, that man endured so much. It made him a bitter person. It's such a shame that he turned away from God. Derek and I have been praying for years that he would return to God. He's a good man, Anna, and always has been. He's just hurting and lost. It's not my place to say anything else. I'm sorry for what I've said already," Maria said. "You should ask Connor."

Anna nodded slowly, at a loss for words. Her mind stormed with questions. What had happened to him?

"I guess you may be able to convince him to start attending church, and that's a start. You and he are...what again?" Maria asked.

"Just friends," Anna replied, understanding that Maria was still trying to understand exactly what the dynamic of the relationship between her and Connor was.

"Mhm." Maria continued to rock the cradle, giving Anna a knowing smile.

"I really tried to get him to come in at the church, but he just got mad at me so I decided to drop it."

"He got angry?"

Anna nodded.

Maria sighed. "I guess he feels that coming to church may bring back painful memories. I mean, they met at church. Church was everything to them."

Anna's mouth had dropped open halfway into that sentence and as Maria absentmindedly continued talking, Anna suddenly realized why Connor had become visibly angry when she tried to use Grace's name to make him come to church. Because she had been ignorantly talking about his wife. Guilt and shame swamped her, and if she could have willed it, Anna would have prayed that the ground open up and swallow her.

Anna reminded herself that as far as Connor was concerned, he was simply doing this because he had put her in danger. His role in her life was simply that of a protector until the current danger was passed. He was not her friend.

His past was none of her business. She had no right to know.

He was a man who wore the ghost of his wife around him like the wedding ring he no longer wore.

*****

Later that evening, Anna offered to clean up the dinner dishes while Derek and Maria went to bed. Because they'd eaten quickly and then left to follow Ella Ruth on yet another uneventful date, they hadn't had time to clean up yet. Liz had watched the children, but they'd told her not to worry about the dishes, saying they'd do them later. Besides, Liz had been feeling tired due to her pregnancy.

Anna hummed as she scrubbed the plates with a sponge. Connor poked his head inside the kitchen. "Let me help."

Anna shook her head. "Don't worry. I've got it covered."

Connor glanced at the sink of soapy plates and the bowl of water set aside for rinsing them. Folding his sleeves, he joined her at the sink. Anna squabbled with him for a few seconds and only relented when it was clear he was not prepared to give up. She also didn't want to disturb their hosts. For a few minutes, both of them worked quietly. Even though there was no pressing need to say anything, Anna still felt curious enough to ask.

174

"So what do you think of church? Was it good to be back?"

He glanced at her and smiled. "It was nice."

She chuckled. "Don't worry, you can say it. It's boring and long. I'd understand."

He shrugged. "It was great. Sure, I didn't understand some of the hymns that were in German, but I understood enough to know what they meant. Derek translated the sermon."

Anna smiled and turned back to the plate in her hand. "I remember the first time I attended a church after I left here. It felt odd to hear piano and guitars and drums after coming from a church that did not allow instruments. It took me a few weeks to understand that not all churches are the same. The church I attend now only uses the piano in their service, and after a while, I started to get used to it."

Connor rinsed a plate and placed it carefully in the rack for drying. He picked up the next one and began to rinse it. Then he stopped and faced Anna.

"I want to thank you for what you said about how I should go to church." He watched as she turned to face him with a slightly confused and embarrassed look. "I needed to hear it. Being in church today helped me."

"You're... You're welcome..." Anna stammered. "I'm really sorry if I crossed a line. I'm sorry if I said something insensitive."

"Thank you. It's not your fault. You didn't know."

"No, I don't know. Connor, what happened to Grace?"

Connor froze, shocked again to hear his wife's name coming out of her mouth. He slowly turned around to look at her, towel still in his hand.

They were probably going to be here for at least another week or so, living in the same house. Now that she knew Grace's name, it was bound to come up in conversation again. Anna was nothing but persistent.

It was time she knew.

"She was my wife. She died a few years ago." And that was all he was going to say for now, even though there was so much more to the story.

Anna dropped the sponge into the sink, and dirty dishwater splashed onto Connor's arm. "I'm so sorry for what I said before church."

"Really, Anna, you did nothing wrong."

"I shouldn't have been so pushy."

"Well, I'm glad you were. It got me back in church. And I'm so glad I went. It made me realize some things about myself, how I've been pushing God away when I needed Him the most. God was always there for me; it was me who wandered away. Like in that song: *Prone to wander, prone to leave the God I love.* That song was what brought me into the church. And you, Anna, what you said."

"I'm so glad to hear that. So, how did Grace die?" Anna asked tentatively.

Connor squeezed his eyes shut. Memories assailed him—the doctor saying he'd done all he could, the feel of Grace's frail hand in his, the hospital monitor beeping when her heart had stopped.

He opened his eyes and shook his head. "I thought I could talk about this, but I can't."

He couldn't. Not here, not now, and especially not with Anna, the one woman who'd made him feel alive again since…

"I'm sorry." Anna took a step back. "I shouldn't have asked."

"It's okay. It was a few years ago, but it's still hard to talk about."

Anna paused, looking as if she was deep in thought with her eyebrows drawn together like that. "So, you're speaking to God again now?"

"Yes. I prayed in church and begged for forgiveness. Honestly, ever since then, I've felt at peace. Like a weight was lifted off me. I know that sounds cliché."

"No, not if it's true. Hearing that makes me so happy."

"Well, I know I have a long way to go. I'm just getting started on my journey. This is just the beginning," he said.

*****

Get a hold of yourself, Anna told herself silently, feeling her face heating. *He's not talking about you and him on a journey. He's talking about his own journey.*

Connor continued, "I remember when Grace died. I was torn to pieces. There was nothing I could do to help." He chuckled mirthlessly. "She'd smile at me and tell me not to worry, that everything would be okay. She was the one suffering, but she showed more strength."

"She sounds like she was an amazing person," Anna said, and she meant it.

"She was." His voice shook with restrained emotion. "I didn't deserve to ever have her. And in the end, I didn't do enough to keep her. I couldn't save her."

Anna frowned. "I don't know what happened, but I'm sure it wasn't your fault, Connor."

He didn't agree with her but didn't answer her. "She was always right except for when she told me from her hospital bed that it would all be okay. She told me that as long as I prayed, everything would work out the way it was supposed to." Connor scoffed. "I prayed and prayed, but He still took her away."

Anna kept quiet, wondering what she could say to help with the pain he was feeling. She knew better than to offer empty platitudes and meaningless clichés. So, she went with the best she had.

"God always answers prayer, but sometimes He gives us answers we don't want."

"Yeah. She died in the end. All those hours spent on my knees by her bedside. Everywhere I went I was always praying. In the end, it meant nothing." He sounded so bitter. She knew he still carried deep emotional wounds.

Anna took a deep breath, swimming through dangerous waters. "I know I'm just someone who was foisted on you and we'll probably never see each other again after this, so I'm not trying to tell you how to feel or what to do. I just think that, from everything you've told me about your wife, I don't think she meant for you to stop praying after she died."

"You were not foisted on me," Connor said after a few seconds of awkward silence. "You know that's not true, right? I mean, I was the one who put you in danger, and I'll make sure you're safe before I leave."

Anna nodded. "I know."

"Good," He made a clicking sound of approval as he turned around. "Because I'm not losing someone again."

The last statement was said more to himself than anything, but Anna understood what it meant, and it all suddenly made sense.

Was he doing this for Grace and not because he cared about Anna? Like he was trying to make up for whatever things he'd done in the past?

And even though Anna understood his reasons, she couldn't help but feel a little heartbroken. No, not heartbroken. Sorry for him. Because why should she feel heartbroken? It was not like she had feelings for him or anything.

And even if she did, it still didn't matter.

It was inconceivable to her that anyone would think there was anything between them. They could not be more different from each other.

"Thank you again for what you said when you told me I should go back to church. It was hard to hear, but I needed to hear it," Connor said.

Lost in her own thoughts, Anna had to blink a few times to get herself to focus on what he'd said. "Of course. I'm just glad that I could help. And that you're not angry with me." He hardly ever opened up to her and had just released a waterfall of emotions on her.

Well, to him it was probably like a waterfall, but to her it was more like a leaky faucet. She wanted to know more, but didn't pry for once.

He smiled at her. "You seem embarrassed."

Anna suddenly grinned at him, flustered. "Do I? Well, how do you feel knowing that you smile more than you did when we first met?"

The smile disappeared from his face. "No, I don't."

Anna grinned and turned back to her plates. "Now who's embarrassed?"

"Why would the fact that I smile make me embarrassed?"

"I don't know. Maybe because you like to act like you're this stoic guy who doesn't care what anyone thinks about him and doesn't think anything is funny."

Connor took the plate she handed to him and dumped it in the water with a little more force than necessary, sloshing water over the side and on both of them.

Anna just grinned more. "Stop being a pansy."

"Oh, now I'm a pansy?" He wrapped his hands around the edge of the bowl and lifted it up slightly. "I wonder what you will call me if I empty this whole bowl on you."

Anna turned and stared at him. "You wouldn't dare."

"Say it one more time."

Anna drew herself to her full height and stared right into his eyes. "I said you wouldn't dare. And you know why? Because you are not the kind of person who would go around pouring water on someone and making her scream so loud that she wakes everyone in the house, including a baby." Grinning at him, she teased him with a nudge of her head. "Come on, I dare you to dump that bowl of dirty water on me."

Connor sighed, putting the bowl down. The sound of Anna giggling made him smile.

"One day, you're going to be alone and I'm going to walk up to you and dump a bucket of water on you," he said, laughing.

Anna's grin just got wider. "Ooh. I'm terrified. So, what do you do for fun when you're not on the run from maniac assassins?"

"I'm restoring a 1966 Chevrolet Chevelle. Bought it three years ago and have been slowly restoring it whenever I get the chance to."

Anna knew from the way he said it that she probably should be impressed by that, but she had no idea what a Chevelle was. "What exactly is a Chevelle? I'm guessing it's a car. Or maybe it's an animal that lives in the African desert."

Connor laughed, which was a rare sound. It was a real belly laugh, and Anna couldn't help but giggle.

"It's a car. Do you know how much it will be worth when I'm done restoring it?"

"No, but I'm almost sure it would cost more than something that functions to take you from one place to another should."

Connor spluttered, seeing the humor dancing in her eyes but still unable to help himself from reacting to the blasphemy she was spewing.

"Who buys a vintage car just so he can drive around in it? That would be like using the Mona Lisa as a sled," he said, throwing his hands up in the air. "Absolutely ridiculous."

"So you don't plan on driving the car once you're done fixing it?"

"Restoring, not fixing. And, of course, I'll drive it when I'm done, but only with the utmost care. Probably mostly to car shows."

Anna raised one eyebrow. She did not understand him at all.

"Isn't there anything you do just because it makes you feel good? It's not something bad, but it's not really important. You just do it because you like to do it," he said.

She smiled as she leaned against the sink to give him a reply. "Nothing I'll spend hundreds or thousands of dollars on."

"What do you do for fun then?"

Anna shrugged. "I read books. Don't have much time for much else. I am a bit obsessed with my work. I go to work, I go to church, and help out in my church. I guess I like to spend what little free time I do have by myself in my apartment. I'm an introvert."

He set down a stack of plates and looked her in the eye. "But I know there's got to be something you've always wanted to do, and I'm not talking about just seeing a movie for the first time. If you could do anything or go anywhere, what would you do?"

Anna stopped scrubbing the pan she was washing, her hand lingering in the dingy dishwater as she looked out the window at the stars blinking over the moonlit fields. "I'd go to Germany."

"What's in Germany?"

"What's in Germany?" Anna asked, flabbergasted. "History, art, amazing architecture, not to mention the Neuschwanstein Castle. I read about it in a book once and always wanted to go. It's beautiful." She turned her attention back to the dishes and started scrubbing furiously. "But I'll probably never make it there. It's expensive, and even if I did have the money, I don't think I'd ever be brave enough to fly on an airplane to get there."

Connor gently grasped Anna's shoulders and turned her toward him. Soap suds dripped off her fingertips onto the floor, but she barely noticed. All she could see, hear, smell, and feel were elements of him—his warm hands on her upper arms, the woodsy scent of his soap, and exactly just how close he was to her at that moment. Most of all, the way his dark eyes looked intently into her own, as if he'd known her for years and could sense every one of her fears that lurked in the deepest corners of her heart.

"Anna Hershberger, I haven't known you long, but I've seen you knock an assassin out with a chair, dodge bullets, learn to drive a car, and help me get further in this investigation than I ever could without you. Not to mention, you've endured my prickly personality for the past several days. I think you're brave enough to do anything you want to do."

Anna smiled up at him, her heart rate hiking. "I don't think 'endure' is the right word. You're not as prickly as you think you are."

"Oh, really." He gave her a mischievous grin.

"In fact, I think it's all for show. I think you have a big heart and don't want anyone to know it."

"I used to."

"You still do, Connor. I don't think that will ever change."

"All I know is, until I met you, I felt…frozen. Cold. And you're like fire."

She gave him a sideways glance, lifting one eyebrow. "Fire can be dangerous."

"If you haven't noticed, I kind of like danger."

Anna smiled. She'd never felt anything like this before. Every cell in her body tingled, buzzed with the need to just be near him. She reached one sudsy hand up to his face, and gently touched his cheek, neither of them caring that tiny soap bubbles dripped down to her elbow and onto his shirt. His hands encircled her back. She took a step closer to him, her heart pounding as she pulled his face closer.

He pressed his warm lips to hers. Her soul soared like a bird that had been trapped in a cage for years and finally set free.

All this time, she'd had no idea she'd been trapped. She'd thought the cage was normal.

All she knew was that they were kissing, and even though her mind could barely conceive the very notion of it, she was kissing him back. Kissing him because she wanted to. Kissing him because it somehow felt right. And for those few seconds, common sense gave way to passion, and emotions overrode that tiny voice in her head that told her all the reasons why this was bad. But just for a few seconds. And then common sense took over again and she pushed herself away from him, her mouth opened in shock.

"Anna," Connor whispered, clearly shocked himself. "Are you okay?"

Anna stared at him for a few seconds. "Yes. I need a moment alone to think things over." She backed away slowly. "I'm sorry. I'll see you tomorrow. I mean, we're kind of both living here, so it's hard to not see each other. Okay, bye." She turned and walked down the hallway.

Connor stood there, blinking, as Anna hurried away. What had just happened?

After a few minutes of stunned silence, he turned around and took care of the remaining plates. Then he made his way to his bedroom and spent most of the night mentally kicking himself in the head, wondering what had gone wrong when he thought things were going so well.

And he spent the rest of the night dreaming about that kiss.

Chapter Twenty-One

Anna hurried into her room, shut the door, and leaned against it. She let herself slide down to the floor.

They'd kissed.

And it had been everything she'd imagined. And she'd imagined it, all right.

But a myriad of thoughts swirled in her head. Even if he wasn't ever an assassin, had he ever killed before in the military or while working for CPDU? She had to know.

And why wouldn't he tell her how Grace had died? Maybe he wasn't over his late wife after all.

But then he'd kissed Anna. So, no, she definitely hadn't been imagining it.

Then when he'd said he still had a long way to go on his journey and it was only the beginning, she'd blushed because she thought he'd been referring to their journey together. Had she been wrong? And why did she have to blush and embarrass herself even more?

And why had she rambled on so much after the kiss?

Anna let her head fall into her hands, wishing she could redo the kiss without making a fool out of herself.

Maybe she'd get another chance.

She hoped so.

He had the dream again. He was driving in his car when he suddenly saw Anna standing in the middle of the road, right in the path of the car. He screamed at her to get away and hit the brakes at the same time, but the car just kept racing towards her. She turned towards him and waved at him, a big smile on her face like she had no fear. Like she trusted him to make sure nothing happened to her. And no matter how hard he tried to stop the car, he couldn't. He swerved the car to the side, not caring at all that it could mean killing himself.

He would do anything to save her. Give his life even. But the closer the car got to her, the more he realized that it didn't matter how hard he tried, he was not going to be able to save her.

And right before his car slammed into Anna, he woke up with a gasp, his whole body dripping with sweat.

It was still too dark to be close to morning, and he fell back to the bed, unable to go back to sleep. It didn't take a genius to interpret the dream.

He wasn't going to lose her. He couldn't bear losing someone he loved again.

Loved? That was a strong word.

He paused and shook his head. Anna was someone he cared about. He wasn't going to stand by and watch as someone he cared about was taken away from him again. Not when it was all his fault that Anna had gotten dragged into this in the first place. He thought back to that day in the parking lot and wished he had not gotten her involved in this mess. He probably could have managed on his own.

Then he realized that would mean he would never have met Anna, and a small part of him was selfish enough to admit that he didn't want that, either.

Now he was thinking about that kiss again. For the first time since Grace died, he was considering the merits of entering a new relationship. And if he was being honest with himself, Anna was close to the most perfect person he could consider doing that with.

He just wasn't sure he was the right person for anyone.

*****

Connor's eyes opened. What was that noise?

Gun in hand, he swung his legs over the side of the bed and silently stepped into the hall. There was a faint light shining in the kitchen, and he could hear the sound of someone rifling around. Instinct took over, and he tiptoed towards the kitchen, stopping by the doorway and hiding behind it. He peeked around the corner, but couldn't see anyone from this angle.

With his gun raised, he stepped into the kitchen.

Anna jumped, dropping the carton of milk in her hand. "What are you doing?" she whispered.

He tucked the gun into his waistband. "Sorry for scaring you like that," he said quietly.

Anna stared at him wide-eyed, her chest rising and falling. She glared at him. "We need to keep it down. There's a baby sleeping down the hall."

"What are you doing up?" he asked.

Anna looked pointedly at the carton of milk. "Getting a drink. Couldn't sleep."

"I doubt your deep and burning desire to have a glass of milk is the reason why you're not sleeping right now."

It took effort for Anna not to smile at his words. It was hard to tell when Connor was being funny, mostly because his face seemed always stuck between a scowl and a blank stare, whether he was telling a joke or staring down criminals trying to kill him.

"I heard a noise in the kitchen and thought I'd come investigate," Connor said.

"You could have shot me," Anna blurted, then regretted it.

"That would never happen, Anna. My finger was nowhere near the trigger."

"Connor, have you ever shot anyone before? Killed anyone before?" she asked before she could change her mind.

"What?" he asked, just staring at her.

"I'm sorry, but I need to know, because of what happened between us. I'm sorry I ran off after we kissed. Look, I just need to know before anything else happens between us."

He turned around and got the mop from the pantry to clean up the mess on the floor. Anna used that time to catch her breath and get her brain to function normally again.

For several seconds he remained silent, seemingly focused on mopping. After a while, Anna wondered if he'd answer her.

"Yes, Anna. I have. When I was in Afghanistan and also while working for CPDU, when a criminal pulled a gun on us. If I hadn't, I'd be dead, and so would my comrades. I know the Amish are against joining the military and all types of violence, even self-defense, so if you still believe that, I understand. But it happened, and it's in the past now."

He said it with such a blank expression, Anna couldn't tell if he was angry or sad. At his words, Anna's heart sank. Now, she knew the truth.

He had killed. And every time she looked at him, it was hard for her to not think about it.

Not to mention the fact that she didn't know how she could be with someone who had such a dangerous job, wondering each day if it would be his last.

"Hey, about what happened earlier—" he began.

"Yeah, I'm sorry for walking out like that. I was just a bit confused. I thought before we kissed that maybe I'd imagined whatever we have between us." She shrugged, holding up her hands.

"No. You didn't imagine it," he said in a low voice, leaning the mop against the counter taking a step closer.

"Well, I thought maybe I had, because you won't tell me anything about Grace."

"I promise, that's not the reason why. It's just hard for me to talk about, that's all. One day soon I'll tell you everything, I promise." He took another few steps until he stood in front of her, then took her hand. "For the first time since she died, I finally can see myself with someone else. You."

Anna looked up at him, tears welling up in her eyes. "So I didn't imagine it."

"Nope, just like I told you."

Anna thought of lying to him. It would be easy.

She could tell him clearly that she had no desire to explore this romance between them because of his job. Anna had no desire to be a young widow, like Maria once was.

She knew Connor well enough to know that the moment she said that, he would leave her alone and never talk to her about it again. To be honest, she was still getting over the shock of hearing him proposing a relationship between them. For so long she had struggled with her feelings for him. It was all a little confusing and staggering. Maybe that was why instead of using any of the excuses she had thought about, she went with the simple truth.

Connor noticed the expression on her face and paused. "What's wrong?"

"Why now and why me?" Anna asked.

Connor looked confused. "What do you mean?"

"You kissed me." Talking about it still made her blush. "And now all of a sudden you are thinking of getting into a relationship with me. Why now and why me?"

Connor thought about her question for a few seconds before he replied. "I want to say I don't know, but the truth is that no one has ever made me think about it before. Since Grace died, I've never allowed anyone to get close enough to me to make me even consider getting into a relationship until you came along."

"So, all a woman has to do is get close enough to kiss you and you instantly start thinking of a relationship?"

Connor heard the bite in her tone but chose to ignore it since he couldn't explain it. "No, that's not it. I started thinking about it even before we kissed. I'm not asking you to walk down the aisle with me tomorrow or anything."

Until that moment Connor had never considered the potential of this turning into a marriage situation. Now that he had, he was equally scared and exhilarated by the thought.

"Then why me?" She got to her feet and folded her arms across her chest, unaware of how removed the posture made her look. "What do you see in me?"

Connor smiled gently, his eyes blazing with affection. "I could tell you what I see, but I don't think it would answer your question. I could tell you how I think you're the strongest and bravest person I've seen in a long time. Your heart of gold put you in a situation you should have never been in." He grinned sheepishly. "The night we met is a very good example. You stood up to me, and you even trusted me, though I was a stranger with a gun. You left everything behind and chose to inconvenience yourself for me." He took a step closer to her. "Most of all, I like that you didn't let my grumpiness change who you are or stifle your spirit. You didn't let my crankiness stop you from being who you are, laughing the way you laugh or seeing the joy in life. Somehow, by doing that you also showed me the joy in life. And now I'm not so grumpy anymore, if you haven't noticed. You even said I'm smiling more."

"And all this you figured out since we met?" Anna asked, struggling to hold on to her will and not give in to his words. How could someone who used to barely talk to her suddenly become this poetic, unlocking the bands around her heart with his words?

Connor looked into her eyes. "Like I said, I can tell you what I see in you and why I like you. But it is not enough to answer your question. It is more than all that. It's intangible. I can't see or touch it. I can't even say what it is. I just know that when I look at you now, I see it. And when I think of you, I feel it."

Anna knew exactly what he meant. Each passing day found her struggling to fight her feelings. She had taken Maria's advice and prayed about it. And when that didn't seem to work, she had taken to praying against the temptation of falling in love with him.

She saw him blink and watched his lashes sweep across those intense eyes. No, God was not answering her prayers the way she wanted this time.

And maybe that was a good thing. Because God certainly knew better than she did.

"I'm sorry," Anna said, then rambled on again. "I just don't want whatever this is to distract us from our investigation, and I know I upset you about church. I'm having a hard time figuring out who you are. You have a really dangerous job, and that scares me. It's complicated between you and God, and we're lying to everyone about being married, and there's a lot of confusing stuff going on right—"

He cut off her words by covering her lips with his.

That shut her up. He chuckled, tucking a loose strand of blonde hair behind her ear. "Then let this be the one simple thing we have going for us right now. I'm falling for you, Anna Hershberger. If you want to wait until this is all over, that's fine. And you don't have to say anything about it now. But I figured I should let you know before you start imagining this isn't real again."

"Okay," she said, smiling. "Okay."

"Good. Glad we established that."

"Well, goodnight then," she said.

"What about your drink of milk?"

"Ha, oh yeah, right. That's fine. I'll just get some water." She quickly filled up a glass in the sink and hurried back to her room.

Connor chuckled again, putting the milk in the fridge as she scampered away.

What an odd pair they made.

Chapter Twenty-Two

Early the next morning, as Maria and Anna cleaned up from breakfast, Maria told Anna stories about her children that were supposed to be funny. When Anna barely reacted, Maria gave her a knowing look.

"All right, what is it?" Maria demanded.

Anna shrugged innocently, continuing to scrub a pot they'd used to cook oatmeal. "What is what?"

"You're barely talking to me; I know you're not listening to me, and you've barely even looked at me today. What's the matter?"

"Nothing," Anna replied too quickly. "Just worried about everything that's happening, I guess," she added quickly so Maria didn't become suspicious.

"Oh," Maria said, looking guilty. "Here I am getting miffed that you were not listening to my stories when you're just worried. I'm sorry. I should not have assumed that just because you seemed fine meant you're not worried."

As she talked on, wringing her hands and feeling bad about herself, Anna couldn't take it anymore. "I kissed Connor," she spat out. "Or he kissed me. I don't know."

Maria pointed at her. "Got you!"

Anna's eyes widened in shock and she dropped the sponge in the sink. "You were playing me."

Maria scoffed. "Of course. I know you better than you think I do."

While that was surprising, Anna suddenly realized something that was more surprising and even shocking.

"You realize I just told you that I kissed Connor, right?"

"Yeah, I guess I should be surprised about that, too." She thought about it for a few seconds. "I don't know. I think I already have it in my head that you two are a couple."

"What do you mean by that?"

"Fight it all you want. The fact that you finally kissed him told me I was not far off the mark."

Anna couldn't help but smile as she remembered the kiss. "I don't know how it happened. All I know is I enjoyed every second of it, even though it was over quickly. Then I ran off to my room like a shy schoolgirl. I kind of ruined it."

"Why?"

"Because it's so complicated. He told me last night he's killed people in the military and while working for CPDU. I'm not sure if I can be with someone who has taken another person's life, even to protect himself or someone else. And his job is so dangerous, what if he gets killed himself? I don't think I could live with that kind of fear."

"He may have had to kill in the military or in self-defense while working for CPDU. Derek did, too, but I learned to accept that part of him. If Connor did, that was in the past. I know we were taught all violence is wrong, even self-defense and military defense. But God calls us to forgive. You have to put the past behind you. Can you accept that part of him?"

And even though Anna had pondered the same question several times in the past days, she still was no closer to a reply. "Maybe, but I'm still not sure I can look past it. I thought I could, but I don't know now. I don't think I can entertain the thought of starting a relationship with him. I mean, maybe if he quit working for CPDU and didn't go back into the military, that might be different. But it's part of who he is. I don't think he wants to give it up any time soon."

And she didn't want to make him.

If she did start a relationship and it ended tragically, she was not so sure she could ever become free of him again. As it was, the thought of the day when they would part made her feel empty inside.

Maria was serious as she leaned forward. "You love him, I can tell. You don't need to deny it. I know you, Anna. There is no way you'd fall in love with someone irredeemable. You don't fall for someone easily. There has to be a reason why you fell in love with Connor. You need to decide if you can accept his past or not, even if you don't know what he's done, and you need to accept him how he is right now."

"So you're saying I should pursue a relationship with him?"

"That's not what I'm saying. I'm saying you should think about it very carefully." Maria smiled. "Sometimes, we're so scared of love that in our head we find reasons why the other person is not suitable for us."

Anna suddenly began to wonder if that was what this was. It was easy to say no and ignore what she felt in her heart. And even much easier to say yes and embrace the emotions she was struggling to control.

"Have you prayed about it?" Maria asked.

"Of course, I have. But I should pray a lot more about it."

"Indeed. So, he told you about Grace?"

"Well, only a little. He told me she was his wife and she died, but he wouldn't say anything more about it." Anna sighed in disappointment, her curiosity eating at her. What had happened to Grace?

"As I said, he will tell you when he's ready. Connor doesn't open up easily. They were so opposite. Grace was fun to be around, and you didn't need to ask for her help before she offered it. I guess you both have that in common."

Anna blushed a bit at the compliment. But she didn't say a word, hoping Maria would keep on talking about Connor's dead wife. A part of her felt guilty about her curiosity. But she couldn't help it.

"I remember the first time I saw you with Connor," Maria continued. "My first thought was how happy both of you looked. Of course, at the time I assumed there was something of a relationship between you and Connor. A part of me was seriously hoping that you were indeed together. It would mean that he had finally moved on from Grace. They were so in love with each other." Maria looked out the window, her gaze soft. "I remember one day Derek said that the only person Connor really smiled for was Grace, and I couldn't agree more. She was the light in his eyes, despite everything he's been through in the military. When Grace died, he lost that light, and I wondered if he'd ever find it."

Anna had nothing to say, and instead felt like an interloper to even have her name involved in something so poignantly sweet. Suddenly, a lot of Connor's actions made sense, and she found herself sympathizing with him. The loss of a loved one was never easy to get over. Anna herself knew this from when she lost her parents. She still grieved them and missed them terribly.

"Seeing you with him made me hope that he had finally found that light again," Maria said.

Anna paused for a few moments. "I hope he finds a person like that again. He surely deserves it."

Maria gave a mischievous smile.

Anna snickered. "Oh, stop it."

"What? I didn't say anything," Maria said with a laugh.

"We aren't together."

"You keep saying that. Too bad. You really do look good together."

Anna forced herself to chuckle at the statement. "I very much doubt that is true. Besides, appearances can be deceiving."

"That is indeed true."

"I think he's still in love with his late wife. I don't know if he will learn to love again," Anna blurted out. Now that she'd finally voiced her fear aloud, she realized the full weight of the words.

"And I know from experience that even after someone's spouse dies, they can learn to love again," Maria said in a somber voice.

Anna touched Maria's arm. Maria's first husband Robert had been killed in an accident when he'd been out looking for his horse in a snowstorm. A woman had hit him by accident with her car and killed him. In fact, Maria had befriended the woman. Her name was Freya Wilson. Anna had become good friends with her, too.

Anna had always been astounded by Maria's willingness to not only forgive, but befriend the woman who'd accidentally killed Robert.

Also, Derek's first wife had been killed by traffickers, and he'd found love with Maria.

"You're right," Anna sighed. "As always."

"One thing I can say, though, is that whether you want to or not, you seem to be having a positive impact on him. In my book, that counts a lot more than appearances." Maria's smile gave way to a serious expression. "Think about what I told you. Pray about it and ask God to lead you. He promised to help us find our direction in life and make important decisions. Trust me, there are few decisions in life more important than the one where you decide who gets your heart. Now, let's get ready to go to my mom's house. I'm sure she can't wait to visit with you."

"And I can't wait to spend some time with your parents," Anna said, standing up to help Maria get the baby ready.

*****

Connor came into the kitchen to find a freshly prepared pot of coffee waiting for him.

Grateful the Amish allowed coffee, he poured himself a cup of coffee and took a sip. It was dark and strong, just the way he liked it. At the back of his mind, he remembered Grace's attempts to prepare coffee. No matter how hard she tried, she just couldn't get it right, and she'd get so frustrated about it. The memory made him smile.

It was quiet. Too quiet. Where was everyone?

Walking with his mug of coffee, he stepped out to the porch. Down the lane, Mary Mast puttered with the row of flowerpots that lined her porch and Gideon Mast sat on a lawn chair reading something. He nodded his head when Mary waved at him and lifted his mug in greeting. Maria and her children were on the porch, and another young Amish woman walked out of the Masts' house with a tray of something—he couldn't tell what it was from this distance. Was that Anna?

Why had she gone out without him?

If something happened to her and he wasn't there to protect her… He didn't even want to think about it.

He was already halfway down the lane before he realized he was not wearing any shoes. Ignoring that misstep, he made his way there and waited for her to lift her head from the tray where she was arranging cookies and teacups.

"Anna, what are you doing here?" he asked, trying not to grit his teeth.

"Hello, Connor. We were just about to have tea. Will you join us?" Mary asked.

"Sounds fun, but I can't. Sorry, Mrs. Mast. I need Anna to quickly help me with something."

"Help you with what?" Anna asked, peering at him.

"Well, it's Liz actually. Come on." Connor was already walking back toward Derek and Maria's house.

"Is Liz okay?" Mary asked, but Connor was already halfway down the lane.

"Oh, okay. Bye, Mary and Gideon," Anna said, scrambling to catch up to Connor.

"What's wrong? Is Liz okay? Did something happen?" Anna asked, and prattled on until they reached the house. Once they got inside, he closed the door behind him and turned around to glare at Anna.

"Are you trying to get yourself killed?" he spat.

Anna frowned. "What?"

"I don't want you leaving without me. I can't protect you if you're not with me."

"But you said that we are safe here."

"Yes, but that doesn't mean you can go gallivanting all around the neighborhood."

"It was just the Masts' house. They're like second parents to me. And what about Liz? Is she okay?"

"She's fine. I only said that to get you to come with me."

He could see Anna's confusion slowly morphing into anger as her face turned red and she scrunched up her nose. "You lied to me."

"I'm sorry about that. But I was upset and worried about you. I knew you might not come with me unless I said that. You can't leave the house without me."

"What? Am I supposed to stay indoors and wait for you to tell me when I can and cannot go outside? Like some sort of pet?" she retorted, throwing her hands up.

"Yes."

Her last statement registered in Connor's mind, and he realized too late the trap he'd fallen in. He gave himself a face palm, feeling like an idiot. Taking a deep breath, he lifted his two hands, asking her to reason with him.

"I'm not saying I want to control you or anything. I'm just saying that it is not safe for you to be walking around town alone when we both know there are people looking for us."

"I am safe here. Besides, stop acting like I can't take care of myself."

He drew himself to his full height. She didn't understand the seriousness of the issue at hand. "Look, Anna I don't want you fighting me on this one. I don't want you just going out anytime you think you want to. Before you go anywhere, you check with me first, and if I don't think it is safe for you, I won't allow you. I'm just trying to protect you, Anna."

By the time he finished his speech, Anna was so furious, she stood frozen for several seconds without saying anything.

"Anna?" Connor moved closer, wondering why she looked like she was about to explode. "Are you okay?"

Anna suddenly released the breath she'd been holding the entire time he was talking. Then she went off.

It was like someone had detonated a grenade.

"No! I've given up everything to follow you around, help you with your injury, and help you on this case. I will not let you tell me when I can or can't go outside. I'm a lot tougher than I look, and I don't need you to protect me. This is my home, and I know it a lot better than you. I wasn't just at the Masts' to visit, I was trying to get information. They're one of the oldest couples in the community, and they know everyone and everything going on here. I'm the one who is getting information here, and without my medical skills you'd have an infection or worse. Without me, you wouldn't be able to shut down this trafficking ring at all. So, before you treat me like a child, remember that!" she shouted, waving her pointed finger at him.

He watched in shock as she whirled around and flounced away, opening the door and slamming it shut. Fortunately, the baby wasn't here sleeping.

What had just happened?

Connor quickly followed her, stopping on the porch when he saw Anna cross the street and head right back toward the Masts' house.

Now furious himself, he turned around and walked right back into the house and slammed the door behind him.

He'd only been trying to protect her. What had he done wrong? Why was she so mad?

They both needed some time to cool down. He was sure when she simmered down and really thought about it, she'd realize that he had only been trying to help.

As he replayed their conversation in his head, he felt more and more guilty with each word that he'd spoken.

"I messed up," he muttered out loud. "I went about it all wrong."

Chapter Twenty-Three

Ever since Maria had made that statement about Anna and Connor looking good together as a couple, Anna found herself increasingly pointing out to herself all the reasons why that statement was hilariously false.

And at this moment, she was doing that now more than ever.

Anna walked up the Masts' porch steps. "Maria, will you come inside with me for a moment?" she asked.

"Sure." She turned toward Carter, who was playing in the driveway. "Carter, stay close by."

"Okay, Mom!" Carter called, jumping rope.

Maria picked up baby Rebecca and went inside with Anna. "Okay, what's wrong? What happened?" Maria asked.

"You wouldn't believe what Connor just said to me. He had the gall to tell me I could not leave the house without his permission." Anna paused for the expected gasp of outrage. Maria didn't disappoint. "I can't believe him."

"Wait, Connor really said you need his permission to leave the house? That doesn't sound like him." Maria tilted her head to one side. "There's got to be more to it than that. What else did he say?"

Anna paused, suddenly realizing that without Maria knowing the full story, it made what Connor did look a lot worse than it really was. Anna told Maria everything that had happened and Maria smiled.

"Seems to me like he's just trying to protect you right now. He could have gone about it in a better way, without lying about Liz, but I think his intentions are good. I know you don't like being told what to do, but he's worried about you. He feels responsible for your safety. But I do understand how you feel. I'd be irked if Derek told me I couldn't leave the house without him. He said that back when I was in danger and he was my bodyguard, but he would never say that to me now because I'm not in danger anymore. And now we're married. So, it all depends on the situation. I don't think he's trying to be controlling. That's not the Connor I know."

Realizing that Maria was on her side, Anna lifted her head up, a scowl on her face as she finally allowed herself to think about what Connor had done.

The door opened and Gideon came inside, a book folded under his arm. He looked up, eyes moving from one lady to the next. An assessment of the situation told him it was best if he removed himself as quickly as possible.

He turned around and escaped back outside.

Maria shook her head at the door, chuckling, then turned back to Anna.

"Again, I think he has good intentions, but he could have handled this a lot better. Still, you can't be mad at him forever. He needs your help."

Anna sighed. A few minutes of reflection had finally made her see where Connor was coming from, but she was still annoyed. "I guess I might have overreacted a little bit."

"Still, you should wait for him to apologize. That way he'll learn a lesson or two. When Derek does something that sets me off, I like to remember how the doctor says more vegetables and less meat is good for his health. Trust me, he comes around pretty quickly when I give him a plate full of leaves for dinner."

205

Anna chuckled. "Connor does like his steak."

Maria nodded. "There you go. But in all seriousness, I can recognize a controlling man a mile away because of my experiences with dating Trevor. Let's see if he is like Trevor or just made a mistake. Hopefully, it's the latter."

Anna nodded, remembering Maria's controlling, abusive ex-boyfriend who'd been arrested for human trafficking. "You're right, Maria. That was so long ago, I almost forgot about that. I trust your judgment."

"Is Anna inside?" Anna heard Connor ask outside.

"Yes. They'll be out in a minute," Mary said.

"He's here already? I guess I'll go and see if he's ready to apologize," Anna said, walking toward the door.

Maria reached out and grabbed Anna's arm. "Not so fast. Make him wait. His behavior might be a warning sign. I do think he is just being protective because of your current situation, but I could be wrong. Maybe he really is controlling. If he acts angry because you make him wait, it could be the first step on a slippery slope. And if he really is controlling, you should back out of whatever relationship you two have right now before it becomes something else."

Anna nodded slowly. "You're right."

A few minutes later, Anna and Maria walked out of the house and stepped onto the porch. "Thank you so much, Mary, for having me over," Anna said.

"Oh, don't be a stranger, darling. I really enjoyed your visit. I guess even Gideon gets tired of me yapping on and on about my roses."

"I do not, dear," Gideon muttered, flipping the page of his book.

"Oh, I love hearing you talk about your roses. I've never seen flowers look so beautiful in my life." Anna patted Mary's arm.

"Oh, thank you, dear."

The tinkling sound of Mary's laughter followed Anna all the way down the dirt lane. When they were close to Maria's house, Anna stopped in front of Connor and glared at him.

"I'm guessing you ladies have been talking about me," Connor said sheepishly, looking up at Maria before bringing his gaze back to Anna.

"Sure, you'll be glad to know that we both agree that you were a big jerk."

Connor sighed. "Okay, I guess you're right. I was a complete jerk back there and I'm sorry."

"I'll give you two a minute," Maria put in, smiling, then dashed into the house.

"Want to go talk in the barn?" Anna offered.

"Yes, thanks," Connor said as they walked toward it. "Truly, I am sorry. I didn't mean to come across like that. But I promised to keep you safe, and I'm only trying to do that. I just couldn't bear it if something happened to you. But I can only protect you when I'm with you, so I'd rather you stick with me. That's all."

They stepped inside the barn, and Connor shuffled his feet as though he was nervous.

"I came on too strong, and it's because I care about you. I can't..." He paused, looking away and scratching his ear. "I can't lose someone I care about again."

Anna had been expecting an apology. She just wasn't expecting him to pour his heart out to her. And for him, as a guarded man who rarely showed his feelings, Anna knew the few words he'd just said was his way of pouring his heart out.

"Well, of course, I forgive you. I understand now. And while we're here, I'll let you know before I go somewhere, just to put your mind at ease."

"Thank you. I'm glad we're on the same page now. Honestly, if anything happened to you, I don't think I could live with myself." Connor looked into her eyes. "Anna—"

"Come on, Anna, we better make dinner so we can be on time for the date," Maria said, walking into the barn, oblivious.

"Oh, of course. You're right." Anna sighed, giving an apologetic smile to Connor. They'd have to sort all this personal stuff out later.

*****

After eating an early dinner, Liz came over again to watch over the children and put them to bed while Derek, Maria, Anna, and Connor went out to follow Ella Ruth and Moses on their date. They once again got in the car, then drove to Ella Ruth's house to wait for Moses to pick her up.

They followed as Moses brought her to another fancy restaurant, and Anna and Maria went inside to keep an eye on them. This time, they sat a few booths behind them, facing away from Moses, like they had before, and ordered a dessert to share.

"I have a wonderful surprise planned for you after dinner," they heard Moses gush.

"Really? What is it?" Ella Ruth asked.

"I'm not telling! You'll have to wait and see. You're going to love it."

Anna and Maria looked at each other with wary glances. A surprise? That sounded ominous. Could this be it? Would Moses finally lead them to where the girls were being kept?

After their dinner, Moses asked for the check, and Anna and Maria hastily set some cash on the table and hurried out of the restaurant before Moses could see them. They got in the car and waited.

"This could be it," Anna blurted as soon as they got in the car. "He says he has a big surprise for her."

"As in, he won't let her look where they are going while he drives the buggy?" Connor asked.

"He didn't say that, but maybe," Maria said.

"There they are," Derek said as the couple walked out of the restaurant and toward their buggy. Moses helped Ella Ruth in, then he got in and they drove down the road.

"Let's see what this big surprise is," Connor murmured as he turned the car around and carefully followed the buggy.

After about fifteen to twenty minutes, they arrived at an art gallery downtown. "What? This is the big surprise?"

"Well, Ella Ruth does love art. She loves to paint. He got her that fancy, expensive art case of supplies," Anna said.

"That's true," Maria said. "No wonder he's taking her to an art gallery. She's probably never been to one before. Of course, she would love this."

Anna couldn't help but sigh in disappointment. "I thought this was going to be it."

"Maybe he doesn't feel like she trusts him enough yet to try anything that big," Derek said.

Connor slowed the car and parked a few spaces away from the buggy in the shadows under some trees.

After a moment, Anna said, "They're taking a while to get out of the buggy. Do you think they're talking?"

"Well," Connor said, rolling down his window. "Maybe not. They usually get out right away. You think we could hear her from here if she said the code word in a normal voice?"

"I don't think so," Derek said. "She might have to shout for us to hear. And if we park any closer, he might see us. Do you think—"

"No! I said no!" they heard Ella Ruth shout from inside the buggy.

"That's her!" Maria cried, but the four of them were already getting out of the car.

"Hey!" Anna called, sprinting toward the buggy. What was Moses doing? Her mind spun with what could be going on, and she hoped she wasn't too late to stop it. "Are you okay in there?"

She reached the buggy, a bit out of breath, and looked up at Moses and Ella Ruth. Derek, Connor, and Maria stood right behind her. "What's going on? We heard shouting and ran over."

"Nothing. It's none of your concern," Moses said haughtily. Ah, finally, his mask of charm was slipping.

Ella Ruth looked as though she was about to burst into tears. And why was her cheek red?

"Excuse me? Maria and I have known Ella Ruth our whole lives and we care about her, so it is our business," Anna shot back.

"Actually," Ella Ruth said. "Moses was not being the gentleman I thought he was. I'm glad you all were nearby."

"What happened?" Connor asked, taking a step forward and glaring at Moses. Maria helped Ella Ruth down from the buggy and Anna put a comforting arm around her.

"What did he do to you?" Anna whispered in her ear.

"He…" Ella Ruth's eyes filled with tears as she whispered back, "He started kissing me and I tried to go along with it but he was moving way too fast, so I pushed him away. Then he hit me in the face." Ella Ruth held a hand to her cheek, her eyes reddening with unshed tears.

"Step out of the buggy, mister," Derek said. "Right now."

"Or what?" Moses spat. "We were on a date, and I kissed her. What's so wrong about that?"

"You did a lot more than kiss me. You hit me! I told you to stop and you didn't listen," Ella Ruth cried, and Anna and Maria pulled her into a hug.

"Get out right now!" Connor shouted.

"Or what?"

Connor whipped out his CPDU badge. He didn't want to do this and blow his cover, but at this point, Ella Ruth wouldn't be going on any more dates with this piece of work anyway, which meant Moses wouldn't lead them to where the girls were any time soon. "If you don't come with us quietly, I'll arrest you for assault."

Moses' mouth dropped open. "For what? Kissing a girl?"

"Well, I know it was more than that, and I'm sure the traffic cameras will agree."

Moses looked around for traffic cameras. Connor wasn't even sure there were any on this street.

"But you're Amish," Moses said, befuddled. "So how can you be a cop?"

"I am a cop, and no, I'm not Amish. And I'm about 100% sure you aren't either. We also know you've been involved with trafficking Amish girls. Come with us quietly and maybe we can work out a deal," Connor said as he and Derek circled in on Moses. Connor pulled out his handcuffs and put them on Moses.

"What? No, man. You've got this all wrong," Moses said as Connor pulled him out of the buggy.

Anna helped Ella Ruth back into the buggy. She was clearly still shaken up. "We will get you home, Ella Ruth," Anna said.

After handcuffing Moses, reading him his rights, and shoving him ungracefully in the back seat of his car, Connor put a second set of handcuffs on Moses' ankles, connecting them to the handcuffs on his wrists. Since this was a regular car and not a police car, this would help prevent Moses from trying to escape or injure Connor.

Connor slammed the car door.

"What are we going to do with him?" Derek asked Connor. "If we bring him to CPDU, the moles will probably alert Korovin that we're onto him and move the location of where they're keeping the girls."

"Right," Connor said, rubbing the bridge of his nose. "I'll have to call Ben or Jeff. I'm not sure. We can't unlawfully detain him." He sighed. "You know, to be honest, I've been thinking about quitting anyway and living a more peaceful life, like you."

"You mean, you want to become Amish?" Derek said, his eyes hopeful. Connor couldn't tell if his friend was kidding or not.

"You'd like that, wouldn't you? Don't push it." Connor laughed. "Sorry, man. I could never be Amish. If you remember, I used to want to be a mechanic a long time ago, but I gave up on that dream when Grace died. Lately, I've been thinking about it again. I'd really like to fix up old cars."

"Wow! I think if the Lord has put it on your heart again, you should pray about it. That would be really great, Connor." Derek beamed.

"Well, for now, we have to figure out what to do with this guy."

Connor's phone rang. It was Jeff.

"Derek, keep an eye on him," Connor said to Derek, then took a few steps away from the car to take the call.

"Jeff? I was just about to call you."

"Connor," Jeff said. "We have Cassidy Hendricks. She's safe. Olivia, Isaac, and Ben are here with me. We're going to bring her somewhere safe now. My friend who was a former Navy SEAL is going to watch over her, so she's in good hands. I convinced her to give me the flash drive, and we've stashed it somewhere no one will find it until we can find out who the moles are and trust CPDU again."

"Excellent."

"That's not all. I told Tucker and Davis I was going to meet up with her, but I think they told Korovin's guys. I think Tucker and Davis are the moles, Connor. How else would they have known? I can't believe I didn't see it. We barely got away. Korovin's men ambushed us in a firefight."

"What? You think they're the moles? But we've worked with them for years. We trusted them."

"And they were working with me this whole time. How could I have been so blind?" Jeff let out a growl of frustration.

"I have news, too. We just arrested a suspect, the groomer who has been luring girls to the traffickers. Derek and I don't want to take him to CPDU because the moles would obviously know we are on to what's going on and move the girls. Do you think you can come get him and bring him to CPDU while the rest of us go get the moles?"

"Yes. The others can drop off Hendricks at the safe location. If we can meet up with the moles and arrest them while your suspect is brought in to CPDU, that would work. The moles will be distracted and we can arrest them before they know the groomer has been arrested. We need to prove to CPDU who the moles are. So, let's set up a trap." Jeff cleared his throat. "We'd need to use Anna as bait. Would she be willing to do that? Would you be okay with that?"

"No. No way," Connor said, shaking his head adamantly.

"What is it? What is he saying?" Anna asked, coming over to see what the call was about.

"Nothing."

"Tell me," Anna persisted, scrunching up her nose.

Connor knew she wouldn't give up. He beckoned for her to lean in. He didn't want to put it on speakerphone here. "Jeff, Anna is here with me."

"Anna, I have an idea to prove who the moles are to CPDU, but we need your help," Jeff said.

"I'll do anything," Anna said, leaning in close to the phone between her and Connor. "I just want to help Katie and Lilly and the other girls."

"This is what I'm thinking. I'll send Tucker and Davis to come and pick up Anna, and we'll let them believe we think they're putting her in witness protection. We will follow Tucker and Davis, and hopefully they'll lead us to Korovin, but maybe not. Either way, once we have eyes on them holding Anna hostage, we call in CPDU for backup. They'll see them holding Anna hostage for Korovin, then we storm the place. Anna, if this works, what they're probably going to do is hold you hostage and use you as leverage to get Connor to bring them the flash drive. If we think you're in any immediate danger, we will come in and get you in seconds. What do you think? We understand if you don't want to—"

"I'll do it." She nodded once and looked at Connor, determination in her eyes.

"You sure?" Connor asked, and couldn't help but admire her bravery.

"Absolutely. Call Tucker and Davis now and tell them I'm ready to go."

Connor kept his eyes on Anna as he replied. "Yes, Jeff. Let's do this."

"Thanks, Anna. Connor, I'm texting you the address where we will meet up before we meet Tucker and Davis. Meanwhile, can you meet me halfway with your suspect so I can bring him to CPDU?" Jeff said.

"Sure. Where do you want to meet?"

"There's a gas station I think that's halfway between us. I'll text you that address too."

Connor ended the call. "You sure about this, Anna?"

"Yes."

"It's risky."

"I know. I don't care. I have to do this."

He just looked at her, admiring the way the moonlight gleamed on her blonde hair. She was by far the bravest woman he'd ever met, besides Grace.

And now was not the time to focus on this. "Well, I better let Derek know what's going on. You can bring Ella Ruth home in the buggy, and I'll come get you after I bring this guy to Jeff. Derek and Maria's house isn't far from the meetup location. That way you and Maria can explain to the Holts what happened to Ella Ruth."

"You're right. Besides, I want to make sure she gets home safely. I'll see you later," she said, returning to the buggy. He hadn't missed the look in her eyes, like she had so much more she wanted to say to him but held back.

Connor updated Derek on the situation outside of the car, away from Moses' earshot.

"How about you go home with Anna and Maria? I'll be going to meet up with the others right after I bring Moses to Jeff, and it could get violent. I know you would probably rather sit this one out," Connor said.

"Yes, thank you," Derek said.

"No. Thank you, Derek. I couldn't have done this without your help. It means more than you know." Connor clapped his friend on the back, then got in the car with Moses.

Now Connor needed to talk to Moses before he left him with Jeff, who would take him to CPDU. If he was lucky, maybe he could persuade him to tell them where the girls were being kept.

He knew that wasn't likely.

216

Chapter Twenty-Four

"What on earth happened back there?" Anna asked as Maria drove the buggy. Derek sat in the back.

Ella Ruth swallowed hard, wiping a tear away. "He told me he loved me, and he listed all the nice things he's done for me and given me. He told me I owed him. So, he tried to kiss me but I pushed him away, telling him I don't want to kiss until marriage. He got angry and tried to undo my dress, but of course with the pins, he couldn't figure out how. Thank God. That's when I was screaming and you came running. A few seconds more and I think..." Ella Ruth burst into sobs, her shoulders shaking.

"I am so sorry," Maria said, reaching for Ella Ruth's hand. "We knew it was risky putting you in this position, but I was really hoping we'd find the girls before anything like this happened."

"It could have been much worse," Ella Ruth said. "We were in the front of the buggy and there were people around. I think that's the only reason why he didn't go any farther than that."

"God protected you," Anna said. "But I am sorry too."

"Some men have terrible intentions," Derek put in.

"But not all," Maria said. "Those are hard to find." Maria turned to smile at her husband.

"It's a shame this ended before he could lead us to where the girls are," Ella Ruth said. "It's all my fault; I blew it!" She buried her face in her hands.

"No, not at all!" Anna cried. "What could you have done? We told you if you felt in danger or if he tried anything inappropriate on you that you would say the code word."

"Well, I knew you wouldn't hear me say cake; that's why I shouted. If I had yelled 'cake' as loud as I could, he'd get suspicious," Ella Ruth said with a small chuckle.

Anna smiled. "Good call. We knew immediately that you needed us."

"But now I've ruined everything!" Ella Ruth cried again.

"No, no. Connor is questioning him now in the car. If Moses knows where the girls are, Connor will get him to talk," Maria said.

"And if not?" Ella Ruth asked.

Anna sighed. "Then we will have to figure out something else."

"Well, after this, none of the other girls are going to want to go on a date with him," Ella Ruth said.

Anna patted Ella Ruth's arm. "And we wouldn't let them. For now, let's just get you back home to your parents. We have some explaining to do."

After dropping Derek off at their house, Maria drove the buggy into the Holt's yard, and Anna's stomach filled with dread. Would Esther and Irvin ever trust her after this, after she'd put their daughter in danger? She wouldn't blame them if they didn't, and she'd known them her whole life.

Anna glanced over at Ella Ruth. Her eye was swollen and red from where Moses had hit her in the face.

"Here goes nothing," Ella Ruth said as they walked up to the door. Ella Ruth opened it and went inside. "*Maam, Daed?* I'm home."

Esther came to the door, holding a book she'd been reading. "Ella Ruth, how was your date with Moses? Oh, dear, what happened to you?" Esther noticed Anna and Maria. "Please, come in."

Ella Ruth had indeed told her parents she was going on dates with Moses, but that was all she'd told them. They believed he was a kind, young Amish man.

It was time to tell Esther and Irvin the whole truth.

They all stepped inside, and Anna closed the door. "We have a lot to talk about, Esther."

"Come inside. Come sit in the living room," Esther said, leading them inside.

"Hello, ladies," Irvin said, also reading a book. "Oh, Ella Ruth!" he said, noticing her swollen face and her distressed expression. He shot out of his chair and came to her side in a moment. "What happened? Where is Moses? Did he do this to you?" With each word, Irvin's voice sounded more like the growl of a protective lion concerned about his cub.

Ella Ruth sat down on the couch with her parents, and Anna and Maria sat on the sofa. "I was on a date with Moses, as I told you before, but he is not the man you think he is."

"It's a bit of a long story," Maria said, then turned to Anna. "Anna, why don't you start?"

Anna nodded and took a deep breath. She explained how she'd come here with Connor and how they'd suspected someone was targeting Amish girls to traffic. Anna told them about Korovin's sex trafficking ring. She explained how they'd arrested Moses and what he'd done, how Ella Ruth had volunteered as bait, how they'd been

219

following her and Moses. She also explained why she had to lie about her and Connor being married. "Connor is investigating this undercover. He works for CPDU, and I'm helping him. We don't know Moses' real name yet, but Connor is hoping the man might know something that could lead us to Lilly and Katie and the other girls they've taken. Ella Ruth bravely volunteered to do this. She said she wanted to do anything she could to find her sisters." Anna beamed at Ella Ruth.

Irvin sighed. "I'm glad you wanted to help, Ella Ruth, but that was very dangerous."

"I assure you, we were watching nearby the entire time. She knew there were risks. When they were in that parking lot, we were parked a few cars away, so that's why it took a moment for us to get to her," Maria said.

"I knew it was risky," Ella Ruth told her parents. "I'm sorry I didn't tell you. I knew you wouldn't let me. I just wanted to help find Lilly and Katie, but instead I ruined everything. Now we might never find them." With those final words, Ella Ruth broke down into sobs again, and Esther held her close while Irvin held his daughter's hand.

Irvin's expression softened. "Oh, my daughter, you did everything you could. Maybe you led them closer to your sisters than you think."

"Connor is questioning that man now. That could be true, Ella Ruth," Maria said.

Esther gave Irvin a questioning look as if asking what they should do, how to react. Irvin looked down at the floor for a moment, deep in thought. Maybe even praying.

"I know I should be angry at the three of you," Irvin said thoughtfully. "Instead, I'm very impressed by your bravery and determination. I should ground you, Ella Ruth, but I don't think that would do any good. And you're right. We probably wouldn't have let you go if you had told us. So, I see why you did what you did." He sighed, looking at Esther.

"I agree," Esther said. "It pains me to think of what could have happened to my darling daughter, but I'm proud of you." Esther held her daughter closer. "I understand you want to help find your sisters, and hopefully, the Lord will bring something good out of this."

"I hope so," Anna said. "And remember, please don't tell anyone about this. Not yet. Just in case there are more men around like this 'Moses'."

"We won't," Esther said.

"So," Irvin said, "that explains why he doesn't speak much Pennsylvania Dutch. He told us he came from a community in New York where they don't speak it anymore. This also explains why he's been coming and going for a while now. And to think we trusted him." Irvin shook his head.

"Yes, it does make sense now. Well, I think Ella Ruth has had quite a night. You should rest, dear," Esther said, patting her daughter's shoulder.

"Absolutely," Anna said, standing up. "Please, let us know if you need anything at all. I'm so sorry for what he did to you, Ella Ruth. I wish we could have stopped it."

"I knew there were risks," Ella Ruth said. "I don't regret anything."

"You're one tough cookie," Maria said. "But it's okay to be upset about it. And please let us know if there is anything else we can do."

"We appreciate everything you're doing to try to find Lilly and Katie," Irvin said, walking them to the door. "Thank you."

"That's one incredible daughter you have there," Anna said.

"They are all incredible," Maria added.

Irvin gave a small smile. The Amish in Unity rarely gave such outward compliments, and clearly Irvin didn't know quite how to react. "Thank you." He nodded. "I know they are."

*****

Connor started the car and drove Moses out of the lot. "Let's start with an easy one, buddy. What's your real name?"

"I'm not talking to you, man," Moses said, staring out the backseat window. "I want a lawyer."

"Look. I'm bringing you to CPDU. We know what you did, but if you tell me the truth, I can put in a good word for you and probably get your sentence reduced if you can give us information that will help us find the other traffickers. Got it?" Connor said, staring the man down in the rearview mirror with an icy gaze. "So tell me who you are and who you're working for."

The man stared back, but only for a moment, then he looked at the floor.

"Okay. Fine. My real name is Joey McCoy. I'm from Unity, but I'm not Amish. I live downtown. I met these guys in a bar and they offered me a job. They asked if I knew the Amish girls in the Amish community and said I'd make a lot of money if I'd set them up to go on dates with non-Amish guys," Joey explained, if that was even his real name. "Look, I have gambling debts and student loans to pay off. I lied and said I knew the Amish girls. I dressed up like an Amish guy and said I was a traveling salesman. I'm not the bad guy here. Those other guys are the ones who did the actual crime."

"Who hired you? I need some names," Connor prodded.

"I don't know their names, man. Sir. They never told me!"

"Really? You expect us to believe that?"

"Yeah, man. They said their names were Bruiser and Brewsky or something weird like that. Nicknames."

"So did you take Katie and Lilly Holt on these 'dates'?" Connor asked, trying not to pull the car over and get his hands on this guy.

"Yeah. Well, no. Not exactly. Brewsky paired me with one of his guys. They called him Adam, but I don't think that was his real name. I introduced Adam to the girls as my friend. He invited them out on the date. We arranged for me to pick them up and drive them to meet him. I dropped them off and that's all. I don't know what happened after." Joey lowered his head.

"You didn't see the red flags?"

"All I was thinking about was the money, okay? I thought they were just going on dates. What is going on here? What did you say about trafficking? Because I don't have any part in trafficking, whatever that is. The girls said they wanted to go!"

Connor squeezed the steering wheel even harder, trying not to explode. "Sex trafficking, Joey. You've been involved in sex trafficking, whether you knew it or not. And that means you'll go to prison for a very long time unless you help us out. Remember, if you give us information, we can put in a good word for you and maybe get you a deal."

Connor didn't believe that this guy didn't know he was being involved in sex trafficking. At best, he knew he was dropping innocent Amish girls off with strange men to do who knows what.

Joey hadn't cared about Lilly or Katie at all. Just like he hadn't cared about Ella Ruth. All he had cared about was the money he'd been promised.

223

"Okay, okay. Let me think. I only met those guys twice. I did overhear them talking once. They mentioned a name. It was something like caravan or karate…" Joey fumbled.

"Korovin?" Connor asked.

"That's the one! Korovin. Who is that?"

"You don't want to know, man," Connor said, shaking his head slowly.

He's the man who'd have Joey killed if he knew Joey blew his cover.

"Where was the exact place where you dropped off Katie and Lilly on their dates?" Connor asked.

"It was a hair salon. It seemed innocent enough to me," Joey said. "That's why I didn't know what was really going on."

Connor didn't buy his innocence act, not for a second. "Hair salons are often used as covers for where girls and young women are sold for sex. Did you know that, Joey McCoy?"

"No, man. I hadn't even heard of sex trafficking before all this."

"A lot of people don't know what it is or that it's going on here in the US. They think just because slavery is illegal that it doesn't happen anymore. There are more people in slavery today than in any other time in history." Connor took a deep breath, trying to calm himself down. The topic got him angry just talking about it. "I think you knew something was going on. But that's beside the point. Let's try this again. Where are the girls being kept?"

"I have no idea. All I did was drop them off at the meet up. Maybe they're still at the hair salon," Joey said. "It was called The Hair Shack or something. If you look it up online, you'll find it."

Depending on where it was, maybe he'd have time to stop by quickly and look around before picking up Anna and meeting up with the others.

Connor pulled into the parking lot where Jeff was waiting to bring Joey to CPDU. Connor got out of the car, approaching Jeff.

"Did he say anything?" Jeff asked.

Connor told him everything Joey had said. "Sorry. I wish I had gotten more out of him."

"He hasn't met me yet," Jeff said with a smirk, opening the car door. Unhitching Joey's ankles from his handcuffs so he could walk, Jeff led him to his car. "Come on. Let's go for a ride."

"Thanks, Jeff. See you soon."

For the first time tonight, hope rose up inside Connor. If someone was there at the salon this time of night, maybe he could find something out. After putting the salon's location into his GPS, he was relieved to see it was just outside the Amish community, minutes from Derek and Maria's house. He'd have just enough time to stop there, then pick up Anna and meet up with the team.

Connor sped to the hair salon. When he arrived just a few minutes before closing time, he nonchalantly walked through the door. The scents of hairspray, hair color, and acrylic nail polish fumes attacked him like a sandstorm, and he had to cough a few times before he could speak. How did people work in this place?

"Can I help you?" a woman behind the counter asked, tapping her long red fingernails on the desk.

"Yes, please," he said. "I was told you have some services that are off the menu."

"What do you mean?" she asked, raising one perfectly-plucked eyebrow.

"I'm not sure what you'd call it here," Connor said, instantly uncomfortable, and unsure of the lingo. If Ben or Jeff were here, they'd know what to say in this type of situation, but he was alone. "You know, maybe downstairs, in the basement, you offer services that are off the menu?"

"Sir, do you mean a wax?" the woman asked, unsuccessfully trying to hide a smirk. "It's okay; you don't have to be embarrassed. A lot of guys get waxing."

"No," Connor retorted, much louder than he'd intended. He lowered his voice. "I do not need a wax." Heat crept up his neck and face, and he wanted to laugh and growl in frustration at the same time. Being here alone without any support was clearly flustering him. "I'm sorry, I'm not being very articulate. Could I just use your bathroom?"

"Sure, honey. It's at the end of the hallway in the back." The woman grabbed a magazine.

Connor walked to the back, fighting through waves of aerosol sprays and the overwhelming smell of acrylic nails. This could not be good for the environment, let alone safe to inhale on a regular basis.

He reached the back of the building where the bathroom was and searched around for other doors. He found a closet, but there were only brooms, hair color, rubber gloves, and mops hiding in there. When he opened another door, he found a staircase leading down to the basement. Bingo.

Connor found the light switch, turned it on, and closed the door behind him. He crept down the stairs, gun drawn, just in case. Though he turned left, then right, there was nothing out of the ordinary that he could see, just some cleaning supplies, boxes of more hair color, and cans of hairspray.

Connor felt along the walls for hidden doors, anything, and investigated every corner of the room, but there was nothing down here. And from what he could see, there was no upstairs to this building, but he'd check to make sure.

He hurried up the stairs and opened the door. Sneaking into the hallway again, he was relieved when no one seemed to notice that he had in fact not been in the bathroom. Poking around, he couldn't find any more doors that led to an upstairs. When he opened the closet door again, he did see a small opening in the ceiling for a crawl space, but there was no way they'd be able to get people in and out through there.

There was nothing here. There wasn't even a sign that the girls had been here and were then moved from what he could tell.

Connor hurried across the salon, back to the front door.

"You sure you don't want that wax, dear?" the woman at the desk teased him, wagging her eyebrows, clearly amused.

"Uh, yeah. Thanks anyway." Connor opened the door and dashed out before he embarrassed himself any further.

Chapter Twenty-Five

"Did you find out anything?" Anna asked Connor as soon as he walked through Derek and Maria's front door. She paused, reading his face. "I'm guessing not much. Shh. Close the door quietly. The kids are sleeping. Maria and Derek are checking on them."

Connor nodded, closing the door softly behind him. He filled her in on the information Joey had given him. "It's just a regular salon," he said. "With a very odd receptionist."

Anna blinked, staring at the framed paintings on the wall that Carter had made. Fortunately, artwork was allowed to be displayed in Unity, because Carter was quite advanced for his age and loved to create countless drawings and paintings. There were several of his drawings and paintings throughout the home.

"Well, we have to go, Anna. We have to meet up with the others to arrest the moles," Connor said, tugging on her sleeve.

The art gallery. She blinked. Memories swarmed through her mind, about the art case that Moses—Joey McCoy—had given to Ella Ruth after she'd told him she loved to paint. Then he'd taken her to the art gallery, but they'd never gone inside.

"Connor," Anna all but shouted. He looked at her in surprise, but she hardly noticed. "You told me that hair salons, nail salons, massage parlors, hotels, and many other businesses are used as fronts for sex trafficking or prostitution. But what about an art gallery?"

228

Connor's eyes widened. "Well, I've never personally heard of it, but I see your point."

"What if Joey is lying and knows more than he says? What if he was taking Ella Ruth to the art gallery because that's where the traffickers told him to take her? What if that's where the girls are being sold and the art gallery is just a front? What if he gave Ella Ruth the art supply case just so she wouldn't be suspicious when they got to the art gallery, because it is something she'd actually like?"

Connor nodded rapidly. "I think you're on to something. The only way we can know for sure is to go in undercover as…interested buyers."

Connor relayed Anna's idea to Jeff on the phone, putting it on speakerphone so Anna could hear his reply.

"I think you could be right, Anna," Jeff said. "But there is no way we can raid the building until the moles are arrested. Otherwise, as soon as we call CPDU for backup, the moles will alert the traffickers and they'll clear out before we can get in. We have to take care of the moles first, then raid the art gallery after. I'm sorry it has to be this way."

Anna sighed. "I understand."

"Hopefully, this won't take long," Jeff said, "and maybe we can rescue the girls later tonight. I just left Joey McCoy at CPDU, and Tucker and Davis were already gone when I got here. I will call the rest of the team and tell them the plan. Thanks."

Connor ended the call and slipped the phone back in his pocket.

"Anna," he began, but she looked away. "I want to promise you that this won't be dangerous, but I can't. Are you sure about this?"

"I know it's dangerous. I'm sure."

229

"Anna," he said her name softly.

He was going to kiss her again. She knew it. She could feel it in the tip of her toes, and even though her head kept telling her to protest or run, she seemed powerless.

As if someone had tossed a bucket of water all over her, she jumped back.

"I can't," she said out loud, shaking her head as if rejecting the voice in her head. "I can't do this right now."

Connor took a step back. "What do you mean? I thought you said you had feelings for me."

"Maybe." Anna forced herself to look at him. "But it doesn't matter what I feel. I know I can never be in a relationship with someone who has killed people. Even if they were terrorists or criminals and you were doing your job or taking orders in the military. It goes against everything I was taught. The Amish are against all violence. And your job is not only violent, but dangerous. And I couldn't live with that fear. And what if you have to kill again in your line of work? I don't want to be the wife of a killer or a young widow."

The realization hit her like a buggy slamming into her. Maybe she had thought of it before, but it hadn't truly hit her until now.

She had said it all out loud. Her stomach sank, like she had made the worst mistake of her life. Something she could never come back from.

Connor's expression morphed from confusion to extreme pain.

Anna pushed down the sick feeling in her stomach and doubled down on her decision. She couldn't go back now. "I'm sorry it has to be this way. But it doesn't matter what I feel for you, I could never live with myself if I—"

"Loved a killer?" Connor asked, his bitter tone twisting the word even further until it was like a hot knife between them waiting to slash and burn whatever was left of the bond between them. "All the time we've been together, talking and laughing…" He took several steps back, eyes still blazing hurt. "You just saw me as a killer?"

"No!" Anna blurted. "I mean, I don't know." She put a hand to her head. Her brain hurt. It had been a long day.

"I don't know what else to say to change your mind about me."

"Nothing," Anna said. "There's nothing more to say. I'm sorry, Connor. I thought I could look past that part of you but I just…can't."

Anna nodded, knowing there was so much he hadn't told her yet, stories of his years with the CPDU and in the military. He might not have shared some memories with her for a long time, maybe not ever. Maybe there were some memories he had that were just too dark to share with her.

Right now, she felt certain she was not willing to accept that.

"Well, right now, we can't talk about this. We need to focus on what we have to do. Let's go tell Maria and Derek," Connor said emotionlessly, as Maria and Derek came out of the kids' rooms and joined them in the kitchen.

"We need to talk to you about something that's come up," Connor said.

"What's going on?" Maria asked.

Connor explained the situation, and Maria gasped. "Anna, are you sure you want to do this? It sounds dangerous," she said.

"Absolutely. I want to do everything I can to help find Katie and Lilly." Anna nodded.

"We have asked so much of you already. Ben got Isaac and Olivia to help us with this, and we have Jeff, and hopefully we will have all of CPDU to help us once we can show them who the moles are. So, Derek, you should stay here," Connor said.

Derek nodded.

"You've both helped so much," Anna said. "There's no way we could have gotten nearly this far without both of you. Thank you."

"We were glad to help," Derek said. "And now at least you think you know where the girls are being held."

"We loved having you here, and I was happy to help with Ella Ruth," Maria added.

"Well, we better get going. We have to meet up with Ben, Jeff, Olivia, and Isaac," Connor said, his tone suddenly business-like.

Maria hugged Anna.

"Anna," Maria whispered as Connor left the room. "Are you two okay? You seem sad, and Connor seems closed off. What happened?"

"I told him…" Anna looked away. "I told him I can't be with him. I thought I could look past that part of him, but I just can't. His job is just too dangerous, and I'm worried he will have to kill again, even in self-defense."

"If you truly love him, Anna, this will work out," Maria said.

"You're a better person than I am, Maria," Anna said, grabbing her friend's hand. "You befriended the woman who accidentally killed your late husband."

"That was God working through me. It wasn't me." Maria squeezed Anna's hand. "You can't do this on your own. You need God to work through you. You need to beg Him for help. We are nothing without

Him. You are so independent, and you think you can do everything on your own, but this time you can't, Anna. Promise me you will pray more about it. And I know you might think he was being controlling when he asked you not to leave the house without him, but I am sure his intentions were sincere and he just wants to protect you. Connor is a good man."

Anna's eyes filled with tears at her friend's profound wisdom. "You're so wise. What would I do without you?" Anna pulled Maria into a tight hug.

"Be careful, Anna. I love you," Maria whispered in her ear.

"I will. I love you too." Anna wiped away a tear and pulled away, then walked out of the house before she completely lost control of her emotions and changed her mind about the mission.

Chapter Twenty-Six

Anna and Connor were on the road again. The silence in the car was thick with anger and tension. Anna had no idea what to say, only that she hated how things had turned out between them. Darkness surrounded the car, the night covering the earth like a black sheet. With no street lights out here, it was hard to see more than twenty feet ahead of the car.

How she hated herself for not accepting all of Connor, even the imperfect parts of his past, and the person he was—dangerous job and all.

When they'd left Derek and Maria's house, Connor had tried to hide his pain in front of them, but he had failed. Maria had told her to keep on praying. Anna had been doing a lot of that since they left the community. With Connor giving her the silent treatment, it was not like she had much else to do.

Only this time, praying was not making her feel better. She still felt miserable.

What was wrong with her? Why couldn't she accept Connor as he is, even the parts of his past that he wanted to forget?

Anna barely noticed when they reached the meeting spot. Connor turned off the ignition and after several minutes scanning the area around him began to talk without looking at her. Then he reached into his pocket and called Ben to relay his location.

He spoke in a clipped tone. "Isaac, Liv, Jeff, and Ben will be here any minute, and we will follow you in a surveillance van. Once this is all over, you can go back to your life."

Anna couldn't leave like this. "Connor. Please, let me—"

"They're here." Connor got out of the car as the surveillance van drove up. Jeff, Ben, Olivia, and Isaac got out of the vehicle.

"Olivia!" Anna called to her longtime friend. Before becoming a police detective with CPDU, Olivia Mast—Maria's cousin—had grown up Amish with them in Unity. Anna had been so focused on her argument with Connor that she'd barely even thought about seeing Olivia again.

"It's great to see you," Olivia said, her short brown hair bouncing as she bounded toward Anna. "I wish we were meeting under lighter circumstances, but I'm really glad to see you. It's been a long time, hasn't it?"

"Way too long," Anna said and turned to Olivia's husband, Isaac. "Hey, Isaac."

"Hi, Anna." Isaac gave a small wave. "Good to see you."

Anna said, "I've been so busy with work, I'm sorry I haven't been in touch."

"Me too; no worries."

"Anna, you know Olivia, Isaac, and Ben. This is Agent Jefferson Martin. Everyone calls him Jeff for short," Connor said.

"Nice to meet you," Anna said to Jeff.

"You too. Wait, how do you know Ben?" Jeff asked, looking from Anna to Ben. "Oh, that's right. Ben worked here with Derek before."

"Yeah," Ben said slowly. "We met once or twice. Sorry I lost touch, Anna. I was super busy with work."

"Yeah, me too," Anna said, feeling the awkwardness getting even thicker in the air. "That's about when I started nursing school, and my parents passed away around that time." She knew she was about to start babbling and wished someone would just interrupt her to make her stop.

"Anna's parents were such wonderful people," Olivia said. "I was so sorry to hear about their passing."

"Thanks, Liv," Anna said, feeling relieved her friend had come to her rescue.

"Anyway," Connor said, breaking the tension, "Enough chit-chat. Let's go over the plan one more time."

Anna winced at Connor's cold tone, but he was right. They had to go over the plan before Tucker and Davis came to pick her up.

A few minutes later, Connor and Anna returned to the car. The other four got in the van and drove away, out of sight. They'd wait a distance away for Tucker and Davis to arrive.

"You don't need to worry about your job or anything. The agency will smooth things over with your employers. I'll see what you're entitled to in terms of compensation for the time and danger I put you in," Connor said as he got in the driver's seat.

"I don't care about that!" Anna cried. "I don't care about any of that. I don't want to leave things like this. You have to understand that—"

"Oh, trust me, I understand perfectly." He finally looked at her. "But don't worry. Very soon you won't have to pretend for my sake anymore."

Anna struggled with all the things she wanted to say, but it was clear he was not ready to listen to her. They sat outside for about fifteen minutes before a car parked right behind them and two men came out.

"Let's go," he said and reached for his door.

"Good to see you, Connor," Agent Davis said with a grin when he saw Connor.

Connor nodded at the two agents. "So, any word on where Korovin might be?"

Davis shrugged. "Last time he evaded the police, he was trying to escape the country on a container ship leaving for Malaysia with a fresh batch of his...um...cargo."

The euphemism was probably for Anna's benefit. When he said the word 'cargo,' Davis was talking about underage girls being trafficked. It was rare for Korovin to be so careless, but Connor figured the man was running scared.

"Where are you taking Anna to?"

Tucker handed a slip of paper with an address scribbled on it to him. "Jeff says to take her to a safe house." He glanced at Anna and gave her a small smile. "After this is all over and Korovin and the other traffickers have been arrested, she can go home. We'll keep a detail on her for two weeks or so. Make sure nothing happens."

Connor nodded. "Thank you." He turned to Anna. For a moment both of them stared at each other, each having so many things to say but no idea how to say them. Finally, Connor stepped away.

"Listen to them and you'll be fine," he told Anna.

The two agents nodded.

"And update me on her situation. Anything happens, no matter how seemingly insignificant, I want to know."

Tucker nodded as Davis walked back towards their car and beckoned at Anna. She looked at Connor for a few seconds, wondering if this was how they were going to say goodbye.

What if this ended badly and these were their last words?

The very thought made his gut clench.

When he refused to meet her gaze, she turned away and began walking towards the car. One stubborn tear escaped her eye.

"Don't worry, we'll take care of her." Tucker nodded at Anna.

Davis came back with a small paper bag. "Jeff said to give you that."

Connor peered inside it and saw a new phone as well as a small stack of bills. Closing the bag back up, he waved at the two men and ambled towards his car. Before he got in, he stopped and turned around to look at Anna. She was watching him, and he wondered what she was thinking.

For a second, his heart softened, and he told himself he should go back and say a proper goodbye. The moment didn't last. He pushed that thought out of his head and got into the car. He drove out of the parking lot, leaving Anna with the two agents.

Soon this would all be over, and then he could start the process of forgetting about this whole mess.

Especially Anna Hershberger.

*****

As Connor followed Anna, Tucker, and Davis, he realized he had made a huge mistake.

He should have never left her side at all. Something just didn't sit right with him. It was a feeling in his gut he couldn't get rid of.

What had he been thinking, letting her be the bait?

His anger had stopped him from thinking clearly, and in his haste, he had placed her in danger. All because she had wounded his pride. Fear struck him as he drove, silently praying that God kept her safe long enough for him to save her. It took everything in him to not hit the gas and catch up to the car, because then they'd notice him following. He had to leave plenty of distance between them.

If anything happened to her, he wasn't so sure he could survive that.

The weight of the gun on his hip felt heavy. But he didn't mind using it if that was what it took to save Anna. He didn't even care if it made her hate him more.

As he drove to the surveillance van to join the others, one thing was for sure.

He just couldn't bear to lose her.

Chapter Twenty-Seven

Liv, Isaac, Ben, Jeff, and Connor parked their surveillance van a good distance down the street from where the supposed 'safe house' was—where Davis and Tucker had taken Anna.

"Okay, put this on," Jeff said, attaching a wire to Connor. "They'll probably check you for wires when you walk in. Once they find this, hopefully, they'll think it's the only one and won't check for this." Jeff used a seam-ripper to open the inside pocket seam of Connor's jacket, then stuck a wire inside. He quickly sewed it back up.

"Where did you learn to sew?" Liv asked.

"My mom," Jeff said proudly.

"Smart woman," Liv said, eyebrows raised. "We'll record everything."

"Remember, we need Korovin, Tucker, and Davis alive so we can get more information from them," Ben said.

The team nodded.

"What's the code word going to be?" Jeff asked.

"Cake."

"Seriously?" Ben raised one eyebrow and chuckled.

"Why not? I like cake. And you can use it in a sentence so many different ways. Have your cake and eat it too, piece of cake, cakewalk…"

"Okay, wise guy. We get it," Ben said.

Connor's phone rang. It was a blocked number. "That must be them," he said shakily, then answered the phone. "Hello?"

"Sinclair," Davis said. "We've got Korovin. I need the flash drive to prove he's guilty. Otherwise, if we turn him in without it, the moles might get him out. I'm holding him here at the safe house. Can you bring it here as soon as you can?"

"Uh," Connor said. "Is this safe? What if he escapes? He's done it before."

"Not this time. We've got him tied up real good, and Tucker is watching him now."

"Is he anywhere near Anna?"

"No, we put her in a different safe house nearby with another agent."

Liar. Conner was quite certain there was no other safe house nearby. And there was probably no other agent working with them, unless there was another mole.

When Connor remained silent, Davis added hastily, "Don't worry, Sinclair. We've got it under control. Just bring the drive here right away so we can turn this scumbag in to CPDU, okay? Do you have it with you?"

"Yeah, I have it here with me. Ben gave it to me."

"Write this address down," Davis said, then rattled off an address. "It's a short drive. If you hurry, you can be here in fifteen minutes."

"I'm on my way."

241

"Thanks, man." The line went dead.

"Now we wait for fifteen minutes," Connor said, toying with the dummy flash drive Jeff had given him. Waiting for those fifteen minutes seemed like waiting fifteen hours, but finally time was up.

"Thanks, guys. Pray for me," Connor said, not wasting any time, then got out of the van.

Connor looked around him. He walked towards the house, making sure he didn't arouse any suspicion. He went up to the door and knocked.

Then he waited. He glanced at the door's peephole and felt someone's eyes on him.

Finally, he heard a click behind the door and it opened to reveal Davis. Connor immediately looked over Davis' shoulder and saw no one there.

Where was she?

"Come in," Davis said, holding Connor's eyes. It was a split second. But it was enough to see the malice there that he'd somehow missed before. "Don't stand out there too long."

Connor stepped inside.

"You've got the drive?" Davis asked.

"Not on me at the moment," Connor replied. He took a look around and found a door that led to the rest of the house. A door also led to the kitchen, but it was open, and it didn't look like there was anyone in there. "I wasn't sure it was safe to bring it with me yet."

"What do you mean?"

"I want to make sure it's safe to bring it here, and that Anna is safe. Cassidy sacrificed a lot to get me that drive, and I want to make sure we keep it safe. Where is Anna?"

"Connor," Davis implored him. "I don't think you understand. We need that drive or Korovin walks because of the moles."

"Oh, I understand." Connor took a position in the corner of the room that gave him a good vantage view of the rest of the room. He spoke loud enough that anyone in the house would have no problem hearing him. Although he guessed that was not necessary. He could bet there were cameras and mics picking up everything he was saying and doing. "Where's Tucker? I want to see Anna and make sure she's okay."

Davis' brow furrowed. "Connor, we've been friends for years. Don't you trust me? I need that drive, Connor, or things could go very bad."

Connor was about to reply when the closed door swung open and Korovin walked in, a big smile on his face. Connor had his gun in his hand in a split second. He would have pulled the trigger if Tucker had not walked out behind Korovin with Anna in front of him, holding a gun to her head.

"Drop it or she gets a hole in the head," Korovin hissed.

Connor lifted his finger away from the trigger and slowly dropped his gun.

"Kick it over," Korovin spat.

Connor reluctantly did as he said, and Korovin picked up the gun from the floor and pointed it at Anna. Korovin walked closer to Connor, clearly confident he had the situation under control.

"I think our friend here understands quite well what is happening," the master trafficker said with a sickening smile. He nodded to Tucker and Davis. "Check him for wires."

"You guys are working with him?" Connor asked Tucker and Davis, pretending to be shocked.

They refused to make eye contact as they patted him down and checked his clothing.

"Got something," Tucker said, holding up the dummy wire Jeff had put on him.

"Take care of it," Korovin snapped, Tucker smashed it under his foot.

Korovin took a few steps toward Connor, dragging Anna along with him. Out of nowhere, Korovin struck Connor in the face with his pistol, and Connor recoiled from the shock.

Korovin spat out, "I should shoot you for that. But I need something from you." He shook his head at Davis. "I thought I told you what was going to happen if you didn't get him to release that drive."

Davis glared at him. "I knew he wouldn't just give it to me. I knew he'd suspect us."

Connor stared him down. "Let Anna go and then we can talk."

"How about I do you one better? I shoot her in the knee and then we can talk?"

Anna's eyes widened, and she squirmed. Connor swallowed.

Korovin smiled. "Yeah, neither of you would like that, would you?"

"You want the flash drive, and I'm going to give it to you. You just let Anna go, and I swear I'll give it to you," Connor said.

"Do you think I'm stupid? You leave here and you'll come back with a whole army." He walked to Anna and grabbed her arm, dragging her forward. Anna winced in pain as his gun dug into her side. "The girl is staying here." The sensation of steel against her made her freeze in place.

Connor looked at Anna, guilt filling him. "No, that's not what I meant. I do have it on me. Here." Connor slowly reached into his pocket and set the dummy flash drive on the floor.

"Go check it. Could be a fake," Korovin said to Davis, who then grabbed a laptop and turned it on. Ben had set up an encryption that Davis would have to hack, which would give them some time—hopefully long enough for CPDU to get here.

Connor swallowed. He didn't have long now.

"What's this? Do you know how to get through this?" Davis turned the laptop to Connor.

"No, man, I have no idea. I didn't set that up. I'm no good with computers."

Davis groaned. "I'll figure it out. Might take a minute."

"Fine. Do it," Korovin said to Davis, then turned to Connor. "Agent Connor, I must admit I was quite eager to meet the man who has come the closest to threatening my business. It would probably have happened sooner if I wasn't surrounded by a bunch of idiots, starting with these two." He pointed to Davis and Tucker. "The mission was simple: give the job of killing Hendricks to some bumbling fool and let him take the fall for it. Somehow, the assassins managed to give it to one of the most stubborn agents I've ever met. That would be you. Then I recruited these two, which was my biggest mistake."

"But we got him and the girl here," Davis whined.

"Shut up!" Korovin screamed, revealing a snippet of his legendary rage. Anna winced. Davis snapped his mouth shut. Taking a deep breath, Korovin curved his lips in a smile directed at Connor. "Like I said, I'm surrounded by idiots. You wouldn't consider switching to the other side, would you? I could use a man like you."

Connor looked past him at Davis and Tucker. "I can't believe you two are working with this disgusting excuse for a human."

Tucker glared at Connor. "Not all of us have the luxury of living in your moralistic driven world. In the real world, money pays for a lot of things."

"At the cost of young girls being trafficked and raped?"

"Yes, Sinclair," Korovin taunted Connor. "Money pays for a lot of things. I wonder if you have a price. Everyone does. Some people prefer to be paid in other ways. For Cassidy Hendricks, it was the joy of helping people. That woman was so obsessed with her work, she would have done anything for those girls. It was easy to use her to gain access to my…merchandise."

Connor cringed at Korovin's choice of words, then he continued.

"Hendricks' diplomatic badge helped pave so many roads for us. All I had to do was pay a few hundred thousand dollars a year in donations." He grinned at Connor. "Sometimes I wonder if she knew where the money was coming from or what was happening."

Connor remembered the anguish on the face of the woman he had seen that night. The pain of knowing how she had been used to build the very thing she had been trying to destroy. He doubted she was ever going to be rid of those demons. They were so much a part of her. Bringing Korovin to justice may never get rid of them, but it would help.

"I got past the encryption," Davis said and Connor tried not to let his shock show.

That wasn't supposed to happen so quickly.

Ben had assured him it would take at least ten to fifteen minutes to get past the encryption, but Davis had zoomed through it. "Wait a minute…" Davis said, furrowing his eyebrows as he stared at the screen. "These are dummy files. There's nothing on here. This is a decoy flash drive!"

Korovin said nothing, just stepped forward and slung his pistol into Connor's head with all his strength, sending Connor to the floor in dizzy waves, even though he'd been expecting Korovin to hit him, or maybe even shoot him. But because Korovin needed Connor to get him the flash drive, Connor had known it wouldn't be fatal.

"One hour," Korovin said. "You don't come back with that drive in one hour and I'll shoot out one of your pretty little friend's kneecaps. In two hours, I shoot her second knee. And if by the end of the day you're not back, I'll simply look for someone else you care about to convince you. Tucker here is going to go with you to make sure you don't call any of your friends for help."

A few weeks ago, Connor would have told Korovin there was no one he cared about. Now, he knew better. He cared about Anna, Jeff, Isaac, Liv, and Ben. He cared about Gideon and Mary, and he would not be able to live with himself if anything should happen to them because of him. He cared about Maria, Derek, Carter, Rebecca, Ella Ruth, Liz, Simon, Katie, Lilly, and all the people in Anna's Amish community. He cared about them and he was going to do his best to save them all.

"Do you understand, Sinclair?" Korovin snapped.

Connor was out of time. He couldn't stall any longer.

He hoped CPDU was outside by now.

"Yes. Piece of cake. I understand."

He watched Korovin give Tucker instructions, and Connor counted the seconds as he waited for his team.

Korovin's eyes darted to the window, and he hesitated.

Had he seen one of Connor's team members? Connor wanted to turn around and look, but he didn't.

As if nothing had happened, Korovin continued talking to Tucker. Moments later, the doors were kicked down as Connor's small team raided the building.

Where was the rest of the CPDU team?

They hadn't made it in time.

A deafening bang shattered the air as a blinding light flashed throughout the house, knocking Connor to the floor. Disoriented, he put his hands to his head, trying to make sense of what had just happened. His ears rang intensely, and for several seconds, his vision went black. He tried to stand but just toppled to the floor.

What had just happened? Had a bomb gone off?

"A stun grenade!" Jeff shouted, followed by the moans of his team members as they tried to get their bearings.

As his vision finally started to return, Connor's eyes darted around the room. "Korovin is getting away with Anna!" he shouted, scrambling to his feet. He hobbled to the other end of the house, where the back door was open, Ben and Jeff right on his heels.

A black car tore out of the back yard, leaving tire marks on the grass.

"No!" Connor screamed. "He took Anna! I promised her nothing would happen to her!" He punched the door frame, bloodying his knuckles, but he didn't even feel it compared to the pain crushing his heart.

"Connor, stop," Ben said. "We'll get her back. We think we know where they are, remember?"

"Right," Jeff said, leading Connor back to the other room. "Let's get Tucker and Davis to CPDU, then we'll get all the girls and women out of that art gallery, including Anna."

Chapter Twenty-Eight

Anna's ears still rang and her vision was still spotty as two strong sets of arms hauled her away like she was a sack of flour. She kicked, fought, and screamed, though she could hardly hear her own screams over the high pitch humming in her ears. She landed on something soft, the seat of a car, and the car lurched forward, swerving out onto the street.

"No!" she screamed. Not *again*!

Korovin had taken her, temporarily disabling the team with his stun grenade and having two of his henchmen haul her away to the car behind the house.

Had any of them seen the car?

Would Connor find her?

Her mind swam with questions, competing with her racing heart as she pushed against the seat, trying to sit up as spots of white danced before her eyes.

"It'll pass, dear," Korovin said with a sneer, sitting beside her, looking unfazed. "I'm so glad I get to add another Amish girl to my collection."

The twisted look in his eye made her sick to her stomach.

"I know you have Katie and Lilly."

"Are those their names? To me, they're numbers six and seven." He gave a short laugh, looking at her up and down. "You're all very pretty. There must be something in the water at that Amish community of yours."

Anna wanted to spit on him, but she was too afraid of what he might do to her. How could any human see precious girls as just numbers, worth less than cattle? She scooted as far away from him as she could, huddling up on the opposite side of the car. Glancing at the door handle, she wondered how seriously she'd be injured if she jumped out of the car going at this speed.

She was willing to take her chances. She'd rather die than be this man's property. Her fingers inched toward the door handle.

"It's locked, buttercup," Korovin said, not even looking in her direction. "Besides, you'd be killed. Maybe paralyzed, if you're lucky."

Her fingers retreating back to her lap, Anna stared at the window, all hope evaporating. "Where are you taking me?" She guessed he was taking her to the art gallery, but there was no way she'd let him know that.

"To be with the others, obviously."

Clearly, that was all the information she'd get out of him.

About ten or fifteen minutes later, the car pulled into the back parking lot of the art gallery driveway and slowed to a stop.

She felt no satisfaction in knowing she'd been right as two more of Korovin's men opened the door and led her toward the back door, a knife held to her back the entire time.

"Make one sound and we kill you right here," one of them seethed into her ear, and she believed him.

Trembling, she let them lead her through the door and into the main room of the art gallery, then through a door that led to a set of stairs. As they went down the stairs, the dank mustiness of the basement filled Anna's nose. She barely had time to glance around before two large hands opened a door and shoved her through.

Anna fell onto a dingy, bare mattress beside a bucket, the only furnishings in the tiny room that had no windows and was no bigger than the mattress itself. In fact, these were not even rooms. They were more like stalls.

Stalls for livestock. For property. Anna shivered, bringing her knees up to her chin as she sat alone.

What's going to happen to me? I was rescued last time before anyone could hurt me, but what about this time? God, please let the team find me and the others before anything happens. Please, let Connor find us, Anna prayed.

"Another Amish girl, eh?" a deep voice said with a cackle.

"Yep. They're the perfect targets. It's too easy."

"She'll make a nice addition. Now we have a trio."

Anna felt bile rising in her throat, and she buried her face in her knees.

"Let's go get some takeout. I'm starving."

Heavy footsteps retreated up the stairs, and the basement door closed.

Silence.

After waiting several seconds, Anna whispered tentatively, "Hello? Anyone in here?"

"Anna?"

The quiet voice was coming from the stall on Anna's right.

"Katie? Is that you?" Anna asked.

"Yes. Lilly is here too, I think on your other side."

"I'm here, Anna," the quiet voice said, barely above a whisper.

Anna's heart wanted to soar because she'd found them, but it broke instead. What had happened to them here?

"Shh," another girl scolded.

"They could come back at any minute. And if they hear us talking…" Katie said.

"Okay. Just know we are going to get out of here. You hear me? I promise we'll get out of here," Anna whispered back.

With every cell in her body, she wanted to believe it. She'd told Connor she'd suspected Katie and Lilly were at the art gallery, now all she could do was pray.

*****

The entire CPDU team had gathered personnel and gone over the plan, then set up their vans and equipment a few blocks away from the art gallery. Derek, Maria, Esther and Irvin were waiting at the police station.

Connor walked with Jeff and Ben into the art gallery. The other agents waited a few moments, then went in after them.

Once again, the codeword was 'cake.'

This place was huge. Connor looked up at the high ceilings and the tall, abstract paintings on the wall. In his opinion, most of them looked like a four-year-old painted them. Then again, he knew nothing about art.

For all he knew, maybe the traffickers had painted them, just to supply a front for their true business.

"May I help you?" a stocky, muscular man in all black wearing a name tag with the name Bill on it stepped up to them.

"Hello," Ben said coolly. "We're just admiring the art work."

Jeff leaned toward the man and kept his voice low. "Actually, we don't care much about art. We heard that a little something extra comes with the paintings. Would you let us see the…merchandise?"

Connor tried not to cringe, but Jeff was playing the part.

Bill's serious expression morphed into a sly, hair-raising smile. "But of course. Right this way, gentlemen."

Not reacting in the slightest, thanks to years of practice in hiding their emotions while working undercover, the three agents followed Bill to the back of the art gallery, where they came to a door.

"Only one at a time is allowed down there," Bill said, looking at the three of them.

Connor looked at Ben and Jeff. Undercover or not, he didn't like this. "I'm not very comfortable with that. We have no idea who else is down there."

Bill crossed his arms and stared him down. "Do you want to see the merchandise or not, mister? One at a time. Who's first?"

Connor's heart hammered; they hadn't been expecting this. Which one of them should go down? Who was the most experienced?

254

Where were the other agents who came in with them? Connor wanted to turn around and look behind him, but he stopped himself.

Connor didn't want to put Jeff or Ben at risk. He blurted, "I'll go."

"Right this way, sir," Bill said without emotion, unlocking the door and going down before him. "Follow me."

Connor didn't like this. He didn't like this at all. Who knew what was down here? This could be a trap for all he knew.

He followed Bill down the rickety wooden steps, and a smell of dampness hit him, becoming worse the lower down they went. There were no windows, the only light coming from a single bare light bulb dangling from the ceiling.

When they reached the bottom of the stairs, there were several small, hastily-built rooms with numbers on the doors. Most disturbing of all, there was a wall with a large, wide glass window, revealing an empty room.

He'd seen this before. This was where the girls were displayed. Connor swallowed back the bile that rose in his throat.

Connor had done several sex trafficking search-and-rescue missions like this before. Yes, it had always sickened him, but not like this. This time, Anna knew the girls. Connor had come to know two of the girls' parents and sister, Ella Ruth. He'd seen the pain in their eyes.

They were counting on him to get Katie and Lilly back.

Connor blinked, trying to focus.

"I'll have them come in, and you see which one you like best, then pick a number. Got it?" Bill said with a sneer.

"Got it."

Connor took a deep breath, almost coughing from the rank air. Bill tapped on the glass, then a door inside the empty room was opened, and eight downcast girls were paraded out, wearing numbers like cattle for sale. Connor fought the wave of nausea that hit him, and for a moment, he had to look away.

Anna was among them, looking every bit as afraid as the rest of them. When she saw him, they made eye contact, but only for an instant before she lowered her gaze. Good, she hadn't reacted to him being there.

Connor had to use every bit of willpower not to break through the glass and carry her out of there. But he couldn't react in any way or show that he knew her.

Connor recognized five of the girls from missing persons' reports that CPDU had gone over before this mission.

And the last two girls to walk out behind the glass were two teenage Amish girls, wearing their dresses and prayer *kapps*—Lilly and Katie Holt. They looked so much like Ella Ruth, he was sure it was them, though he'd never seen a photo of them. Connor was surprised to see that the traffickers had them continue to wear their traditional head covering.

Though Connor had seen similar situations before with girls and young women standing behind that glass with numbers around their necks, it was like a vicious kick to the stomach. They were pale and sullen. Their eyes were sunken in, with dark circles, full of hopelessness. At this point their fear was probably gone, and they were probably just trying to survive, if that.

"Those two are Amish. Pretty, eh?" Bill then proceeded to make several vulgar comments, which Connor tuned out. He'd deal with him later.

Lilly and Katie looked as though they'd given up. Powerless, dejected, and defeated, they seemed as though they'd accepted this was their new life as they stared off at nothing.

Then Katie reached for Lilly's hand and squeezed. They looked at each other, and the look they shared looked almost hopeful. As though they were silently telling themselves that even though they were trapped in this hellish reality, they still had each other.

"Hey, no touching!" Bill shouted at them, and Katie and Lilly let go of each other's hand. Bill turned to Connor. "Those two are sisters, always hugging and talking. Hard to choose from all of them, eh?" he said with a sickening laugh.

It was time these traffickers—Connor was sure there were several lurking around the building—got what was coming to them.

"Actually," Connor said, "it's a piece of cake. I'm taking all of them."

Bill laughed out loud, bending over and wheezing from the effort. "You must be loaded, man."

Well, he wasn't, but his gun was.

Immediately, Ben, Jeff, and the other agents shot through the lock on the door and stampeded down the stairs. Bill tried to run, but Connor tackled him to the floor and handcuffed him to the railing on the stairs, ignoring the searing pain where his stitches were.

"You'll be sitting in a cell for a long time, you scum," Connor seethed into the man's ear. There were so many things he wanted to say to this man, but now was not the time.

Mayhem ensued as the rest of the CPDU team invaded the building. Screams sounded upstairs as everyone in the building was rounded up. Even though some people browsing the art gallery might have had no idea what was truly happening here and thought there were only paintings for sale, they would still be questioned at CPDU.

The girls behind the glass panicked as the sound of gunshots tore through the air. Some tried to run, but some dropped to the floor. Anna bolted out of the room, chasing after a panicked Katie who had run into the line of fire.

"No!" Connor shouted at them. "Stay in there! It's safer."

Panic contorted Anna's features as her eyes darted around the room and bullets shot through the air. She grabbed Katie's arm, pulling her back to the room.

"You could get shot! Get back in there!" Anna ordered.

Ben was running into the room where the other girls were.

"Tell them we're here to rescue them," Connor told Ben, but Ben was already on it. Who knew what they were thinking, after what they'd been through?

Several of the girls burst into tears, especially Lilly, who was screaming for her sister to come back. The rest of them sat on the floor, holding each other. He wanted to tell them he knew their family, and everyone who was waiting for them was worried about them, but right now he had to focus on their safety.

As Connor ran toward Anna to help her get a struggling and disoriented Katie back into the room, a searing pain exploded in Connor's shoulder. Warm liquid oozed down his vest, and his vision tunneled as the pain overtook his entire body.

"Anna," he murmured, stumbling, reaching out to her. No matter how much he willed his body to move, he felt as though he was walking through sludge, unable to get to her. Anna still hadn't made it back to the room with Katie as they tried to get around the fighting and violence.

Korovin, the trafficking leader, stepped forward and stood in his path between Connor and Anna, pointing a gun right at his head.

Chapter Twenty-Nine

Anna dropped to the floor, covering her head with her hands. The sound of hand-to-hand combat and gunshots assailing her as Connor tackled Korovin to the floor.

Two more shots popped off, the first one smashing the glass of the viewing window and the second one shattering an old, dilapidated wooden coffee table into splinters right next to Anna's head. The officers were busy with the other traffickers who were trying to either run or fight them off. There must have been more than they'd expected.

As Anna finally got Katie back into the room, she looked back at Connor. His shoulder was bleeding profusely. He must have been shot.

"No!" she screamed, but no one seemed to hear her over the noise. He'd been wearing a bulletproof vest, but his shoulder was exposed.

Korovin stepped between her and Connor, aiming a gun at Connor's head.

Fear gripped Anna, and she looked around for what she could use. Her hand found one of the legs of the table and she grabbed it.

Anna jumped to her feet and lifted the wooden table leg.

Korovin was surprisingly strong for how thin he was, and as he punched Connor, Anna's stomach wrenched. The pain subdued Connor even more, and his eyes closed.

"Please!" she screamed at Korovin. "Don't kill him! Please!"

As if the word 'please' would have any effect on him at all, even if he could hear it above the melee.

The gun in Korovin's hand didn't move, and as his finger shifted towards the trigger, Anna looked at the wooden table leg in her hand.

"I said don't kill him!" she yelled out, voice shaking in fear.

Korovin turned to her and stared at her for a moment, then dismissed her and aimed the gun at Connor's head. Connor moaned in pain, his hand clutching his bleeding shoulder. Anna was not going to let him kill Connor right in front of her.

As Korovin faced Connor with the gun and had his back turned to her, Anna lifted the table leg high into the air, then struck Korovin in the head with all her strength.

Korovin swayed, then stumbled, his eyes fluttering. But he wasn't down yet, so Anna swung the table leg again. It connected hard with his head, sending him crashing to the floor.

Now he was down. Anna checked his vitals, making sure he was truly unconscious and not faking it.

Anna flew towards Connor, praying he was still alive.

Anna immediately took off her jacket, wadded it up, and pressed it on the wound. The bullet had gone clean through. The sounds of fighting and gunshots finally subdued, and Anna looked up to see all the traffickers down, either shot or in handcuffs.

Connor said in a cracking voice, "Because of you, these girls are safe now."

"We all did it together," Anna said, tears dripping down her face and onto Connor's vest.

"Not without you," Connor said. His eyes drooped, then closed completely. Was he…? Surely a shoulder bullet wound wasn't fatal.

Anna felt for a pulse. Weak, but still there.

Someone gently took Anna's shoulders, helping her up and leading her out of the room. She looked back at Connor.

"He'll be taken to the hospital right now," Ben said, coming to her side and walking with her and the other girls up the stairs, as the light from the open door above made them all squint. "He'll be okay. And he was right. We couldn't have done this without you. You're all going to be okay."

In the parking lot outside the art gallery, EMTs, officers, and agents assisted the rescued girls and women. Anna looked around in a haze, still in disbelief at everything that had just happened.

She'd been kidnapped by traffickers. Again. Then God had rescued her. Again.

Connor was unconscious as he was put into an ambulance. The doors closed and he was driven away.

There was so much she wanted to say to him. Now she'd have to wait until he came out of surgery.

He'll be okay, she thought. She wanted to cry, scream, and throw herself on the ground, but she couldn't. Anna just looked around as an EMT also brought her into an ambulance. She remained silent, too stunned to feel any emotion at all.

What had just happened?

*****

At the hospital, an EMT helped Anna out of an ambulance. Irvin, Esther, Derek and Maria ran toward the ambulances, and caught sight of her.

"Anna!" Maria called. "Are you okay?"

"I'm shaken up, but I'm not hurt," Anna said. "Connor's been shot."

"No!" Derek cried.

"Is he…?" Maria asked.

"He was shot in the shoulder, so he should be okay."

"What about our girls? Are they hurt?" Irvin asked.

"They didn't seem visibly injured," Anna said. "Although, they will probably still need to be treated for physical conditions. Their mental and psychological recovery might take much longer than their physical recovery." She shivered, not even wanting to imagine what had happened to them before she'd been taken there herself. "I don't know which ambulance they were in."

"My daughters!" Esther cried. "I have to find my daughters," Esther said, rushing across the parking lot, surprisingly fast for her age.

"Esther," Derek called, and finally, Esther stopped. "You should know your girls might not be the same after this. They've just endured serious trauma. You might not fully recognize them."

"What do you mean? They're my children," Esther said, tears flowing down her face as she finally stopped, and Anna's own eyes stung with tears. Anna didn't have children of her own, so she couldn't even imagine what Esther was feeling now, but maybe one day she would.

Derek walked up to Esther. "I'm saying they have probably changed. I've seen it many times with human trafficking survivors. They might not be the same lively, energetic girls they once were. The light in their eyes might be gone for a while. It's going to take some time for them to heal. If you run up to them and hug them, they might not react the way you're expecting. I just wanted you to know before you go over there."

Irvin came over to his wife and put his arm around her, a rare show of physical affection for an Amish married couple. "Whatever happens, I am right here for you and our daughters, Esther. They are in the Lord's hands. They have been all along."

"They are my daughters," Esther said. "They will always be my daughters. In a small way, I can relate to them. When I was raped, I thought my life was over. I think the light from my eyes was gone for a while too. What I endured was probably nothing compared to what they have gone through, but not for one second will I lose hope that they will be restored to the girls they once were. It is all in the Lord's hands. I accept whatever He decides."

Anna didn't even try to stop her tears from coursing down her cheeks. "We're all here for you, Esther and Irvin."

Esther nodded, then walked with Irvin across the parking lot, looking for their daughters. With every step they took, Anna said a prayer. *Please be with them, Lord. Please let Connor be okay.*

"There they are," Derek said, pointing.

Esther and Irvin bolted toward Katie and Lilly, who were coming out of an ambulance. Anna watched from a distance as Esther recklessly threw her arms around both of her daughters.

Holding her breath, Anna watched as Katie and Lilly didn't respond at first. But after a second, they both dropped their blankets and hugged their mother in return. Irvin also joined the group hug, and instantly they were all crying.

Anna wiped away her own tears. "I'm so glad they're together again."

"It may be a long road to recovery, but one day they'll be whole again," Maria said.

"Thank you that everyone is okay, Lord," Anna whispered, her eyes stinging with tears again.

For now, she had to be there for the Holts. It might be hard for Katie and Lilly to go back to their normal lives after what they'd just been through, but one thing was for sure. The Holt family had the entire Amish community supporting them, whether it be by bringing them meals or praying constantly.

And even though Anna was no longer technically Amish, she would be just as supportive, doing whatever she could.

In Unity, the Amish were always there for each other, especially in times like these.

Now, Anna had to find Connor.

Chapter Thirty

A few weeks ago, Connor would have prayed for death if it meant he got to be reunited with his Grace. Now, he was not so sure he wanted to go just yet. He had unfinished business.

He had saved Anna, so that couldn't be it. Besides, Ben would take care of her. Not that she would need it. She was strong and capable of taking care of herself. After all, she had gotten him to care. Still, he couldn't fathom leaving her just yet. But not because he thought she still needed saving.

No, he still needed saving.

This was all because of Anna. She had given him a reason to live again, and he was not ready to let go just yet. He was not ready to leave her.

*****

After Connor's surgery, Anna went to visit him in the out-patient surgery unit. She'd been overcome with relief when she'd been told the surgery had gone well and he would make a full recovery.

Anna quietly let herself into the hospital room. When she saw Connor in the hospital bed, memories of when they first met rushed back to her.

266

Again, a bullet wound united them.

"Hey," Connor said as one of the nurses helped him sit up. "You stayed."

Anna nodded, surprised to find her tongue wooden in her mouth. The nurses finished with their check up and left, telling Connor to press the call button if he needed anything.

"What happened to Korovin?" Connor asked. "I think he shot me. Or maybe it was one of the other traffickers. I don't know. I didn't see who did it."

"He was arrested along with the other traffickers. They're being questioned at CPDU in Portland now. Ben gave one of the copies of the flash drive to CPDU as evidence. Hopefully, there are no other moles. So far, the drive has been safe, so we think that there are no others," Anna explained, sitting next to his bed.

Connor settled back into his pillow, finally feeling relaxed. "Good. I'm so relieved. Hopefully, we can finally get this whole thing wrapped up."

"Well, Korovin, Tucker, and Davis aren't saying much. CPDU thinks there are still more places like the art gallery where girls are being held captive."

"Ugh. Korovin won't say anything, but Tucker and Davis might if they get offered a deal."

"Let's hope. Olivia has a concussion, so she'll be here for a few days, but she'll be totally fine. Actually, while she was having her tests done, they found out she's pregnant," Anna said, excitement in her voice.

"Wow, really? That's great news," Connor said. "I'll have to congratulate them."

"They're super excited, and the baby is doing well, but she'll be staying for a few days to have some more tests and make sure everything is okay. How are you feeling?" she asked in her nurse voice. "And hey, I thought bulletproof vests were—you know—bulletproof. But your shoulder wasn't covered anyway."

"Actually, they're bullet-resistant, and yes, only the torso is covered, so the rest of the body is exposed. I've had worse than this, as you know." He gave her a grateful, knowing smile. "The nurse said you stayed here the whole time. Thanks."

She shrugged awkwardly. "It was the least I could do. You saved my life."

He cocked his head to the side. "Actually, you saved my life when you hit Korovin over the head with that… What was it?"

"A broken table leg." She chuckled. "I guess we're even."

"A table leg? Wow. Anna, I'm sorry for putting you in danger. I promised not to let anything happen to you, and I failed you."

"What?!" Anna exclaimed. "How did you fail me?"

"I let Korovin take you. I'm so sorry, Anna. When he used that stun grenade, we were all immobilized long enough for him to get away with you in that car. It destroyed me. I promised I wouldn't let anything happen to you."

"No one knew he had a stun grenade."

"Well, if it weren't for me, there is no way you would have been there." He stared at his bed sheet. "And if that's why you're still here, because you think you owe me, you don't."

That was why he thought she was still here with him?

Anna stared at him, all the anger, frustration, fear and pain of the last few hours suddenly coalescing into one big stick of dynamite.

And his last statement was the match that had lit the fuse.

Anna folded her hands and glared at him. "That's not why I'm still here. That's your plan, isn't it?" she asked, slowly nodding her head. "You're going to do all these things for me so that I feel guilty and fall in love with you?"

"What?!" Connor lifted his head and immediately winced in pain.

"Sit back and calm down," Anna scolded him immediately, still looking concerned as she fluffed the pillow behind him. It was a nurse habit.

"I wasn't trying to make you feel guilty," Connor replied.

"Then why does it feel like you do?" She looked away. "Why else would you try to take the blame when it was you who got shot trying to save me? Even after all the mean and stupid things I've said and done. Right from the beginning. Like when I ran to the police even though you warned me not to."

"I was a stranger and you were scared. I think your decision is understandable."

"And when I called you a killer," Anna continued, not really listening to him. "Only, when Korovin was about to shoot you, I swear I wanted to shoot him. I was so mad and angry at him that it didn't matter what I believed. I just wanted to make him stop attacking you and hurt him for injuring someone I love. And that scared me. I didn't realize I could be so…evil. Instead, I knocked him out with a wooden table leg."

"Anna!" Connor said, but she still wasn't hearing him.

"The thought that you could die was like a metal claw in my heart, ripping and ripping until I thought I'd die from sheer panic. Then the ambulance took you. And as if God was not done laughing at me, I got to talk to Ben and Jeff, and they reassured me again that you

269

never were an assassin. They told me about the times you shared in Iraq, how you fought off and killed several terrorists and saved their lives when they were trying to capture them. They said if it weren't for you, they might be in their prisons now or dead. They said you're their hero."

She moved closer. "I grew up being taught that murder, killing, or any type of violence is wrong, even self-defense. The Amish don't believe in self-defense. They don't condone any type of violence, no matter what. So, the fact that you've killed, even to save your friend's life, is hard for me to grasp and accept. But God also commands us to love and forgive."

"I understand, Anna. It's hard for me to accept sometimes, too. I wish I could block those memories forever, but it's in the past. It's not who I am anymore. I just want you to know that even though I did kill in the past when I was in the military and CPDU, I'm done after this, Anna. I'm putting this life behind me and never looking back." Connor held her eyes as he said it, wanting her to know and believe this. "Yes, I had to kill terrorists when they attacked us while I was in Iraq, and I see their faces every day. I have had to use my gun when traffickers and other criminals pulled their gun on me and my officers. It still haunts me, but I can't go back and change it now. I just wanted you to know that. It's up to you if you want to accept that part of me or not. I just need you to know."

"Really?" Anna asked, squeezing his hand.

"Really."

"I'm ready to accept that. I'm ready to accept all of you, everything about you," she said, tears spilling onto the hospital sheets.

Connor stared at her for a long time. "So, you love me?"

Anna nodded without hesitation. "Yes. No one ever told me it was going to be this scary. Or that the thought of losing you would be my biggest fear now." She moved even closer. "Even with all that fear, the joy of seeing you alive right now is overwhelming. I love you, Connor."

He wanted to say something, but she wasn't done.

"In the beginning, it was easier to deny what I felt since I thought you were this bad person who killed for money. I thought you were a criminal. And even as everything I learned about you pointed to the exact opposite, it was easier to believe that you were this horrible person than admit that I was falling in love with you. I've given my heart away before, and it didn't work out. So, I pushed you away. Until the shield I hid behind was broken. Until you convinced me to trust and love again."

It was an honor she was giving to him, and Connor's heart pumped wildly in his chest. Looking at her, he wondered how he could have been so blessed to have found love again. He wondered how she could ever think he'd do anything to hurt her.

She was his life and his love. She gave meaning to his life, and he fought for the right words to reveal this truth to her. And when the silence between them began to stretch too long, Anna looked away. "I'm sorry. That was a lot. I understand if you don't—"

"I couldn't save her or the baby," he blurted out, taking a deep breath when she turned back to him.

"Baby?" Anna whispered.

"When Grace was pregnant, we found out she had cancer. The doctors told her she should abort the baby so she could start getting chemo treatments. She refused, saying she and the baby were in God's hands, and she said that abortion is murder, no matter the reason. The baby was born too early, and she only survived a few hours. Her name was Amelia. There was nothing I could do. Then, after the baby was born, they tried chemo treatments for Grace. The cancer had progressed too much. Grace died while I was holding her hand, telling me to keep on trusting God."

Connor's eyes filled with tears, and his voice cracked with emotion. "If she had aborted the baby, she probably would have survived. But I don't think either one of us could have lived with that. She kept telling me we had to trust God, but they both died anyway. That's why I wasn't on speaking terms with God after that."

"Connor, I'm so sorry. I had no idea…" Anna choked back a sob, not even able to imagine the grief he must have endured.

"I know it's not like I could have done anything. But the fact that she had to die; I felt like that was my fault somehow, and that I couldn't save her. Maybe because I didn't have enough faith, she died. Then you came into my life, and all of a sudden, I was left feeling like I couldn't save you, either. You have to realize that when I met you, I didn't care for anything or anyone in the world anymore. I was living life recklessly enough in the hope that it would end sooner rather than later. Then I met you, and first you gave me a reason to care. Then you gave me a reason to live. And just when I thought that was all, you gave me a reason to love again."

He reached out and took her hand. "You made me believe in myself again, and for that I'll always have you to thank. I love you, Anna. I know that now. And I'll do everything in my power to make you happy." He paused and looked at her. "Are you crying?"

"Yes. Sometimes I do that when I'm happy, but it's been a long time." Anna smiled as she reached down and hugged Connor tightly. She made no move to wipe the tears that ran down her face. They were tears of joy because she had never felt so happy.

Happy that he lived. And happy that he loved her.

"You know, I heard you say to yourself that you thought I was cute," Connor teased. "That day that we met in the hospital where you worked."

"You heard that?" Anna blushed. "I thought maybe you did, but wasn't sure—"

"Oh, yes, I heard you talking to yourself. That was when I knew you were different, in a good way. And I secretly thought you were cute, too, and annoying as all get out."

Anna playfully swatted him on the arm.

"Hey, isn't there a rule about being nice to patients?" Connor laughed. "I'm going to report you." His expression turned serious. "I don't think you're annoying anymore. For the most part."

"Same goes for you, Connor Sinclair." Anna bent down and kissed him. "For the most part." She savored the feeling of his lips on hers, closing her eyes.

*****

After Connor healed, they went back to the church in Unity. Anna had asked the bishop if she could explain to everyone what had happened along with Maria, Derek, and Connor, and he'd readily agreed.

After the service ended, Anna stood up. "I'd like to take a moment to talk to you about what happened. I'm sure you've all heard by now," she said as the four of them made their way to the front of the sanctuary.

Anna took a deep breath, but she didn't feel nervous, which surprised her. She had a good feeling. These people were understanding, and hopefully, they'd understand why she lied.

And if not, she would accept that. She didn't regret what she'd done. If she hadn't lied to them, Katie and Lilly might not be sitting with them in that room at that moment.

Anna explained, "I'm sure by now you've figured out Connor and I are not actually married. And I'm sorry to say we are not rejoining the Amish. I hope you see we had to lie for two reasons. One, Connor needed to stay in Derek and Maria's house with us so he could protect us, so we knew in order for that to happen we had to pretend to be married. Obviously, we stayed in different rooms. And secondly, we had to pretend to be Amish so we'd blend in and wouldn't scare off whoever was targeting the girls in this community."

"She's right," Connor said. "Now we know who it was: Joey McCoy, who at the time had been pretending to be an Amish salesman named Moses. If he had known we were not Amish, he might have gotten suspicious that we were on to him and run. Then we may never have found the art gallery where all the abducted girls were being held."

"We will never know if it would have worked out any other way. I hope you understand why we lied to you all. We didn't want to. I felt terrible about it, but I hope you see it was for the greater good. We apologize and we hope you forgive us," Anna said.

"I want to also be up front with everyone and let you know I helped Connor monitor and follow Ella Ruth when she went on her dates with Joey McCoy. All we did was make sure she was safe. We didn't want to put her in any danger. I did not use violence at all," Derek explained.

"Ella Ruth put herself in danger by going out on dates with Joey McCoy," Maria said. "She was the reason we found the art gallery."

"We couldn't have done it without her," Connor said, smiling at Ella Ruth. "She was very brave and wanted to do anything to help find her sisters."

"We hope you can forgive Connor and me for lying to you, especially me. I was the one who let you all think I was planning on rejoining the church. And I am sorry for that." Anna looked at all the faces she'd known for all of her life, trying to find a hint of what they were thinking.

Katie and Lilly sat with Esther on the women's side, all holding hands.

Bishop Byler stood up. "From my perspective, I think these four had just cause for lying. I don't normally condone lying, but sometimes it is necessary. Rahab lied to the soldiers when they searched her house and she hid the spies on her roof. She was doing it to protect them and was rewarded for it. I don't see any reason to shun Maria and Derek, and Anna never officially joined the church. They were doing what was right, and because of it, we now have Katie and Lilly Holt back here with us."

"Amen," Gideon said, also standing. Mary stood up on the women's side of the church, followed by Irvin, Esther, Liz, and Simon. Within a few moments, the entire church was standing.

"Clearly, we all forgive you. Most of all, we thank you, along with Liv and Isaac, who are still in the hospital. We will also no longer shun them," Bishop Byler said. "Anna and Connor, we welcome you back here any time you'd like. We hope you come to visit again soon."

Anna smiled, staring at the bishop in shock, joy overflowing within her. After the crowd dissipated, Esther and Irvin approached them.

"How are Katie and Lilly doing?" Anna asked.

"Actually, quite well, considering what they went through," Esther said, glancing at her daughters, who were talking to their friends. "When we brought them home, they were a bit overwhelmed by all their siblings being so excited they were back. For the first few days, they were very withdrawn, constantly clinging to each other. They had to have testing done at the hospital, which was hard on them. But they are having counseling, and we know the entire church is praying for them. It may be a long road to a full recovery, but we'll be there for them every step of the way."

"We want to thank you again for helping bring them home," Irvin said, looking at each of them. "There are no words for how grateful we are. Also please tell Olivia and Isaac thank you as well. We heard Olivia was injured and Isaac is still at the hospital with her. And she's pregnant? How wonderful!"

"Yes, she is. Isn't that great? We're so happy for them," Anna said.

"She's doing better now, and the baby is fine. She's resting, and they're running more tests to make sure the baby is continuing to do well," Maria added.

"We're so glad Katie and Lilly are home safe," Connor said.

"We were so happy to help," Derek put in.

"Well, I hope you come back to visit often, Anna and Connor. We've gotten quite used to seeing your faces around here," Esther said.

"Oh, we will," Anna said, grinning. She glanced at Connor. "We hope to see you all again very soon. This place will always be my home."

Epilogue

Anna slammed her locker door shut at the Unity Hospital, where she had recently started working in order to be closer to the Amish community. Ever since Katie and Lilly had returned home, Anna and Connor had been visiting almost every weekend, spending time with Maria, Derek, and all of their friends there who were really more like family.

In fact, Anna and Connor had been talking about how nice it would be to build a house right next to the Amish community.

Taking a deep breath, Anna smiled. She felt at peace. There was so much joy in her life. Before, she'd felt so empty.

She quickly sat down to take off her nurse shoes and slip on her date shoes—white ballet flats. High heels were for the birds. She'd rather be comfortable than risk tripping over her own two feet. Yes, she was a practical kind of woman and nurses are on their feet too long not to take good care of them, even when off duty, as far as Anna was concerned.

Looking in the mirror, she smoothed out the skirt of the floral sundress Connor had bought for her at the department store when they'd first began their journey together. That seemed like years ago, and at the same time, it seemed like only yesterday.

Anna had been saving the dress for this special occasion: seeing a movie for the first time.

She was about to turn around and head out when a ringing sound made her pause. Sighing, she retrieved her new phone from her bag, not surprised to see that it was Connor calling. He was one of the few people who had her number.

"I'm already on my way down," she said after answering the call and putting it to her ear.

"I know," he replied, a smile in his voice. "Just got tired of standing here and not seeing you. I just thought I'd settle for hearing your voice instead."

Anna went still in the middle of the locker room, blushing at his compliment. "I already told you, you can't keep saying these things to me. I don't know how to…" She took a deep breath. "I don't know what to say back."

"There's only one thing you need to say."

Anna's lips curved in a smile. "I love you," she said, pouring the entirety of her feelings into those words.

"Good. Now, let's go so we can kick off this special day."

Anna scowled. "I don't see how me going to the movies with you is such a big deal."

"I think the fact that this is the first time you'll be seeing a movie with me makes today very special indeed." He chuckled. "But it's more than that. Just get down here."

Anna smiled as the call ended. She slipped the phone into her purse and looked again, making sure she was not forgetting anything, then decided it didn't matter if she was forgetting something. The only thing that mattered was the man waiting for her. She left the locker room and walked towards the elevator that would take her downstairs.

He was waiting right outside the door for her. Connor smiled when Anna practically skipped to him and hugged him before smiling up at him.

"Wow. You look beautiful. Is that the sundress I got you at the store when we first met?" Connor asked, grinning at her.

"Yes. That was the day you told me I had to chop off my hair." Anna smirked playfully.

"I'm so glad you refused," Connor said, running his fingers through her long, blonde hair. Anna smiled blissfully as he pulled her in close. "Really, Anna, you look breathtaking," he whispered into her ear.

"Thank you," she said shyly and kissed him. It still made her heart rate hike just as much as their first kiss, if not more.

"How was your day?" she asked as they made their way through the parking lot where his car was parked.

"Great," he replied. "We managed to track down more of Korovin's traffickers. We rescued the girls from the Romanian ship, and now they are in after care where they will receive counseling and medical attention."

The information on the hard drive had proved very useful in bringing down Korovin's empire, an empire so vast it would take months to sort through the mess it had left behind, from prosecuting people implicated by the drive to saving the victims of the monster. It had even incriminated the dirty police officers, including Officer Barrett. They later on found out that at the motel, the stolen car had been located, and it had been a corrupt police officer who had told the assassins of Connor and Anna's whereabouts. That officer had also been arrested.

It infuriated Connor when he saw the dastardly acts that Korovin and all the people working for him had committed. After wading through all that filth, Anna was the breath of fresh air he needed. She kept him grounded, reminded him that there was still good in the world and gave him a reason to keep fighting.

Connor was also training to become a mechanic in the evenings. Once all the loose ends from this case were wrapped up, he planned on handing in his resignation at CPDU in exchange for a more peaceful life.

Anna had to admit, she couldn't wait.

"How was your day?" he asked, squeezing her hand as they walked unhurriedly towards his car.

"Okay," she replied. "Mr. Watson wandered away from his room again and it took like an hour before I found him in a supply closet two floors down, building forts from the supply boxes."

"Well, sounds like he was having fun."

"Yeah. I just wished he would tell me so I wouldn't be so worried about him. Anyway, his daughter finally arrived today so I don't need to worry so much about him anymore. Doesn't mean I won't, though."

Only Connor knew she would still worry, because that was the kind of person she was. She was kind and caring. And he was so in love with her. He suddenly took her hand and stopped walking, turning around to face her.

"Now, let's get in the car. I'm taking you somewhere, and it's a surprise. When we get closer, you have to close your eyes," he said, a glint of mischief in his eye.

"Where are you taking me?" she asked.

"No telling. Now, let's go," he said with a smile, opening the door for her.

As they got closer to their destination, Connor said, "Now you have to close your eyes. No peeking."

"This is silly," she said, but kept her eyes closed. When they arrived, he helped her out of the car with her eyes still closed.

"Okay. You can open your eyes now."

She looked around. They were at the hospital in Portland, where she used to work. Where they met.

"Do you remember this place?" His hand made a sweeping motion as she looked around the hospital parking lot.

Anna glanced around, and her lips curved in a smile. "Of course, I do. It's where I first met you." She turned to her left. "That was the corner where you were when you called out to me. Wait, you know all this."

Connor nodded. "Yes, I do. I also know that it is the place where I met the woman who saved my life. And even though I don't know much, I know that there is no way I want to spend the rest of my life away from you. I want you by my side, right here with me. I want your face to be the first thing I see when I wake up in the morning and the last thing I see when I go to bed. I want to be there for you, by your side. Helping you, supporting you through whatever it is you want to do. I want to make you happy. I want to make you laugh. It is why when I thought of it, the perfect place I could think of to ask this question was here. Right where I first met you."

Anna's eyes widened at his words and even more when he got down on his left knee. In his hand he held a ring, the band around it shining gold and a sparkling diamond in the middle of it.

"Anna, will you marry me?" Connor asked, his eyes shining with joy and hope.

She had known he was going to ask her to marry him for some time, but she was still stunned.

Anna had decided her answer a long time ago. She had prayed about it and the answer she had gotten had been reinforced every time his smile made her belly flutter or he said those things that make her want to smile, blush, and cry all at the same time. Like right now.

"Yes! Yes, Connor." She took the hand he held out. "I'll marry you."

He got to his feet and slipped the ring on her finger, smiling when she admired it.

"I love it." She looked at him. "But even more, I love that now I get to call you mine forever."

Connor grinned. "Now look at who is being romantic."

Anna kissed him, not caring who was watching or could see them. "I guess I learned something from you then."

Connor laughed. "Come on, darling. Let's go see your first movie. As promised."

Anna leaned her head on his shoulder, smiling. He'd promised much more to her than a movie, and she couldn't wait to see it all unfold.

"As promised."

About the Author

Ashley Emma knew she wanted to be a novelist for as long as she can remember, and her first love was writing in the fantasy genre. She began writing books for fun at a young age, completing her first novel at age 12 and publishing it at age 16. She was home schooled and was blessed with the opportunity to spend her time focusing on reading and writing.

Ashley went on to write eight more manuscripts before age 25 when she also became a multi-bestselling author.

She now makes a full-time income with her self-published books, which is a dream come true.

She owns Fearless Publishing House where she helps other aspiring authors achieve their dreams of publishing their own books. Ashley lives in Maine with her husband and children. She plans on releasing several more books in the near future.

Visit her at www.ashleyemmaauthor.com or email her at amisbookwriter@gmail.com. She loves to hear from her readers!

FACT: **There are more slaves now than ever before in history, including over 2 million children trapped in sex slavery.** Over 12.3 million people worldwide have become victims. Operation Underground Railroad has rescued over 4,100 children from slavery and has arrested over 2,300 sex traffickers. And yes, slavery is happening in your hometown, and it is the fastest growing criminal industry in the world.

Donate here to join the Abolitionist Club and help support rescue missions to free more children from slavery:
https://my.ourrescue.org/product/DONATE-ONETIME/become-an-abolitionist

OPERATION UNDERGROUND RAILROAD

If you enjoyed this book, would you consider leaving a review on Amazon? It greatly helps both the author and readers alike.

Leave your Amazon review here:

https://www.amazon.com/Amish-Assassin-Romantic-Suspense-Detectives-ebook/dp/B084R9V4CN/

Thank you!

GET 4 OF ASHLEY EMMA'S AMISH EBOOKS FOR FREE

www.AshleyEmmaAuthor.com

Download free Amish eBooks at www.AshleyEmmaAuthor.com, including the exclusive, secret prequel to Undercover Amish!

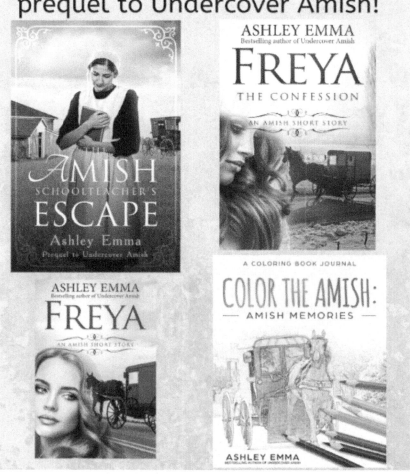

Other books by Ashley Emma on Amazon

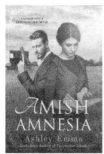   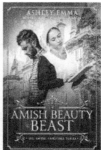

Coming soon:

 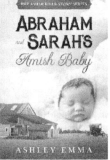

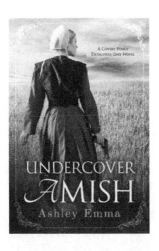

UNDERCOVER AMISH

(This series can be read out of order or as standalone novels.)

Detective Olivia Mast would rather run through gunfire than return to her former Amish community in Unity, Maine, where she killed her abusive husband in self-defense.

Olivia covertly investigates a murder there while protecting the man she dated as a teen: Isaac Troyer, a potential target.

When Olivia tells Isaac she is a detective, will he be willing to break Amish rules to help her arrest the killer?

Undercover Amish was a finalist in Maine Romance Writers Strut Your Stuff Competition 2015 where it received 26 out of 27 points and has 455+ Amazon reviews!

Buy here: https://www.amazon.com/Undercover-Amish-Covert-Police-Detectives-ebook/dp/B01L6JE49G

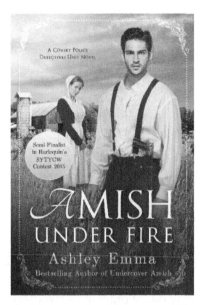

After Maria Mast's abusive ex-boyfriend is arrested for being involved in sex trafficking and modern-day slavery, she thinks that she and her son Carter can safely return to her Amish community.

But the danger has only just begun.

Someone begins stalking her, and they want blood and revenge.

Agent Derek Turner of Covert Police Detectives Unit is assigned as her bodyguard and goes with her to her Amish community in Unity, Maine.

Maria's secretive eyes, painful past, and cautious demeanor intrigue him.

As the human trafficking ring begins to target the Amish community, Derek wonders if the distraction of her will cost him his career…and Maria's life.

Click here to buy: http://a.co/fT6D7sM

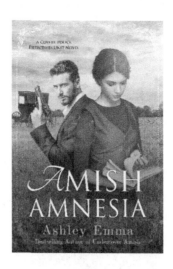

When Officer Jefferson Martin witnesses a young woman being hit by a car near his campsite, all thoughts of vacation vanish as the car speeds off.

When the malnourished, battered woman wakes up, she can't remember anything before the accident. They don't know her name, so they call her Jane.

When someone breaks into her hospital room and tries to kill her before getting away, Jefferson volunteers to protect Jane around the clock. He takes her back to their Kennebunkport beach house along with his upbeat sister Estella and his friend who served with him overseas in the Marine Corps, Ben Banks.

At first Jane's stalker leaves strange notes, but then his attacks become bolder and more dangerous.

Jane gradually remembers an Amish farm and wonders if that's where she's from...or if she was held captive there.

But the more Jefferson falls for her, the more persistent the stalker becomes in making Jane miserable...and in taking her life.

Buy here: https://www.amazon.com/gp/product/B07SDSFV3J

FREE EBOOK

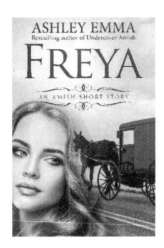

After Freya Wilson accidentally hits an Amish man with her car in a storm, will she have the courage to tell his family the truth—especially after she meets his handsome brother?

Get it free: https://www.amazon.com/Freya-Amish-Short-Ashley-Emma-ebook/dp/B01MSP03UX

FREE EBOOK

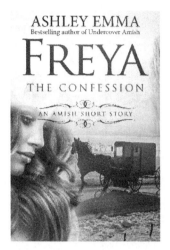

Adam Lapp expected the woman who killed his brother accidentally with her car to be heartless and cruel. He never expected her to a timid, kind, and beautiful woman who is running for her life from a controlling ex who wants her dead.

When Freya Wilson asks him to take her to his family so she can tell them the truth, he agrees.

Will she find hope in the ashes, or just more darkness and sorrow?

https://www.amazon.com/Freya-Confession-Amish-Short-Forgiveness-ebook/dp/B076PQF5FS

Ever wondered what it would be like to live in an Amish community? Now you can find out in this true story with photos.

https://www.amazon.com/Ashleys-Amish-Adventures-Outsider-community-ebook/dp/B01N5714WE

Excerpt from Amish Alias

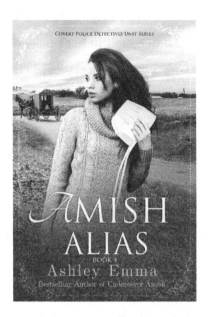

(This Series Can Be Read Out Of Order Or As Standalone Novels)

Chapter One

"Mom, are we there yet?" nine-year-old Charlotte Cooper asked from the back seat of her parents' van. Her legs pumped up and down in anticipation. Mom had said they were going to a farm where her aunt lived, and she couldn't wait to see the animals. The ride was taking forever.

"Just a few more minutes, honey," Mom said from the driver's seat.

Charlotte put her coloring book down and patted the lollipop in her pocket Mommy had given her for the trip. She was tempted to eat it now but decided to save it for the ride home. She hoped it wouldn't melt in her pocket. The van was hot even though she was wearing shorts and her favorite pink princess T-shirt. Charlotte shoved her damp blonde curls out of her eyes.

The van passed a yellow diamond-shaped sign that had a black silhouette of a horse and carriage on it. "Mommy, what does that sign mean?"

"It's a warning to drive slowly because there are horses and buggies on the road here."

"*What?* Horses and bugs?"

"No." Mom smiled. "They're called buggies. They're like the carriages you've seen in your storybooks. Except they are not pumpkin-shaped. They are black and shaped more like a box."

Charlotte imagined a black box being pulled by a horse. If she were a princess, she would like a pumpkin carriage much better. "Why are there buggies here?"

"The folks who live in this area don't drive cars."

They don't drive cars? Charlotte thought. "Then what do they drive?"

"They only drive buggies," Mom said.

How fast do buggies go? Charlotte wondered. *Not fast as a car, I bet.* "Why would anyone not drive a car? They're so much faster than buggies."

"I know, honey. Some people are just…different." Mom glanced at Charlotte in the rear-view mirror. "But being different isn't a bad thing."

Charlotte gazed out the window. Even though they had just passed a pizza place a few minutes ago, all she could see now were huge fields and plain-looking houses.

There was nothing around. This looked like a boring place to live. What did people do to have fun here besides play outside?

A horse and carriage rumbled past them on the unpaved road going in the other direction. A girl wearing a blue dress and a white bonnet sat on the top seat, guiding a dark brown horse. She looked just like a picture Charlotte had seen in her history book at school. "Look, Mom." Charlotte pointed at the big black box on wheels.

"It's not polite to point, Charlie."

Charlotte dropped her hand to her side. "Why is that girl dressed like a pilgrim, Mom? She's wearing a bonnet. Are we near Plymouth Plantation?"

Mom didn't answer. Maybe she was too distracted. She seemed really focused on the mailbox up ahead.

"We're here," Mom said and turned onto a long driveway.

Charlotte gaped at the chocolate-colored horses in the fields and the clucking chickens congregating in the front yard. The van bounced over bumps on the gravel path leading to a huge tan house with bright blue curtains hanging in the windows. The dark red roof had a large metal pipe coming out of the top with smoke coming out of it, and behind the house stood a big red barn. Charlotte wondered how many animals were in there.

Mom parked the van and helped Charlotte out. "I'm going inside to talk to your Aunt Esther. I don't want to bring you inside because... Well... You should just wait here. I won't be long."

"Can I walk around?"

Before Mom could answer, a young boy about Charlotte's age walked out of the barn. He saw them and waved.

"Can I go play with him?" Charlotte asked.

"Hi!" The boy ran over. "I've never seen you around here before. Want to go see the animals in the barn?"

"Can I go in the barn with him?" Charlotte asked her mother.

"What's your name?" Mom asked the boy. "Is Esther your *Maam*?"

"I'm Elijah. No, she's not my mother. My *Maam* and *Daed* are out running errands, so I'm playing here until they get back. My parents are best friends with Esther and Irvin. I come here all the time. I know my way around the barn real well."

Mom crossed her arms and bit her lip, then looked at Charlotte. "I suppose you can go in. But stay away from the horses."

"We will, ma'am," said Elijah.

Charlotte and Elijah took off running toward the barn.

They ran into the dim interior and she breathed in. It smelled like hay and animals, just like the county fair she had gone to last fall with her mom and dad. To the left, she heard pigs squealing. To the right, she heard sheep bleating.

Which animals should we go see first? Charlotte wondered, tapping her toes on the hay-covered floor.

Elijah leaned over the edge of the sheep pen, patting a lamb's nose. He was dressed in plain black and white clothing and a straw hat. His brown hair reached the collar of his white shirt. He even wore suspenders. Charlotte glanced down at her princess T-shirt and wondered why he didn't dress like other kids at her school. Every kid she knew wore cool T-shirts. *Why are the people here dressed in such plain, old-fashioned clothes?*

Charlotte stepped forward. He turned around, looked at her, and grinned. "So what's your name, anyway?"

"I'm Charlotte. Well, you can call me Charlie."

"Charlie? That's a boy's name."

"It's my nickname. I like it."

"Suit yourself. Where you from?"

"Biddeford, Maine. Where are you from?"

"I live in Smyrna, Maine."

"Oh." Charlotte raised an eyebrow. Smyrna? Where was that?

Elijah smiled. "It's a bigger Amish community in northern Maine."

Charlotte shrugged. "Never heard of it."

Elijah shrugged. "Want to pet the sheep?"

"Yeah." They climbed up onto some boards stacked along the edge of the enclosure. Several of the animals sniffed their fingers and let out high-pitched noises. "They sound like people," Charlotte said. "The lambs sound like babies crying, and the big sheep sound like adults making sheep noises."

They laughed at that, and when the biggest sheep looked at them and cried *baaa* loudly, they laughed even harder.

Charlotte looked at the boy next to her, who was still watching the sheep. A small smear of dirt covered some of the freckles on his cheek, and his brown eyes sparkled when he laughed. The hands that gripped the wooden boards of the sheep pen looked strong. She wondered what it would be like if he held her hand. As she watched Elijah tenderly stroke the nose of a sheep, she smiled.

When one lamb made an especially loud, funny noise that sounded like a baby crying, Elijah threw his head back as he laughed, and his hat fell off. Charlotte snatched it up and turned it over in her hands. "Wow. I've never held a straw hat before. We don't have these where I live. I thought people only wore ones like these in the olden days."

Elijah shrugged. "What's wrong with that?"

"Nothing." Charlotte smiled shyly and offered it back to him. "Here you go."

Elijah held up his hand. "You can keep it if you want." He smiled at her with those dark eyes.

Charlotte got a funny feeling in her stomach. It was the

same way she felt just before saying her lines on stage in the school play. She knew she should say, "Thank you," like Mom had taught her. But she couldn't speak the words. Instead, she took the lollipop out of her pocket and handed it to him.

"Thanks," Elijah said, eyes wide.

"You're welcome."

Elijah gestured to Charlie's ankle. "Hey, what happened to your ankle?"

Charlie looked down at the familiar sight of the zig-zagging surgical scars that marred her ankle. "I've had a lot of surgeries on my ankle. When I was born it wasn't formed right, but now it's all better and I can run and jump like other kids."

"Does it hurt?"

"No, not anymore. But it hurt when I had the surgeries. I had, like, six surgeries."

"Wow, really?"

"Charlotte!" Mom called. "We have to leave. Right now."

"Thanks for the hat, Elijah." Charlotte turned to leave. Then she stopped, turned around, and kissed him on the cheek.

Embarrassment flushed Elijah's cheeks.

Uh oh. Her own face heated, Charlotte sprinted toward her mother's voice.

"Get in the car," Mom said. "Your aunt refused to speak with us. She wants us to leave."

Charlotte had never heard her mother sound so upset. She climbed into the van, and Mom hastily buckled her in.

"Why didn't she want to talk to us, Mom?" Charlotte said.

Mom sniffed and shook her head. "It's hard to explain, baby."

"Why are you crying, Mom?"

"I just wanted to talk to my sister. And she wanted us to go away."

"That's not very nice," Charlotte said.

"I know, Charlie. Some people aren't nice. Remember that."

The van sped down the driveway as Charlotte clutched the straw hat.

"Why are you going so fast?" Charlotte said and craned her neck, hoping to see Elijah. She saw him standing outside the barn with one hand holding the lollipop and the other hand on his cheek where she'd kissed him. He was smiling crookedly.

Mom looked in the rearview mirror at Charlotte.

"Sorry," Mom said and slowed down.

Charlotte settled in her seat. She hoped she'd see Elijah again, and maybe he'd be her very own prince charming like in her fairytale books.

But Mom never took her to the farm again.

Chapter Two

Fifteen years later

"Hi, Mom," twenty-four-year-old Charlie said, stepping into her mother's hospital room in the cancer ward. "I brought you Queen Anne's lace, your favorite." She set the vase of white flowers on her mom's bedside table.

"Oh, thank you, honey." Mom smiled, but her face looked thin and pale, a bright scarf covering her head. "Come sit with me." She patted the edge of the bed, and Charlie sat down, taking her mother's frail hand.

"You know why Queen Anne's lace are my favorite flowers?" Mom asked quietly.

Charlie shook her head.

"Growing up in the Amish community, we'd get tons of Queen Anne's lace in the fields every summer. My sister, Esther, and I would try to pick as much as we could before the grass was cut down for hay. At the end of every August, we'd also check all around for milkweed and look for monarch caterpillars before they were destroyed. We'd try to save as many of them as we could. We'd put them in jars and watch them make their chrysalises, then watch in amazement as they transformed into butterflies and escaped them. I used to promise myself that I'd get out into the world one day, just like the butterflies, and leave the Amish community behind. I knew it would be painful to leave everyone and everything I knew, but it would be worth it."

"And was it?" Charlie asked, leaning in close.

"Of course. It was both—painful and worth it. I don't regret leaving though. I never have. I miss my family, and I wish I could talk to them, but it was their choice to shun me. Not mine." Determination still shone in Mom's tired eyes. "I had already been baptized into the church when I left. That's why I was shunned. I still don't understand that rule. I still don't understand so many of their rules. I couldn't bear a life without music, and the Amish aren't allowed to play instruments. I wanted to go to college, but that's forbidden, too. Then there was your father, the Englisher, the outsider. It was too much for them, even for Esther. She swore she would never shun me. In the end, she turned her back on me, too."

Mom stared at the Queen Anne's lace, as if memories of her childhood were coming back to her. She wiped away a tear.

"And that's why she turned you away that day you took me to see her," Charlie concluded.

"Yes. Honestly, I've been so hurt, but I'm not angry with her. I don't want to hold a grudge. I can't decide if we should try to contact her or not to tell her I'm..." Mom's voice trailed off, and she blew out a lungful of air. She shook her head and looked down. "She wouldn't come to see me, anyway. There's no point."

"Really? Your own sister wouldn't come to see you, even under these circumstances?" Charlie gasped.

"I doubt it. She'd risk being shunned if she did." Mom patted Charlie's hand. "Don't get me wrong. I loved growing up Amish. There are so many wonderful things about it. They help each other in hard times, and they're the most tightly knit group of people I've ever met. Their faith is rock solid, most of the time. But most people only see their quaint, simple lifestyle and don't realize the Amish are human, too. They make mistakes just like the rest of us. Sometimes they gossip or say harsh things."

"Of course. Everyone does that," Charlie said.

Mom continued. "And they have such strict rules. Rules that were too confining for me. Once your father taught me how to play the piano at the old museum, I couldn't understand why they wouldn't allow such a beautiful instrument that can even be used to worship the Lord."

Mom shook her head. "I just had to leave. But I will always miss my family. I'll miss how God and family always came first, how it was their priority. Life was simpler, and people were close. We worked hard, but we had a lot of fun." Mom's face lit up. "We'd play so many games outside, and even all kinds of board games inside. Even work events were fun. And the food… Don't get me started on the delicious food. Pies, cakes, casseroles, homemade bread… I spent countless hours cooking and baking with my mother and sisters. There are many things I've missed. But I'm so glad I left because I married your father and had my two beautiful daughters. I wouldn't trade you two for anything. I wouldn't ever go back and do it differently."

Gratitude swelled in Charlie's chest, and she swallowed a lump in her throat. "But how could Aunt Esther do that to you? I just don't understand."

Mom shrugged her frail shoulders, and the hospital gown rustled with the movement. "She didn't want to end up like me—shunned. I don't blame her. It's not her fault, really. It's all their strict rules. I don't think God would want us to cut off friends and family when they do something wrong. And I didn't even do anything wrong by leaving. I'll never see it their way." Mom hiked her chin in defiance.

What had her mother been like at Charlie's age? Charlie smiled, imagining Mom as a determined, confident young woman. "Well, your community shouldn't have done that to you, Mom. Especially Aunt Esther, your own sister."

"I don't want that to paint you a negative picture of the Amish. They really are wonderful people, and it's beautiful there. You probably would have loved growing up there."

Charlie shook her head with so much emphasis that loose tendrils of hair fell from her ponytail. "No. I'm glad we live here. I wouldn't have liked those rules either. I'm glad you left, Mom. You made the right choice."

******

Elijah Hochstettler trudged into his small house after a long day of work in the community store with Irvin. He pulled off his boots, loosened his suspenders, and started washing his hands, getting ready to go to dinner at the Holts' house. He splashed water on his beardless face, the trademark of a single Amish man, thinking of his married friends who all had beards. Sometimes he felt like he was the last single man in the entire community.

He sat on his small bed with a sigh and looked around his tiny home. From this spot, he could see almost the entire structure. The community had built this house for him when he'd moved here when he was eighteen, just after his family had died. The Holts had been looking out for him ever since.

His dining room and living room were one room, and the bathroom was in the corner. It was a small cabin, but he was grateful that Irvin and the other men in the community had helped him build it. Someday he wanted to build a real house, if he ever found a woman to settle down with.

Another night alone. He wished he had a wife. He was only in his early twenties, but he had dreamed of getting married ever since he was a young teenager. He knew a wife was a gift from God, and he had watched how much in love his parents had been growing up. He could hardly wait to have such a special bond with one person.

If only his parents were still alive. Even if Elijah did have children one day, they would only have one set of grandparents. How Elijah's parents would have loved to have grandchildren. At least he had Esther and Irvin Holt. They were almost like parents to him. But even with the Holts right next door, he still felt lonely sometimes.

"At least I have You, Lord," Elijah said quietly.

He opened his Bible to see his familiar bookmark. His fingers brushed the waxy paper of the lollipop wrapper he had saved from his childhood. He had eaten the little orange sucker right away, since it was such a rare treat. But even after all these years, he could still not part with the simple wrapper.

Maybe it was silly. Over a decade had passed since that blonde *Englisher* girl had given it to him. How long had it been? Twelve years? Fifteen years? Her name was Charlie, short for Charlotte. He knew he'd never forget it because it was such an odd nickname for a girl. He remembered her laughing eyes. And the strange, exciting feeling she had given him.

307

Over the years, Elijah had been interested in a few girls. But he'd never pursued any of them because he didn't feel God calling him to. He never felt the kind of connection with them that he'd experienced with that girl in the barn when he was ten years old. He longed to feel that way about a woman. Maybe it had just been feelings one only had during childhood, but whatever it was, it had felt so genuine.

All this time, he'd kept the wrapper as a reminder to pray for that girl. For over fifteen years, he'd asked God to bring Charlie back into his life.

As he turned the wrapper over in his calloused hands, he prayed, "Lord, please keep her safe, help her love you more every day, and help me also love you more than anything. And if you do bring her back to me, please help me not mess it up."

He set down his Bible and walked to the Holts' house for supper.

The aroma of beef stew warmed his insides as he stepped into the familiar kitchen. Esther was slicing her homemade bread at the table.

"Hello, Elijah."

"Hi, Esther. I was wondering, do you remember that young girl named Charlie and her mother who came here about fifteen years ago? She was blonde, and she and her mother were *Englishers.* Who were they?"

"I don't know what you're talking about." Esther cut into the bread with more force than necessary.

"It's hard to forget. Her mom was so upset when they left. In fact, she said you refused to speak to them and made them leave. What was that all about?" He knew he was prying, but the words had just tumbled out. He couldn't stop them. "And I remember her name was

Charlie because it's such an odd name for a girl."

"It was no one, Elijah. It does not concern you," she said stiffly.

"What happened? Something must have happened for you to not want to talk to her. Will they come back?" he pressed, knowing he should stop talking, but he couldn't. "It's not like you at all to turn someone away at the door."

"It's a long story, one I don't care to revisit. I do not suspect they will ever come back. Now, do not ask me again," she said in such a firm voice that he jumped in surprise. Esther had always been a mild and sweet woman. What had made her so angry? Elijah had never seen her act like that before.

Elijah knew he was crossing the line by a mile, but he just had to know who the girl was. "Esther, please, I just want to know—"

Esther lifted her head slowly, looking him right in the eye, and set her knife down on the table with a thud.

"Elijah," she said in a pained, low voice. Her eyes narrowed, giving her an expression that was so unlike her usual smiling face. "The woman was my sister. I can't talk about what happened. I just can't. It's more complicated and terrible than you'll ever know. Don't ask me about her again."

******

The following night, Dad got a phone call from the hospital while they were having dinner at home. Since Dad was sitting close enough to her, Charlie overheard the voice on the phone.

"Come to the hospital now. I'm afraid this could possibly be Joanna's last night," the woman on the phone told them.

"What's going on?" Zoe, Charlie's eight-year-old sister asked, looking between Charlie and their father. "Dad? Charlie?"

Dad just hung his head.

Charlie's eyes stung with tears as she patted her younger sister's hand. "We have to leave right now, Zoe. We have to go see Mom."

As Dad sped them to the hospital, Charlie said, "Dad, if you're going to drive like this, you really should wear your seat belt. I mean, you always should, but especially right now."

"You know I hate seat belts. There shouldn't even be a law that we have to wear them. It should be our own choice. And I hate how constricting they are. Besides, that's the last thing on my mind right now. Let's not have this argument again tonight."

Charlie sighed. How many times had they argued about seat belts over the years? Even Mom had tried to get Dad to wear one, but he wouldn't budge.

They arrived at the hospital and rushed to Mom's room.

It all felt unreal as they entered the white room containing her frail mother. Charlie halted at the door.

She couldn't do this.

She felt her throat constrict, and for a moment her stomach felt sick. "No, Dad, I can't," she whispered, her hand on her stomach. "I can't say goodbye."

"Charlie, this is your last chance. If you don't, you'll regret it forever. I know you can do it. You are made of the same stuff as your mother," he said and pulled her close, stroking her hair.

Compliments were rare from her father, but she was too heartbroken to truly appreciate it.

He let out a sob, and Charlie's heart wrenched. She hated it when her dad cried, which Charlie had only seen once or twice in her life. Zoe came over and wrapped her arms around them, then they walked over to the bed together.

They held her hand and whispered comforting words. They cried and laughed a little at fond memories. Her father said his goodbyes, Zoe said her goodbyes, and then it was Charlie's turn.

She did not bother trying to stop the flow of her tears. Sorrow crushed her spirit, and no matter how hard she tried she could not see how any silver lining could come from this. Was God punishing her for something? Why was He taking her beautiful, wonderful mother?

"Charlie, I love you," her mother whispered and clutched her hand with little strength.

"I love you too, Mom," Charlie choked out.

"Please promise me, Charlie. Chase your dreams and become a teacher."

"Okay, Mom. I will."

"I just want you to be happy."

"Mom, I will be. I promise."

"Take care of them."

"I will, Mom." She barely got the words out before another round of tears came.

"Thank you. I'll be watching."

Charlie nodded, unable to speak, biting her lip to keep from crying out.

"One more thing. There's something I need to tell you. Please tell your Aunt Esther that I forgive her. Promise me you will. And tell her I'm sorry. I am so sorry." Mom sobbed, and Charlie saw the same pain in her eyes she'd seen all those years ago after they left the Amish farm.

"Why, Mom? Sorry for what?"

"I lied to you yesterday, Charlie, when I said I wasn't angry with her. I didn't want you to think I was a bitter person. Honestly, I have been angry at her for years for shunning me. It was so hard to talk about. I'm so sorry I didn't tell you the whole story."

"It's okay, Mom. I love you."

"I love you too. Tell Esther I love her and that I'm sorry. I forgive her. I hope she forgives me too…" Regret shone in Mom's eyes, then her eyes fluttered closed and the monitor next to her started beeping loudly.

"Forgive you for what? Why does she need to forgive you?" Charlie asked, panic rising in her voice as her eyes darted to the monitor. "What's wrong? What's happening?"

"Her heart rate is dropping," the nurse said and called the doctor into the room.

Charlie's heart wrenched at the sight of Zoe weeping, begging Mom not to die. Dad reached for Mom.

"Mom!" Zoe screamed.

"I'm sorry," the nurse said to Dad. "This could be it."

The doctor assessed her and slowly shook his head, frowning. "I'm so sorry. We tried everything we could. There's nothing more we can do. We will give you some privacy. Please call us if you need anything. We are right down the hall."

Charlie stood on shaky legs, feeling like they would give out at any moment. The doctor continued talking, but his words sounded like muffled gibberish in her ears. He turned and walked out of the room.

Charlie squeezed Mom's hand. "Mom? Mom? Please, tell me what you want Aunt Esther to forgive you for." It seemed so important to Mom, and Charlie wasn't sure if Dad would talk about it, so this could be her last chance to find out. If Mom's dying wish was to ask Aunt Esther's forgiveness for something, Charlie wanted to honor it.

Mom barely opened her eyes and mumbled something incoherent.

"Joanna, we are all here." Dad took Mom's other hand, and Zoe stood by Mom's bed.

Then Mom managed to whisper, "I…love…you…all." Her eyes opened for one fleeting moment, and she looked at each of them. She gave a small smile. "I'm going with Jesus." Her eyes closed.

The machine beside them made one long beeping sound.

She was gone.

Zoe cried out. They held each other as they wept.

Charlie's heart felt literally broken. She sucked in some air, feeling her chest ache, as if there was no air left to breathe.

When they finally left the hospital, she was in a haze as her feet moved on auto pilot. After they got to the apartment, hours passed before they finished drying their tears.

What would Mom say to make her feel better? That this was God's will? Charlie knew that was exactly what she'd say.

Why did God *want* this to happen?

Why didn't He take me instead? Mom was so…good, she thought glumly.

Her whole life she had been taught about the perfect love of Jesus and His wonderful plan for her life. Why was this part of His plan? This was not a wonderful plan.

She fell on her bed, put her head down on her pillow and sighed. "God...please just help me get through this. I don't know what to think right now. Please help me stop doubting you and just trust You."

Someone knocked on the apartment door. When neither her father nor Zoe got up to see who it was, Charlie dragged herself off her bed and went to the door, opening it.

"Alex!" she cried in surprise.

Her ex-fiancé stood in the doorway in his crisp police uniform. Dad and Zoe quickly came over to see what was going on.

"I need to talk to you, Charlie," he told her with determination. He glanced at Charlie's dad and sister. "Alone."

"Not going to happen, Alex," Dad said, stomping towards Alex. "In fact, you broke my daughter's heart. You cheated on her. If she doesn't want to talk to you, she doesn't have to."

"This is terrible timing, Alex. My mother just passed away," Charlie told him, tears constricting her voice. "You should go."

"I'm really sorry. But I've got to tell you something important, Charlie," Alex insisted, taking hold of Charlie's arm a little too roughly. "Come talk to me in the hallway for one minute."

"No." Charlie shoved him away.

"Charlie!" Alex yelled and pulled on her arm again, harder this time. "Come on. I wouldn't be here if it wasn't really important."

"Enough. Get out of here right now, Alex. And don't come back, you hear?" Dad's tall, daunting form seemed to take up the entire doorway. He loomed over Alex threateningly.

The police officer backed away with his hands up and stormed down the stairs.

Charlie let out a sigh of relief. He was gone. For now.

******

If you enjoyed this sample, check out Amish Alias by Ashley Emma here on Amazon:

https://www.amazon.com/Amish-Alias-Romantic-Suspense-Detectives-ebook/dp/B07ZCJBWJL

Made in United States
North Haven, CT
04 October 2024

58349782R10183